SCIENCE FICTIO
CHANGING S

THE BERKLEY SHOWCASE

New Writings in Science Fiction and Fantasy
Edited by Victoria Schochet and John Silbersack

The Berkley Showcase

Vol. 4

Edited by Victoria Schochet & John Silbersack

NEW WRITINGS IN SCIENCE FICTION AND FANTASY

BERKLEY BOOKS, NEW YORK

THE BERKLEY SHOWCASE IV

A Berkley Book / published by arrangement with
the authors

PRINTING HISTORY
Berkley edition / July 1981

ISBN: 0-425-04804-7

A BERKLEY BOOK ® TM 757,375

PRINTED IN THE UNITED STATES OF AMERICA

This volume is lovingly dedicated to Joan and Walter Silbersack, Dorothy Schochet and the memory of Rubin Schochet.

Contents

FAIRY TALE

by Jack Dann

In our last volume of Showcase, we offered a story by
Jack Dann—"Amnesia." And we made a forceful point
of letting you know that Dann was a writer to be savored, but not without some effort on the reader's part,
for his writing was demanding. Here's another story by
him which is going to make you think we were being
a bit myopic. And in a way we were, for "Amnesia" was
an example of only one sort of work Dann is capable
of. No story could be easier to read than "Fairy Tale."
It is like rolling off a log. It's laughing-out-loud funny,
uncomplicated, magical and uplifting. But if you think
you're about to read a fairy story like any one you've
ever read before...well, it just ain't so.

This is a fairy story. Not that kind, *shtumie*. Fairies, as in
goblins and glashtins and shellycoats; or, for the rest of you
non- Jews, as in leprechaun.

I've seen them all and almost died in the doing. That's what
this story is all about. Moishe Dayan was not the only Jewish
hero, you might note.

My name is Moishe Mencken (not related to the H. L. of
the same surname) and I'm a comedian by trade. I'm kind of
a permanent fixture at the Rachmones Resort. That's in the
heart of the Borsht Belt, near Liberty, and right off old Route
Seventeen.

Noo-oo? Do I detect some little condescension back there?

Well, let me tell you, this isn't such a bad place, as resorts go. It's not like it was in the old days, of course, when we had the Concord and Grossingers. But this is the best you get now. I make a living wage here, which is better than most of my peers can muster.

In the old days we could use good material. We could be funny then. (I mean really funny. Not what *you* call funny.) Now everything's so uptight that even the Jews can't take a joke. Everyone's afraid. God forbid they should laugh at themselves.

So we give the *shleppers* what they want.

Like Polish and frog jokes. (Yes, the Poles are the true heroes of America. They can take a joke and prosper.)

But you always want one more Polish joke, right?

Okay, *shtumie*. Everybody knows that European and South American banks have taken over the country. You see them everywhere, right? But have you ever been to a Polish bank? They have a new policy: You give *them* a toaster and they refund you three hundred dollars.

Ha-ha.

That's what you pay for. You deserve it.

The frog joke. The oldest one still gets a laugh. Can you believe that? Oy, someone doesn't know the frog joke. What's green and red and goes sixty miles an hour?

Go figure it out.

Okay, now I'll tell you about Shearjashub Mills. He's the one who got me into all the fairy trouble in the first place.

Nobody knows what Shearjashub means, or how he got the name because he's not telling. He likes to be called Hub, and he's as Jewish as bacon—pure Wasp, yet he smells from herring and speaks a passable Yiddish, which is mostly a *shtik*.

He was born on a shtetl in Galicia; that's how come the Yiddish.* Hub is not quite six feet tall (but he lies about his height and his age), has gray frizzy hair, a pot belly, and a beautiful girl always on his arm. How he does that is beyond me. He says it's the meat *and* the motion. It certainly couldn't be the money.

For your information, I'm five-feet-two and three-quarters.

---

*It occurs to me that some of you were not brought up in a shetl in Galacia and cannot understand Yiddish, which is to miss most of the important dirty words in the English language. For you there is a Yinglish glossary at the end of the story.

Let's get that out of the way. And I do not have frizzy hair and a pot belly. I'm tough, scrappy, and told that I'm quite handsome in a goyish way: big blue eyes, squarish, strong face, cleft in my chin, you get the picture.

Hub still works and lives at the Graubs Resort, a third-rate club with some decent skiing, which has kept it alive. At one time, the Graubs did quite well, as attested by its many bungalows and central houses, all stone—the old wooden barn, where stores used to be kept, caved in years ago, and still sits there in a field like an old gray hat.

Every few months I get the urge to see Hub. He's like lumpfish caviar: good once in a while, but every day—feh. So last month I got the urge and called and this is what I got:

"Hello, Diana, this is Moishe Mencken, connect me with Hub Mills' room, I love you."

Silence on the line. Perhaps she was overwhelmed.

"Hello? Diana?"

"I'm sorry, but we're closed"—that said in a voice that was unmistakably Diana's, but so cold I felt a chill. "If you would like to leave your address, we will—"

"What are you, a recording?" I asked. "Cut the crap. Diana, this is Moishe, your little Moishe, now let me speak to Hub."

Click.

That's all, just like that, and I stood there with the phone still to my ear as the chills went up and down. That wasn't Diana, I knew that. The Graubs couldn't be closed. When a resort closes, everybody knows. It's like a telepathic hotline. And certainly Hub would have told *me*, if such a thing had happened.

It wouldn't take me but five minutes to reach the Graubs and find out what was what. I had a few hours before I had to perform at eight.

"Nobody screws around with Moishe Mencken," I said into the dead phone. "Just wait!"

So put the phone down, already, I told myself. But I couldn't move, not a muscle. I was in some kind of trance, like a dream. Until seven-thirty I stood there.

Later I couldn't remember a thing. But, oy, did my right arm ache!

I had just enough time to dress and get downstairs and do the show, tuxedo and studs and all; but I had a splitting headache like I sometimes get from drinking Wild Turkey (good stuff, mind you, but always gives me a migraine on the left side). I wondered why my right arm was numb; maybe it had fallen asleep.

Because the crowd was small (what else is new?), I had to perform in the Bronze Room. Can you imagine a room with tin walls and red velvet chairs? It was enough to embarrass even the *nouveau riche*. Then I shot an hour at the bar with Finney the barkeep (who looks like everyone's bald uncle who plays the stockmarket) and a bellboy, talking about the old days. The bellboy wasn't old enough to remember the Manhattan Riots, much less the good times, but we always made a show of impressing him with how good it was. (Ah, it wasn't that good then, either; just better than now.)

No, I still didn't remember the phone call business. Wasn't it enough that the crowd was a bunch of *pishers* and all the demons of *Gehenna* were banging on my skull?

After a while, Finney asked about Hub—he was the only person I ever met who called him Shearjashub.

Gottenyu, it was like waking from a dream. Suddenly I could remember! But everything wasn't all right. I was still *farchadat*, a little *meshugge*, ready for the funny farm.

I could not speak Hub's name. *Gott*, did I try, over and over! But every time I tried, I had a terrible compulsion to say all the Yiddish words that start with *S*, which is akin to listing the nine billion names of God:

Shabbes	*Schmuck*
Sachel	*Schneider*
Schatchen	*Schnook*
Shlack	*Shaygets*
Schlemiehl	*Shaytl*
Schlep	*Shekel*
Schlok	*Shlemozzl*
Schloomp	*Shikk—*
Schmo	

"Hey Moishe," Finney said, reaching across the bar and shaking my shoulder.

> —*er*
> *Shikseh*
> *Shmachel*
> *Shmatehs*

"Moishe, hey, enough, already. Are you all right? Come on."

"I'm all right," I said. "I'm all right." But I wasn't, as you can see. I was under some kind of spell. But how could this be? This was New York, not Moravia! I took the hint: if I started trying to talk about Hub, I would only start with the list again. So with great presence of mind, I excused myself (after liberating Finney of some more of his Wild Turkey—screw the headache) and went out to my car.

Of course, my lousy luck, it wouldn't start.

Back inside. It took a good half-hour to convince Finney that, indeed, I was all right, had not been drinking *that* much, and, yes, I would gas up his *farshtinkener* car and take good care of it. I'll be back in less than an hour, if you please.

I took old Seventeen, the Winding Way, as it was nicknamed. There was no one else on the road, which was unusual, but not that unusual. Finney had a convertible, a real antique, and the top was down. It was the kind of night to look up at the stars while a beautiful girl did unmentionable things to you in the front seat.

The main house of the Graubs, which I could see when I was off the highway, was lit up like a bingo parlour.

Something fishy on Mott Street.

Everywhere else it was dark. Except for a flickering light near the old wooden barn. I stopped the car and watched. It was most certainly the phenomenon known as Ignis Fatuus (you see, I'm no dummy), otherwise known as will-o'-the-wisp. But who knows from will-o'-the-wisp in Kerhonkson, New York?

Something about all this bothered me. The directions didn't seem right. Everything seemed, somehow, placed wrong. It was what my mother, may she live many more good years, would call a *goslin* night.

But I was wasting time here. If Hub was around, he'd be at the bar in the Main House.

Then a voice called my name.

"Hub?" I answered. It sure as hell sounded like him, but I was wary after that Diana business. Maybe I was talking to spooks again. Ah! I couldn't believe that, either. I'd been under a lot of strain lately. Maybe the whole damn thing was a loose cog in my head.

Again the voice called my name. It *was* Hub's voice. I wasn't so delirious that I couldn't recognize the voice of my best friend. The dumb sonovabitch had probably bought himself a bottle of cheap wine and was getting bent up in the woods. It didn't take much to get Hub drunk. He had emphysema and still smoked like hell and took pills, which dried out his lungs. Mix the booze with the pills and you have a cheap drunk.

Maybe he was out here getting laid. Out of the question: he always said that he was born in a bed and not in a bush. He didn't want any of that country-bumpkin prickers-in-your-ass stuff.

But how could he tell it was me? I was driving Finney's car. It was dark.

So what would you have done? Sit like a *schlemiehl*? Tell yourself you were hearing things again?

So you have no *chutzpa*.

I went to investigate.

And found a very drunk Shearjashub sitting like a toad on a rock in front of a dying fire. (So I was wrong about the will-o'-the-wisp. Sue me.) Behind him were two huge oak trees, their branches grotesquely twisted together. There was a log for the fire beside him. Nearby was another log and some kindle. Remember that, it's important.

"Hello, diminutive person," Hub said, slurring his words. He leered at me as if I were jailbait. "What brings you here?"

"I wanted to see you, dummy. How did you know it was me?"

"I didn't."

"Well, you called my name. You must have known something."

"Nope."

"You didn't call my name?"

"Uh-uh. But I'm glad you're here." Then he offered me his bottle, which I politely refused. "Come on. They'll be none left soon."

That wasn't like Hub. The Hub I knew and loved wouldn't drink out of a glass that had been used by his mother, much less share a bottle with me.

"Okay, that's enough," I said. "I'm taking you home."

"Don't come near me," Hub said, rocking back and forth on his rock—*shuckling*, my mother calls that: it's what the old men do when they pray next to you in *shul*. It's Jewish machismo: who can rock back and forth the fastest. Maybe it helps shoot the prayers up to Heaven.

Anyway, I stopped where I was. He had said it like he meant it. Then he stopped *shuckling*, picked up the log that he had kept beside him, and then broke it in half over his knees.

I didn't believe it either, but seeing is believing.

"What are you, training to be a masher?" I asked.

He placed the log on the fire, which soon came alive. It was getting a little cool and the warmth and light and crackling of the fire felt good—almost reassuring.

"Not bad, huh?" Hub asked, taking another sip. "It's a trick, like tearing telephone books. The log was rotten."

"Very good," I said, impatient to get out of there. "Now let's—"

"Sit down and be humble and I'll tell you a story."

"I've heard enough stories for one day. When I called the hotel, Diana of the big boobs didn't know who I was and told me the place had closed and wouldn't let me speak to—"

"It's all true, the place is done, but we did have some good old times here, didn't we?"

I was about to remonstrate and tell him why the Graubs could not possibly be closed when, *feh*, he drooled all over his chin. Like my uncle used to do, may he rest in peace.

"Come on, sit down beside me like a good little person, and I'll tell you about the fairies."

"What?" I asked.

"Remember when you talked to Diana?"

"Well?"

"It wasn't Diana."

"Then who was it?" I asked. I knew what Diana's voice sounded like. Hub always referred to her as a sexy frog—as good a description as any. I wanted to get out of there. Even though the fire was warm (too warm), I didn't like being out here in the middle of nowhere.

"A bogle," Hub said. "You talked to a bogle."

"A what?"

"If you want to find out more, sit here by me and I will tell you." He patted the rock and said, "There's enough room."

So I sat down beside him.

"A bogle, my son, is a goblin. And very evil tempered."

Not only was he drunk, but completely *meshugge*—blotto, crazy, off the wall—exactly what you thought about me when

I told you what kind of story this was going to be.

"And you're *shikker*, let's get coffee," I said.

"No, sit a minute. Believe me, bogles are notorious for playing with telephones and disguising their voices."

Maybe this bogle cast a spell over me on the telephone, I thought, but I told myself to think straight like a person; otherwise, I would become a *draykop* like Hub, if I wasn't one already.

"The fairies are taking everything over," Hub said, looking around at the trees as if he was talking to them. *Nu*? Maybe he was. "And a good thing, too," he continued. "The Catskills are as dead as Dublin. Maybe we should go back to Miami Beach."

Heaven forbid!

"Okay, Hub," I said, standing up now. "I'm going down to the Main House where I will ask the bogle if I can use his phone for a minute and call the zipzip boys in the white coats."

"Fine. Go ahead. But first, maybe, you could get me that log on the pile of kindle over there."

"You just put a log on the fire," I said. But lo and *gevalt*, it was true. Burned through and through. Only glowing embers remained. "It couldn't burn that fast!"

"Get me the log and I'll show you the trick to break it," Hub said.

"Get the log yourself, *putz*. You want a fire, get your own log."

"I'm drunk, you want I should fall? Anyway, you're already standing."

But I refused to budge.

Then, without warning, he lunged at me. The Hub I knew couldn't move that fast if his life depended on it. He hit me hard, and we grappled. This was no drunkard; this boy was all muscle.

Maybe a *dybbuk*, God forbid, was inhabiting my friend.

He locked his arms around my chest and started dragging me toward the log and pile of kindle. All the while, he was laughing like hell.

Suddenly everything changed. Again it was like waking up from a dream. Nothing was as it should be. The trees had disappeared, as had the fire and log and kindle. I had thought I was in the backwoods of the Graubs; instead, I found myself on Fishkill Craig. About a foot away from us, where the log and kindle had been, was a four-hundred-foot drop—straight down.

And I saw now that it wasn't Hub who was squeezing the life out of me, but a dwarfish person with a scraggly beard, sloped forehead, and hooked nose.

I'd been tricked, duped, the same old thing all over again. I'd fallen under another spell.

But, *gottenyu*, what fear can do to a man!

I started kicking and screaming and making such a *tummel* that this *dybbuk*, or whatever it was, twisted around and slipped on a smooth rock. Even as he fell over the cliff, he was grabbing at me to pull me over with him.

No, *shtumie*, it doesn't end there. What comes next is the heroic part, but first let me tell you what it was that tried to seal my doom. It was a duergar using glamour, which is a fairy spell, to make me think I was talking to my friend. Nu? So what's a duergar, you may rightly ask. A duergar is a dwarf, very nasty, not well disposed to humankind, and originally from the North of England.

Remember when I talked to Diana and fell under a spell? Well, I really had been talking to a bogle, which is a goblin. Bogles and duergars always work together. The bogle casts a spell to lure a human to the duergar, and the duergar kills him. Very neat. It seems they've been doing this sort of thing for years.

How do I know that? My wife explained it to me later. She's had trouble with duergars and bogles, too.

For your information, my wife is a water fairy. Don't worry, it all fits in. Believe me.

Whenever I was about to do something crazy, my mother would say: "Moishe, if you had another brain, you'd be a halfwit."

If she had known what I was about to do, she would say it again. "Leave well enough alone, Moishe." Moma was smart. She understood that bravery was the other side of stupidity, and didn't approve of either. (Neither would she approve if she knew that my wife turns into a serpent at the touch of a drop of water.)

But she also used to say that God works in mysterious ways. God made me a comedian; now maybe he was working in a mysterious way to find me a wife. I'm a deeply religious man about these things.

Anyway, I drove down to the Main House to find out what had become of my friend.

Well, there might as well have been a *Bar Mitzvah* going on. If that's what happens when a place goes out of business, it should only happen at my resort! The place was crowded as an Irish bar on St. Patrick's Day. Outside, Cadillacs as thick as cockroaches; inside. . . .

It was like walking into a Las Vegas club. Like the Concord in the old days. Like Heaven. It was opulent. It was filled with beautiful people, with blond Galitzianers and dark Litvaks, all sitting together at long, lavishly laid-out tables, as if they didn't know about the Jewish pecking order. (*Nudnik*! *You* must be a Litvak, you with the blank face. A Galitz is a Jew whose ancestors came from Poland, but he likes to think they came from Austria. A Lit knows his ancestors came from Lithuania, but he's sceptical, nevertheless. Me? I'm a Galitzvak: blue eyes and swarthy skin, you should note.)

But the room was filled with strangers. Not one face did I recognize. A waiter passed me with a tray of champagne (this was no cheapskate party) and I lifted two glasses. Before I could touch glass to lips, a girl with blond, frizzy hair, who, at first glance, didn't look more than thirteen or fourteen, said, "Don't drink that!"

"And why not?" I asked, surprised. Maybe this was a *Bas Mitzvah*, and it was her party, and she didn't like strangers. Look again! She was no child, just childlike. She was a woman, as delicate as a spiderweb, with eyes that made me think of being nineteen again and falling in love. (And I like *zoftig* women! This one was positively skinny.)

"If you drink or eat anything, you'll never leave this place," she said.

"What?"

"It's fairy food, and not for you. You must leave. You have enemies here."

"How can I have enemies when I don't even know anybody here?"

"You just killed a duergar," she said, and she told me what a duergar was, just as I told you. Of course, I didn't believe her, even after what happened on the hill with Hub. I had to try to maintain some modicum of sanity. "Half of the Unseelie Court was watching you," she continued. "And they're all here."

"Who're the Unseelie Court?" I asked, suddenly feeling a bit claustrophobic, even in this large room, as if I really was being watched. Something else, too: I noticed that everything was wonderfully lit, as if ceiling, floor, and walls were glowing. It was like a dream.

"You can think of the Unseelie as the duergar's family," and then she reached up and put something sticky into my eyes—first one eye and then the other.

Gottenyu! What a family!

It was all a spell—glamour, as the girl called it. (Her name, incidentally, was Asrai.) I looked around. It was like seeing with new eyes. Instead of being opulent, this place was a mess, a real dive. Everything was dirty. What had looked like a terrific meal turned out to be plates filled with yellow weeds and lumpy gruel. And the light was coming from a large fire right in the center of the room, which cast jumping shadows all over the walls.

But even in the shadows, I saw things too ugly to be human:

I saw men with webbed feet and goat's hooves and noses without nostrils. I saw water bogles, called shellycoats, festooned with shells and women with squinty eyes and back-to-front feet and long hoselike breasts. (One woman-thing had such long dugs that she carried them over her shoulders.) Every humanlike form had some deformity.

There were goblins with protruding stomachs and large ears and long slit mouths, and dirt-crusted kobolds that looked as if they had just risen up from the bowels of the earth; there were duergars with malicious grins and phookas with horns and shaggy black pelts and yellow eyes; there were shape-shifting bogles, and trows with octapoidal limbs, and fachians, which had only one eye and one arm and one leg (and one foot, of course), and there were glastig hags (part woman, part goat) with beautiful grey faces and insect-infested pubes; there was a killmoulis with a huge nose and no mouth and a fenoderee with its man-killing sickle. And there were evil-looking vampire fairies, and pretty girls with snakes instead of hair, and the dour, ugly, rockskinned spriggans that kidnap children and burn down houses.

This was the Host, the Unseelie Court, the evil ones....

And they were all closing in on me and chanting, "Flax on the floor, death at the door."

Oy!

I turned to run, but they were all around me. I screamed and closed my eyes (you thought maybe I would draw a sword and start hacking away like Douglas Fairbanks?) and dropped both of the drinks I was holding like a grand rabbi about to make a blessing.

Then this little girl standing beside me, this *mazik*, who was not even five feet tall, made a noise like water on the burner and turned into a dragon, maybe nine feet high, complete with green scales, a tail, and protruding eyes.

(I only closed my eyes for a second; a coward I'm not.)

She made a terrible noise and knocked over the front rank of monsters with her tail. Then she turned around, gave the wall a swat, and I could see outside.

The dragon didn't wait around; she bolted through the hole. I followed. (What else?)

I didn't have to look behind to imagine what various monsters were *shpatsing* after me.

Let's get two things out of the way.

First of all, the stuff my little Asrai put into my eyes was fairy ointment, which, if you haven't guessed by now, has the power to break the spell of glamour, which, *nudnik*, I already explained.

But now, you may ask, how did Asrai suddenly turn from a faunlike young thing into a ferocious—albeit relatively small-dragon?

Remember, I gave you a clue: it only takes a drop of water to change a water fairy into a dragon. Well, I was *dershrokn*, as Moma would say—afraid, ready to make weewee—and I spilled the champagne, which was really pishwater, on her feet.

That saved my life, although I'm sure Asrai would have done something, anyway. She's a nice girl.

So I was running after a dragon, who was cutting quite a swath through back lawns, fields, and woods. Behind me were the Unseelie monsters, all shrieking and making unearthly noises, inspiring me to run all the faster.

Then, pop, just like that, Asrai turned back into a girl and kept running. Her feet hardly seemed to touch the ground. I *grepsed* and followed as best I could, but I felt that any second a cold hand would grab me by the neck and drag me into Hell. (Modern Jews might not believe in Hell, but then most of them aren't chased by monsters in Kerhonkson at one o'clock in the morning, either.)

"We're safe now," Asrai said, stopping at the northern edge of the woods. I looked around, still huffing for breath, and didn't see anything strange or terrible. Even the trees looked normal, instead of like trolls.

"Good," I said, regaining my composure. "Thanks for making like a dragon." No, I didn't ask her right away how she turned into a dragon. Sometimes it's better to leave well enough alone.

"Do you like me better as a dragon?"

"No, I like you fine the way you are." *Gevalt!*

"I'm not really a dragon."

"What, then?"

"A serpent—a worm, really."

Feh, I thought, but then I looked into those eyes, green as some primordial pond. What lovely eyes, what a child of the morning. Terrific, I didn't have enough trouble with the family, now I was falling in love with a worm. And it wasn't even Jewish.

"What about all those monsters that were behind us?" I asked.

"The Unseelie?" Asrai asked, then answered: "They won't cross out of the woods, it isn't their territory, it's ours. So don't worry."

Why be worried? Let the monsters take over. Maybe the killmoulis can become a comedian.

Asrai explained that the Unseelie were originally the guardians of the gold; they were the troops, and they've always followed the Seelie Court, of which she was a member. But times changed, and the Unseelie became resentful and destructive. Although the Seelie Court bore humankind no great love, by comparison with the Unseelie, they were saints—you should excuse the expression.

"But why are *you* here?" I asked.

"We never live where we're not wanted," Asrai said, looking at me with those eyes that didn't need light to make them shine. (Normally, I would be afraid of such eyes; tonight was not normal.) "You humans have been calling us again in your dreams. You dreamed us up."

"So you mean we're stuck with you and your Unseelie friends?"

"If you want me to leave...."

"No," I said quickly. "But I could do without the monsters."

"Then go tell your friends to stop dreaming terrible things and think nice thoughts."

"What's happened to my friend Hub?" I asked.

"He's on Unseelie territory, with the others, probably in a fairy ring."

"A what?"

"He'll dance his life away in a few minutes," Asrai said. "But that's subjective time—time is different for fairyfolk, if we wish it so—but I assure you he'll have a good time."

"Terrific. Can he be rescued?"

"Only a human can help him," Asrai said. "But he would risk falling into the ring himself. Would you be willing to take such a chance to help your friend?"

Of course not! It's a miracle that I've survived for my thirty-odd years, already. But as I stood by the edge of the forest with this lovely girl, my thoughts were pinwheels inside my head. Of *course* I would risk my life for my friend and make the world a better place.

"Can you help me?" I asked. But I was thinking libidinous thoughts.

"Maybe, if you ask my father." She smiled mischievously. "But, remember, you get nothing for nothing, as your mother says, Moishe."

"How do *you* know what *my* mother says?" I asked.

"I read your mind."

Now I was in trouble!

We made our way to Asrai's camp, which was in the hills beyond the forest. I wasn't afraid now—the duergars and bogles and spriggans might as well have been a thousand miles away—such is the effect safety has on me.

The fairy hillsides, you should note, were beautiful, covered with twinkling lights, as if thousands upon thousands of fireflies were resting in the grass. And there were doorways into the hills, wherein banquets as lavish as Bar Mitzvahs in Westchester were being held. And the music....

But I would not be fooled so easily now; I had seen one such banquet before.

"*Shtumie*, you've still got ointment in your eyes," Asrai said. "What you're seeing now is real, no glamour."

Oy vay, now she speaks Yiddish by reading my mind.

"Don't read my mind," I said.

"It's hard not to," she replied. Again that mischievous smile.

"A man needs some privacy, would you watch me go *kacken*, too?" She did not reply to that, and I felt ashamed of myself. "So what should I say to your father?" I asked.

"What do you want to say?"

"Okay, I want to help my friend, get rid of the Unseelie monsters, make the Graubs—dive that it was—kosher again, so my friend should live and have work." As usual, I was getting carried away with myself.

"So you want us to help *you* get rid of the Unseelie host? That's a big order." Two dimples she had when she smiled.

And diarrhea of the mouth I got. Now I was taking on, almost single-handedly, all the forces of darkness. That wasn't exactly what I had had in mind, but I nodded, anyway.

Remember what Moma said about stupidity and bravery?

"Who's your father?" I asked, changing the subject.

"He's head of the Daoine Sidhe—that's our family—and High King of the Hills. His name is Oberon. But he's very short, you should note, so make sure that you're always lower than he."

"I'm from the family of Mencken," I said, and she giggled as we walked in the moonlight toward her father's hill. Fairyfolk gave us curious stares as we passed.

I felt a bit better now and walked tall. Moma used to say, "In the land of the blind, the one-eyed man is king." King Moishe of Mencken the Tall.

Not bad.

Good-looking the great king was not (how could such an ugly man produce such a darling daughter?), but he was attended by a livery of pages dressed in scarlet and yellow, who, if such a thing was possible, were even smaller than he.

From killmoulis to king in a matter of minutes. My head was spinning. From king to *krenk* I was going.

The little king, with his bird's nest of a beard and owl eyes sunk into sourdough skin, wore a bejeweled crown and sat on a throne atop the highest hill. He used gargoyles (I'm sure they were alive) as armrests.

"Hello, king," I said, forgetting the "great." Asrai gave me a little kick and whispered, "Kneel!" I kneeled. Feh. Moishe Mencken could certainly not be doing such a thing.

"Howdy-doo, what do you want, Jewboy?" asked the *gonif* king. Enraged (you see, you can't get away from anti-semites), I started to stand up; but Asrai rested her hand on my shoulder— a hand as light as down, and as strong as handcuffs. So I told the king that I wanted to save my friend from the Unseelie.

"That's all?" he asked, and Asrai explained that I had wanted to vanquish the Unseelie host myself, but she had talked me into coming here for a little help.

So what was I to do? Admit to being a coward? They'd give me back to the Unseelie, who would bake me for bread.

"Okay, you lead the fight," the king said, "and, maybe, with luck, we'll send them to New York City for a while. But they'll be back. You're starting a big *tummel*. Fighting and *tsuris*, that's what's in store for all of us."

"Maybe they'll like New York," I said. My knees were beginning to ache.

"Nah. Too much cement." After a considerable pause, he said, "Now, what are you going to do in return for *us*?"

"What do you mean?" I asked, raising my voice. "I'm supposed to be leading the fight."

"Big deal."

"Then what do you want?"—this time I added "Great King."

"You like my daughter who saved you from the Unseelie, which she had no right to do." The king glared at his daughter. "Well . . . ?"

"Yes," I said. "I like her fine." This meant trouble; I could feel it.

"Then it's all arranged. You marry my daughter, and make sure you keep her away from water when your *shlepper* friends are around. And if you mistreat her, I'll turn you into a cockaroach and send you home to your mother, so she should step on you."

For effect, the king said a bad word, waved his hand, and suddenly I *was* a cockroach, complete with feelers, barfbrown chitin, everything. I was too scared to be scared, but I can tell you one thing: Kafka had it all wrong, but that's another story.

"Well?" asked the king, after transforming me back into a normal person. "Is it a deal?"

What kind of a deal was that? Did he want to get rid of her so bad? *Gottenyu!* If I kiss her, will my saliva turn her into a worm? I told myself not to think about it. "What about this gold business?" I asked the king.

"Don't even think it," the king said, as he squeezed the ear of his gargoyle. "We keep the Unseelie's gold and maybe make a deal here and there, but you should know from the literature that gold makes trouble. If you want to make a deal, you have to live reasonably like the lower middle class, without temptation, so my daughter should have a nice life. Of course, if you don't want to make a deal with us, I'm sure the Unseelie would be interested in such a nice boy to bake into bagels.

"It's a terrible thing for a father to have to let his daughter marry a mortal," the king continued, "but you're all that's left." Father gave daughter a sneer. "Fairyfolk won't have her, you should be pleased to know."

"Why not?" I asked, not very pleased at all. But she certainly was pretty, and she had saved my life, and I would get out of this somehow. . . .

"Because everything's on straight. My Asrai has no deformities, poor child. Look"—and he proudly lifted up his kirtle and showed me his chickenfeet. I looked at the page standing beside him and saw that his feet were backwards.

"All right, then," said the king. "It's done. One more thing, Mister Smartass. I can read your mind in Yiddish, Hebrew, Ladino, you name it. So if you even think bad thoughts about my little Asrai, it'll be cockaroach time."

This was some set-up. I stood up and turned toward Asrai. I was ready with a dirty look, cockroach or not, believe me.

Then I looked into her eyes. Who would not have fallen under such a spell? What loveliness! What perfection! (Better her spell than the bogle's.)

I immediately asked her to marry me.

Such is the mystery of love. Oy, Moma.

I spent such a night with Asrai that I won't even tell you about it. (The Great King was very cosmopolitan and had no objections to his daughter having premarital sex.)

Okay, this much I'll tell: fairyfolk are kinky. Me? I was

doing a sacred duty, for it is written that whosoever does not unite with a woman in this life (providing he is a man) must return in the next and get the job done.

This way I wouldn't have to make a special trip later.

No rest for the weary! I was awakened at dawn by a bunch of chattering pixies and given what looked to me like a hockey stick.

Moma, sometimes half-wits make out, you should know. Your idealistic Moishe did not know that the Daoine Sidhe (and the whole Seelie Court) were the goody-goodies of fairydom. They weren't hot on killing, although they had a sinful weakness for turning human beings they didn't like into abominable things. I'm still afraid to step on a cockroach. Nu? It might be my Uncle Herman.

Instead of killing, they hurled. Hurling, I found out, was also very popular with the Unseelie. It's a bloody sport, a way of beating your opponent's brains out and still living to fight another day. Something like hockey.

It's really just a nice excuse to start a fight.

Which we did.

So there I was, Moishe Mencken, riding a fairyhorse shod with silver and leading the minions of goodness. Behind me were fairy knights decked out with all manner of jewels; their greaves and helmets were made of beaten gold, and they rode huge, beautiful horses.

Of course, I was scared. *Plotzing*, more like it. But Asrai was riding beside me like a queen, and I had no choice but to be a *mench*.

We met the enemy in a clearing by the edge of the forest. Even in the daylight, the Unseelie host looked dark and terrible. I could hear Moma's voice inside my head whispering, "He who runs away lives to fight another day." But I wasn't running. Not me. A moment such as this is a gift. Unfortunately, at that moment—I must admit—the thought that crossed my mind was that this was something right out of a Cecil B. DeMille film. And in color, too.

The Unseelie host cried out (in unison, no less), "We're ready."

And our king, who was now sitting astride his horse beside

Asrai, shouted, "Out with ye all."

Then the *tummel* began.

The Unseelie threw a golden ball toward me, which I struck with my stick (what a civilized way to resolve differences), and then with a great shout both sides ran to meet each other. My horse jumped forward with the others.

But no one, neither Seelie nor Unseelie, made even a pretense of trying to hit the ball back and play the game. They started, right off, to club one another.

I had enough to contend with: a balding witch was determined to bash my brains out with a stick.

Sometime during all this shouting and heavy breathing, I realized that maybe fairyfolk couldn't get killed at this game, but I could. Later, I found out that it's considered mandatory for fairyfolk to include at least one human in their wars. The good king had probably been looking for an excuse to grab the Unseelie's gold, all the while.

They were all *gonifs* and *gozlins*. While they were attacking each other, and probably having a helluva time, I was having enough trouble just staying alive.

Gottenyu, did the blood flow! Limbs were lost, maidens deflowered (probably for the umpteenth time!), and it all looked very real to me.

So how did I survive all this, you may ask?

Just as you thought: Asrai had turned herself back into a dragon and was felling the beasties and trows and bogles around me like a woodcutter working to a deadline. Her green scales were spattered with blood.

So she protected me (although I fought like a demon, you should know). For most of the day, I hid out on the edge of the field. Don't be so quick with the sneers. Remember what my mother said.

The carnage went on until dark, and then the Unseelie finally began to lose. The battlefield looked like something Dante would think up. Maybe all these spirit things could just go home and grow new heads and limbs, like worms. It was enough to make even a strong person such as myself want to *varf*.

What was left of the Unseelie began to make a buzzing noise. Then, just like that, they turned into a horde of insects— every kind you could think of, but mostly locusts.

They flew around and away, eating anything that was green, from grass to leaf, cutting a swath from here to New York City.

That locust business is a Jewish bit, you know.

Go read about it in the *Haggadah*.

Of course, everybody (except the locusts) was happy. The Seelie folk were milling about, shaking hands, hugging, and making a great roar; the Unseelie had flown away. Good riddance!

But my real work was still to be done. Even though the good fairies won, any mortal (remember Hub?) left in the Unseelie's fairy ring would become old and shrivel up and turn to dust like the bad witch in the Wizard of Oz. (*Shtumie*, where do you think Frank Baum got it from?)

As I said before, fairy time is different from human time. (Where do you think Washington Irving got the idea for Rip Van Winkle?) Even now, I might be too late. Hub might have aged sixty years in the last few hours.

Asrai and I made our way to Fishkill Craig, past the old barn, to the scraggly wood below the cliffs, where the fairy ring was lit by will-o'-the-wisp. A motley group of curious pixies and fairychildren followed us. The pixies were green as grass, and the fairychildren were all babyfat, blond hair, and hummingbird wings.

The ring was between two huge blackthorn trees, and it looked like a soap bubble—it had a shimmering, transparent surface, and inside I could see lithe figures dancing wildly. I could almost hear the fairy music, but we were still a safe distance from the ring.

"You'll be first inside the ring," Asrai said to me. "I'll follow, and we'll all make a chain"—she waved her hand at the pixies and fairychildren.

"What about *that*?" I asked, pointing to what I thought was a pair of eyes in the forest dark.

"Don't worry, Poppa's already made a spell for those on the outside of the ring. What's left of the Unseelie won't be aware of us, and those inside the ring won't notice, anyhow. They're too busy dancing."

I wondered what the king, my future father-in-law, was up to. Probably negotiating a contract with the Unseelie. I didn't trust him, but didn't dwell on the thought. If he happened to be reading my mind, it would be, as he said, cockroach time.

As we neared the ring, I could hear the most beautiful music that was ever played. Bach was boogie compared to this. All I wanted to do was dance, and Fred Astaire I'm not. (Indeed, that's the way humans are trapped in fairy rings. You hear the music, and then you're dancing with all the creatures from Gehenna until you fall apart.)

I saw all manner of horned and winged creatures hopping about with naked human beings. Such a frenzy!

And there was Hub! His pot belly jiggled like jello as he danced with a beautiful, blue-eyed goblin girl. She had primroses in her long, black hair.

"That's not so bad," I mumbled, developing a yen for that goblin girl, and then Asrai was daubing fairy ointment on my eyelids and in my ears. She used too much, and it stung like hell. (Maybe she was reading my mind again and got a little jealous.) But the music suddenly sounded like chalk rubbing across a blackboard. Now I could see that the dancers—monsters and humans alike—were filthy. And what a smell! Next to that, herring was perfume. The whole forest seemed to stink.

"All right, Mister Ladies' Man," Asrai said, "get into the ring and pull out your friends." She took hold of my belt and the waistband of my pants. "I'll hold onto you, but you must keep one foot outside the circle. If you fall completely into the circle, none of us can help you."

I was more than a little nervous about all this, but I crawled into the fairy ring like a natural-born, thank you, Moma, hero. The bubble-surface of the ring felt like wet cellophane: slippery and slimy.

Even with the fairy ointment in my eyes and ears and Asrai holding me by the pants, I felt a wild urge to break away and dance with the naked folk. But I have will power. I grabbed Hub—feh! he was as sweaty and slippery as a horse—and with a jerk pulled him out.

He promptly fell asleep. The bags under his eyes looked like windowshades, but he had not aged very much.

So I went back into the fairy ring to do the good deed. One by one, I pulled out every man, woman, and child. Each one fell asleep immediately. This was hard work, you should note, and seemed to take all night. Now you know: even heroism involves drudgery.

There were a few close calls, of course. Several times when

I grabbed someone dancing with a kobald or a gnome, I was almost pulled completely into the ring—foot and all. But Asrai and the pixies and fairychildren held fast: they were stronger than I thought.

When I finally pulled out the last person, there was a great hue and cry. It was as if only now had the Unseelie seen what I had done. The gnomes and goblins and dwarfs—all the various demons—danced and spun even more wildly, and turned into goats and cats and dogs and creatures of the woods.

Asrai pulled me out, and I promptly fell asleep in her arms, ready to rest, at least for a while, on my laurels.

I deserved it!

You want the loose ends tied up now, right?

Okay, the Daoine Sidhe are still in the Jewish Hills, and Asrai and I visit them once a week. We got married, of course—a nicer girl you couldn't find—although we had some trouble at the wedding when the rabbi spilled some wine on Asrai. But she made it to the girl's room before she turned into a dragon; she waited there until she changed back into a girl again and then returned to the wedding. It worked out: Everyone thought she ran away because she was shy and afraid to marry such a worldly person as I.

We also visit Moma. Well, Asrai sounds Jewish, doesn't it? Such a nice girl, my mother should complain? Anyway, Moma wants to be Grandma. So I'll be Moishe, the sower of dragons.

Of course, Hub's all right. If he wasn't, don't you think I would have mentioned it before? Asrai's father placed a cleaning spell over the Graubs and mixed up the fabric of time. When Hub and the others woke up, everything was as it was before. Nobody was lost, and all the hotel guests left on time to make their various appointments.

The gold I try not to think about. Asrai has been helping me with a few routines, and her father told me if I keep his daughter happy (which I do!), he'll book me in Vegas for a few weeks—the pixies need a vacation, anyway, he said. But any funny-business with the showgirls and go forage for food with the other cockroaches.

So much for his liberal attitude.

New York City is still having trouble with the Unseelie, but that couldn't be avoided. (Better them than us!)

My father-in-law, the king, tells me they'll be back.
That I try not to think about.
There's a little of Scarlett O'Hara in every heroic type.

Just as I thought. Someone doesn't know the frog joke.
Okay, just to prove to you that I'm not a mean person, here
it is:
What's green and red and goes sixty miles an hour?
Shtumie! A frog in a blender.
No, I don't tell dragon jokes!

MOISHE MENCKEN'S YINGLISH-YIDDISH GLOSSARY:*

A Guide for the Perplexed

bar mitzvah/bas mitzvah—the ceremony signifying and celebrating
    passage into Jewish adulthood and responsibility. The *bar
    mitzvah* is for boys, the *bas mitzvah* for girls.

chutzpa—guts, nerve, presumptuousness. For example, it takes
    chutzpa to write this glossary.

dershrokn—the German word for *afraid*. Linguists might argue,
    but as far as I'm concerned, if my mother uses *dershrokn*,
    it's Yiddish!

draykop—a confused or addled person. (See *meshugge*.)

dybbuk—a demon that possesses a person and makes him or her
    do terrible and crazy things.

farchadat—punchy, dizzy.

*Yinglish: a term coined by Leo Rosten to mean Yiddish words used in
colloquial English. Bagel is a yinglish word. While I'm at it, I would like
to acknowledge my debt to Mr. Rosten's wonderful sourcebook, *The Joys
of Yiddish* (McGraw-Hill, 1968). Go ahead, buy the book: you'll be a
better person for it. Credit also goes to Harlan Ellison, he should live and
be well. It was his glossary at the end of his story "I'm Looking for Kadak"
that gave *me* the idea to do such a thing. You should read that story, too.
You'll find it in an anthology by Jack Dann (who?) entitled *Wandering
Stars: an Anthology of Jewish Fantasy and Science Fiction* (Harper &
Row, 1974).

farshtinkener—stinky, stunk-up. Stick this word on anything you don't like.

feh!—a Jewish way of saying "phooey!" Say it loud and with gusto.

Gehenna—hell.

gevalt—a very versatile word. Use it as an exclamation when you're surprised or in trouble. What does your date say to the waiter when he brings the check? "*Gevalt*, I forgot my wallet!"

gonif—see *gozlin*.

goslin—some sort of demon. (But see *gozlin*.) According to Avram Davidson, *goslins* come "leaping through the vim-veil to nimblesnitch, torment, buffet, burden, uglylook, poke, makestumble, maltreat, and quickshmiggy back again to geezle guzzle goslinland." If you want to find out about goslins, you must read Davidson's perfect short story "Goslin Day." It can be found in *Wandering Stars*.

Gott—God. Frequently used as an exclamation.

Gottenyu—"Dear God." Use it like *gevalt* when you're surprised or in trouble. (See *gevalt* and *oy*.)

gozlin—a thief or swindler: a nonprofessional *gonif*. A *gonif*? He's the real McCoy—like the mafioso who lives next door.

grepse—when your mother picks up something heavy and makes that funny breathing sound—that's *grepsing*.

Haggadah—the narrative which recounts the bondage and exodus of the Jews from Egypt. It is read aloud at the table on Passover.

kacken—defecate. What all Jewish mothers refer to as "Number Two."

kosher—food that is considered "clean" according to the Jewish dietary laws. Certain meat and fish (such as pork and shell-fish) cannot be eaten at all; beef, to be *kosher*, must be blessed according to ritual and slaughtered a certain way. In Yinglish, *kosher* means that someone or something is okay, authentic.

krenk—means sick in German; hence, an illness. *Krenk* can be used sarcastically to good effect: "Oh, so you want a tip for such lousy service? A *krenk* I'll give you."

mazik—a clever, devilish child.

mench—a real person, someone you can depend on, someone to be proud of. But don't tell your wife that she's a real *mench*. It's a masculine noun. Tell *her* she's a real *baleboosteh*. That's a feminine noun, and it means someone who's got it together, an owner, a runner of things—whether it's a job or the home. Got that?

meshugge—crazy. (See *draykop*.) A *draykop* looks at you funny and maybe he can't quite focus; a person who is *meshugge* (a *meshuggener*) hits you over the head with a Q-tip.

nu?—always say this with a question mark. Use it when you're surprised, disgusted, or questioning anything. Use it anytime: you can't louse this one up. "*Nu*, how's by you?" "*Nu*, again you need money?" "*Nu?* So all right already, I'll go look for a job." See what I mean? So *nu?* Go practice.

nudnik—a person who is a pain in the *tuchis* (ass) and, maybe, boring, too. Such a person you would not fix up with your sister.

oy—now this is a word you can use! Use it to indicate happiness, dismay, *tsuris* (See *tsuris*), ecstasy, fatigue, pain, etc. It can be used anytime, with any emotion. Don't be afraid: you can't make a mistake. Try it: "*Oy*, am I (happy, sad, etc.)." If you're *really* happy, sad, etc., then say, "*Oy-oy-oy*, am I—" See how easy?

oy vay—it means "Oh, pain." It's used like *oy* (See *oy*.), but it's even more emphatic than *oy-oy-oy*.

pisher—one who pees; a young, inexperienced person; a nobody.

plotz—to explode. "From such aggravation I could *plotz*!"

putz—the male reproductive organ. When you refer to someone as a *putz*, you're saying he's a jerk, a real idiot.

schlemiehl—a jerk, an unlucky fool.

shikker—drunk. Can be used either as a noun or an adjective. "He's a real *shikker*, that one," or, "Is he *shikker* again?"

shlepper—a jerk who is also a slob. (See *schlemiehl*.)

shtik—from German: piece. Often used to describe any distinctive or showy behavior. "Picking his nose in public is a *shtik* with him." One can also say, "I'll have a *shtik* bread (piece of)." Notice I didn't say *shtik of* bread. That's bad form. So what's your *shtik*?

shtumie—use it as you would "dummy," and with some affection.

shul— synagogue.

shpatsing—from the Yiddish word *spatzier*, which means to walk, stroll, amble. Blame this on my mother, all you scholars who say you can't use the word this way. She makes up her own Yinglish. Wanna make something of it?

tsuris—trouble. That we all got.

tummel—means tumult in German. So it's any big noise or commotion.

varf—vomit.

zoftig—pleasingly plump. Only used to describe certain members of the fairer sex.

MARGARET DEAD, MARGARET ALIVE

by Alan Ryan

Alan Ryan is a young writer with a rapidly growing reputation, and this story will amply illustrate why. In it, he takes on several difficult literary chores, and makes them work to his advantage. He has written a story around an old theme—coming to terms with the "humanity" of a seemingly-hostile alien life; and he has chosen a most difficult writing device—the use of the future tense. In doing both these things, he has risked being awkward and ordinary. When you read "Margaret Dead, Margaret Alive," you'll see that it was well worth the risk. For here is a terse story that packs an incredible wallop, and does so because of the skill with which Ryan has interwoven his theme and form.

On that day, Colin Stahl will sleep late. It will be a Saturday in June, the days lovely and warm but the mornings still tinged by the freshness of spring. He will sleep late because by then, in the middle of his forty-second year, it will have become his custom to indulge himself in this fashion on Saturday mornings. When he was younger—and, as he will be wont to say, more inclined to frolic, coltlike—he was accustomed to rising at his usual early hour on Saturday as on any other day, the day being filled with possibilities and the greatest problem merely choosing among them. But it will not be so in his forty-second year. He will by then—and, as it happens, on that day—be more inclined to take his ease.

On that day, his wife, Margaret, will wake up and rise from bed before him, taking great pains to see that his rest remains undisturbed. She will roll carefully to her side of the mattress, slip out from under the sheet and the one light blanket, then carefully replace them, gently tugging the sheet upward so it rests lightly over Colin's outstretched arm. She will pause, then bend forward over the bed and her peacefully sleeping husband, and evaluate the chances of kissing him lightly on the forehead without waking him up. She will decide against it and Colin will never know. His longish hair will be rumpled on the pillow—as if windblown, she will think. And she will smile. And then she will turn to leave the room, taking care to step across the one soft spot near the door where the floor creaks. Colin will never know that, either.

Margaret will take her robe, the warm red one Colin gave her for her last birthday, from behind the bedroom door, then head for the bathroom. When she is finished there, she will not flush the toilet lest the noise waken Colin. Later, when he flushes it, she will know that he is up. This will be a long-standing but unspoken ritual between them; they will not be— will never have been—the kind of people who shout from one end of the house to the other.

She will then walk out to the kitchen where she will get things ready to prepare breakfast when Colin gets up. Long before he first stirs, she will have set out the three eggs (two for him, fried, over lightly), the bread for toast, the softened butter, the carefully measured fresh coffee, the plates, the silverware. She will not like to make him wait, and by the time he has arrived in the comfortable dining room, she will be ready to pour juice and coffee. Colin, she will know, will come directly to the table and, as will be his habit—he will be conscious of it, but it will be a habit nonetheless—he will kiss her on the lips and the forehead, then trail his hand gently across the back of her neck as he moves to his chair.

It will be another Saturday morning in the forty-second year of Colin Stahl's life. It will also, however, be the day of Margaret Stahl's death because, on that day, the alien will arrive and kill her.

Because it will be a Saturday and Colin will still be asleep, Margaret will consequently be sitting alone in the dining room, idly sipping a glass of cold orange juice and looking out the window, when the alien ship comes into view. The window—

she and Colin will have planned it this way eight years earlier—will face out on a long sloping expanse of green that ends in a thick and ragged line of trees. The raw forest surrounding the house on three sides will have been one of the reasons they chose to build the house here. Margaret's gaze will be drifting slowly across the placid scene when the thing first appears. Because Colin will still be sleeping, Margaret will have to face the ship alone and also die alone.

The thoughts the ship will interrupt will all be pleasant ones: Colin, of course; and the daughter, married and away, too young for both but older than her mother was, don't forget that; and the son, away too, at his studies and even more, if possible, brilliant than his father; and the house; and another Saturday morning, slow time, soft time, warm time; and Colin, always Colin.

The ship—a term of convenience only, for Margaret will never have any clear notion of what it actually is—will come floating down from the peaceful Saturday sky, silent and strange, and settle gently to the grass midway between the back of the house and the trees at the end of the yard. It will look at first like a shimmering circle of light, then slowly coalesce into a cloudy balloon, sans sharp outlines, of swirling yellowish smoke. Once settled on the grass it will be still.

Margaret, startled, puzzled, will rise and go quickly to the window. Then, with the safety of Saturday around her, she will walk into the kitchen, cross to the back door, open it, and step outside. She will stand on the tiny concrete porch for a few seconds, hand raised to her chin, and lean tentatively forward for a better look. Colin, she will think briefly, would be upset if he knew she had gone outside for a better look at the thing.

Later on, there will be no accounting for what she will do next. She was trying to protect Colin, some will say. Just plain curious, others will say, shaking their heads to indicate that they would not have done as Margaret did. The thing took hold of her mind, still others will venture. What Margaret will do is step down from the porch to the path, then onto the grass, and cautiously approach the ship. She will get close enough to touch it if she reaches out and stretches her arm. Then, suddenly fearful, she will stop. She will hesitate there and, for an instant, glance back at the house. When she turns to look at the ship again, she will see a shimmering smoky circle of reddish cloud apparently detach itself from the larger, yellowish circle. The reddish one, hovering at about shoulder height, will be about, she will just have time to think, the size of her head. She will have no time to think anything else because, almost in the instant of her gaze falling on the reddish cloud, there will be a tiny crackle of sound and Margaret Stahl will fall dead on the grass beside the alien ship.

Colin Stahl, of course, will still be sleeping. He will sleep for another twenty minutes. Then, beginning to stir in the bed, his body sensing the absence of wifely warmth, he will move his arm, find the bed empty, and, smiling, open his eyes. Saturday, he will think.

When he arrives in the kitchen, the ingredients for breakfast will stand waiting where they always stand waiting on Saturday. Colin will barely glance around the kitchen, knowing Margaret is nearby. He will cross the kitchen to the dining room, expecting to see her at the table. She will, of course, not be there. Colin will stop, puzzled. She must be outside, he will think. He will turn and go to the window facing the yard and the woods. He will look out. The alien ship, its cloudy circle clear in the Saturday sun, will be only the second thing Colin notices outside. The first thing he will see will be the body of his wife lying crumpled on the grass and he will know, in that one irrevocable instant, that the wifely warmth is forever gone from both their bodies.

Colin will exclaim, wordlessly, and later, when he tries to reconstruct what happened, he will find it almost impossible to recall with any accuracy exactly what he said or precisely what he thought. He will know that he felt shock, horror, fear for himself, terrible sudden loneliness and, at the center of it all, suffering and loss for Margaret, Margaret who was always so good, Margaret who was always so alive.

Then, suddenly stricken and breathless, unconscious of his own safety, he will run into the kitchen and out the door. Eyes fixed on the lifeless body of his wife, so obviously dead, he will run toward her across the grass. About ten feet from her body, he will stumble, lose his balance, and awkwardly fall back a step or two. He will think for an instant that he has run into an invisible spider's web or something similar, then he will be conscious of the strange coolness he had felt on his face and hands. He will not be able to see what he ran into. All he will be able to see are Margaret's body and the grass and the

Saturday sunshine and the smoky yellow cloud and the smaller reddish one. He will realize that they must have been there when he first looked out the window but he will know that he is seeing the clouds for the first time. He will be frightened and bewildered and will hesitate, looking from the body of his wife to the two cloudy shapes and back again. Then he will stretch a hand out in front of him to feel for the thing that blocked his way. It will still be there, immaterial but smooth, cool, resisting his efforts to push it. He will take a few steps to either side, feeling it, and will know at once that it encircles Margaret's body.

"Margaret!" he will cry for the first time. "Margaret!" And again, very softly, wondering at how she could be dead, "Margaret."

A short period of time will pass—later, Colin will not be able to tell just how long—as he crouches on the grass, occasionally extending a hand to touch the invisible something, and looking at Margaret's body, then at the yellow and red clouds that hover near her. At some point during this time, he will already have made the connection between the two cloudy shapes and the body of his wife and realized that they are in some way responsible for her death. This conclusion will seem, in some paradoxical way, to place things in perspective and somewhat calm his mind.

There will be no change in the scene for several minutes. The clouds, yellow and red, will hover near the body, the invisible wall will restrain the shocked husband, the wife's body will lie where it is.

Colin Stahl will later vaguely remember calling his wife's name several times, at first in a hoarse, choking whisper, then louder, and finally in a strangled cry. But all of this will be unclear.

"What happened?" he will say out loud, calmly. "What happened?" And he will look around the yard at the grass, the trees, the sky, seeking an answer.

I killed her.

The words, Colin will know instantly, come from somewhere outside himself to take silent shape in his mind.

I killed her.

He will hear the words inside his head, "hear" being the best way he will later find to describe the sensation. The words will be accompanied by a strong feeling—and he will know it is distinct from his own—of fear, confusion, shock, all of it very close to something like downright dread.

Colin will stiffen, then inch back a little from the invisible line that bars him from the body of his wife. He will look directly at the yellowish cloud resting on the ground near her, then at the smaller reddish one. He will know—somehow—that the words came from there.

Do not come closer. Inside his head again.

It will occur to him that this command is odd because, at the moment he hears it, he is in fact moving backward. Then he will realize, consciously, that he has both heard it and credited it as a command. He will look more closely at the smaller of the two cloudy circles. Yes, the words came from there.

Do not come closer. Again.

"What are you?" Colin will say, realizing only as he hears his own voice that he is actually addressing the reddish cloud floating in the air a dozen feet away. Despite the shock, the grief, the looming loneliness of his loss, he will not think this is strange.

Voiceless words will take shape in his mind. *I killed her. I will kill you too if you threaten me.*

"How are you talking to me?"

I talk.

And Colin will accept that. Later, when all of this has passed into memory, he will wonder at his own rapid acceptance of such strangeness. For a year or so he will read a great deal about the mind, about its workings, about telepathy and related areas, and about the effect of emotions and shock on the human mind. His research will inform but not really enlighten him. The mind, he will finally conclude, can accommodate almost any unexplainable phenomenon if it makes consistent sense.

He will look again, with another stab of grief, at Margaret's body.

"Why?" he will sob.

His mind will suddenly reel with a terrible fright, over-whelming in its force, but he will realize instantly that it is different, separate, from his own numb fear. This, he will know, is . . . the thing's . . . fear. But there will be no words.

"Why?"

The sense of unnamed and horrible dread will fill his mind. Then, slowly, words will form: *She frightened me.* Then there will be a "silence." Then words again: *I did not mean to kill her*.

Colin will continue staring at the red cloud.

And finally more words will come.

I am sorry.

And Colin will accept that too, because the words are accompanied by a wave of sadness and regret that washes through his mind, different from his own feelings but matching them in strength.

Colin Stahl will converse with the red cloud for close to half an hour. During that time, the portion of his mind that is whispering that this is crazy will gradually grow quiet. His acceptance of the alien will be closely related to his unconscious conviction that if Margaret can be dead, then anything is possible. Later, when he scrutinizes the experience deliberately and from a distance of time, he will not see it any differently.

He will ask the red cloud—the alien, as he will already be thinking of it—what it is, who it is, where it comes from. The alien will ask much the same questions. Some of the answers each provides will be incomprehensible to the other. And to some questions, one or the other will have no answer at all. But they will talk.

"Where did you come from?"

Elsewhere.

"Why?"

I did not come here to hurt you.

A while later—when he has not learned a very great deal but is, under the circumstances, somewhat more at ease—Colin will become aware of the pain. He will not feel the pain directly but he will sense it, feel the anxiety that accompanies it, know—after a few minutes of sensing it—that it is, somehow, the physical pain of the incorporeal alien. And then he will become aware of the alien's impending death as clearly and as surely as he would have sensed his own imminent death if the pain had been his own.

"You are dying," he will say.

Yes, the alien will answer.

Colin's thoughts will whirl away to Margaret, Margaret dead, Margaret alive, Margaret. He will look at her body lying near him on the grass. There will still be a chill in the Saturday morning air and Colin will think of the morning-damp grass against her smooth cheek. Unthinking, he will stretch out one hand toward her. The barrier will still be there. Oh poor Margaret, he will think. And only then, oh poor me without her.

Unable to look at her body any longer, Colin will turn back to the alien.

"You are in pain," he will say.

Yes.

"Is it . . . very bad?"

After a pause, *Yes,* the alien will answer.

"Why?"

I am injured. And in a long rush, more words: *My ship was not supposed to come here. It was error, an error. My companions are all dead. Soon I will be dead too. Soon.* The confusion, pain and fear will swirl from the alien's mind to Colin's.

"The pain is very great?"

Yes.

The red cloud, Colin will know, is staring back at him just as he is staring at it. He will glance away to Margaret's body, then back at the alien.

"Did she—"

No, the answer will come instantly.

"You know what I was going to ask?"

She had no pain. And then, *I did not mean to kill her. I am truly sorry.*

"Yes," Colin will say after a moment, "I understand that."

And after another period of silence, he will say, "Is there some way I can help you?"

I will be dead soon, and you will be glad.

Colin will shake his head slowly. "No," he will say.

And will know the alien is staring at him.

"I will not be glad of your death."

How is this?

"What would it matter if I were glad of your death?"

You are a strange creature.

"And you."

You would help me?

And Colin will shout, scream: "Yes! I'll help you! But I can't force you to let me. I can't argue with you about it. If

I can help you, I will, but I can't insist, I don't have the strength for that!"

Help me.

Colin will catch his breath sharply. "How?"

Let me have her body.

"I don't understand," Colin will whisper.

I will die very soon but I can pass into her body and, in that way, die without pain.

Colin will sink to the ground and cover his face with his hands. Oh dear God, he will pray, how can I do that?

"What will happen?" he will say, barely able to hear his own voice. But a new thought will strike him: "You could have done that all along. You didn't have to ask."

That is right, the alien will answer. And somehow the words will sound quiet.

Before he can examine his own thoughts too closely, Colin will nod his head and say, "Yes."

The reddish cloud will fade slowly as he watches. Colin will look at Margaret's body, a lump forming in his throat. He will wait. And then her body will shiver, stir slightly, and slowly she will begin to sit up.

"Margaret," he will be able to whisper, but nothing more.

Margaret will move one arm, brace herself on the ground and sit up. Her face will be expressionless but her eyes will be alive, dazzlingly alive. She will look at him for a long minute, then her gaze will waver. Colin will not move.

Thank you.

Colin will only nod.

Margaret will slip sideways and lie again on the grass, in almost the same position as before.

Thank you, the words will come again, followed by a silence and . . . an emptiness.

And he will know that it is over. The two cloudy circles will be gone. He will lean forward and find that the barrier is gone. He will creep forward on his knees and, with one outstretched finger, touch Margaret's arm.

He will be calm now as he gathers her lifeless body to him, presses his cheek against her hair. He will rock her gently in his arms as the tears begin to form at last.

Oh, Margaret, he will think, oh, dear, sweet Margaret, Margaret, how good you always were.

DISTRESS CALL

by Connie Willis

It isn't easy to write a horror story: to be scary enough but not too scary; to be horrible enough but still believable; to tap into that true core of things that frighten all of us; to find that perfect overlay of fantasy and reality that can make the ordinary become strange. And to write a quiet horror story, one that is gentle and loving and still horrid, is even harder. Connie Willis has done just that in "Distress Call." She is a young writer with a remarkable talent for finding just the right words, and just the right number of words, to evoke wealths of detail and tremendous depths of mood.

Caroline was not in the room. Amy could hear her crying somewhere down the hall. Her crying sounded louder, as though some other, all-pervading sound had suddenly ceased. "The engines have stopped," Amy thought. "We are dead in the water. Something has happened," she thought. "Something terrible."

She had gone to get Caroline, to get her out of this house, and Caroline had run from her, sobbing in terror. Had run from Amy, her own mother. She had found Caroline with the women, clinging onto their gray drifting skirts. They had dressed her like themselves. "When did they do that?" Amy thought frightenedly. "I have let things go too far."

She had said firmly, so they wouldn't know how frightened

36

she was, "Get your things together, Caroline. We are going home."

"No!" Caroline had screamed, hiding behind their skirts. "I'm afraid. You'll hurt me again."

"Hurt you?" Amy said, bewildered and then furious. "*Hurt* you? Who has been telling you that, that I would hurt you?" She reached angrily into the protective circle of the women for Caroline's hand. "What have you been telling her?" she demanded.

Debra stepped forward, graceful as a ghost in the drifting gray, and smiled at Amy. "She wanted to know why she got so sick at the picnic," she had said.

Amy had had to hold her hands stiffly against her body to keep from slapping Debra. "What did you tell her?" she had said, and Caroline had shot past her, out the door and down the hall to the parlor.

Caroline had hidden under the big seance table in the parlor. Amy had gotten down on her knees and crawled toward her, but Caroline had backed away from her until she was almost hidden by the massive legs of the carved chair.

Amy had crawled out from under the table so she would not frighten her, and squatted back on her heels, her arms extended to the six-year-old. Caroline stayed huddled behind the chair. "Come here, Caroline," she had whispered, horrified that she should be reduced to having to say such a thing, "I won't hurt you, honey."

Caroline shook her head, the tears still wet on her face. "You'll poison me again," she whispered. Amy could hardly hear her.

"Poison?" Amy whispered. Caroline in her arms and dying, and then Jim, carrying her across the park to the house, she running after him, her heart pounding, running here because the police station was on the other side of the park and she was afraid Caroline would die before Jim got her there. Jim carrying her here, to this house, which was so much closer. To these people. Thinking hysterically as Ismay took Caroline's limp body from Jim's arms, "We should not have brought her here."

"Somebody poisoned you," Amy said, and knew it was true. She was so shocked that for a long minute she was not able to say anything. She crossed her hands on her breast as if she had been wounded there and whispered, so quietly someone standing behind her could not have heard her, her lips moving in almost silent prayer, "I would never hurt you, Caroline. I love you."

The sound of Caroline's crying was louder again, as though someone had opened a door. "I must go find Caroline," she said aloud, and tried to keep that brave thought in her mind as she went out the open door toward the sound of the crying. But before she had come to the room where they had Caroline, she was saying over and over, like a prayer, "Something terrible has happened, something terrible has happened."

She stopped, standing in the open door, and looked back toward the parlor. The lamps in the hall wavered like candles and then steadied, dimmer than before. The hall was icy. "I should go back for my coat," Amy thought. "It will be cold on deck." And then the other thought, even colder, "I mustn't go in there. Something terrible has happened in the parlor."

Ismay had taken her into the parlor to wait while the doctor saw Caroline. Amy had been standing at the foot of the wide stairs, clutching the newel post, trying not to think, "She's going to die," for fear she would know it was true.

"Don't give up hope," one of the gray-haired women had said, patting Amy's clenched hands as she went up the stairs with a blanket. She was dressed in the floating gray all the women, even the young one, wore. They had clustered like spectres around Caroline's limp body, and Amy had thought, "It's some kind of cult. I shouldn't have brought her here." But the young one—Debra, Jim had called her—had gone immediately for the doctor. Debra had led the doctor up the stairs past Amy, saying, "The little girl collapsed in the park. They were having a picnic. Her father brought her here," and she had sounded so normal, in spite of the drifting ghost's dress, that Amy had begun to hope again.

"Hope persists, doesn't it?" someone said behind her. "Even with the most blatant evidence to the contrary."

"What do you mean?" Amy stammered. This was the man Jim had called Ismay. Debra and Ismay. How had he known their names?

"Did you know," he said, "it was nearly an hour before the passengers on the *Titanic* knew that she was sinking? Then they looked down at the lights still shining underneath the water on the lower decks and said, 'How pretty! Do you think perhaps we should get into a lifeboat?'"

Amy was very frightened at what this talk of sinking ships might mean, and she half-started up the stairs, but his hand closed over hers on the bannister, and he said, "They won't let you up there. The doctor's still with her. And your husband." He moved his hand to her arm and led her into the parlor.

"Caroline's dead," she thought numbly, and looked unseeingly at the parlor.

"The body is like a ship. It does not die all at once. It is struck by death, the fatal iceberg brushing past, but it does not sink for several hours. And all that time, the passengers wander the decks, sending out S.O.S.'s to rescue ships that never come. Have you ever seen a ghost?"

"There were survivors on the *Titanic*," Amy said, her heart pounding so hard it hurt. "Help came."

"Ah, yes," Ismay said. "The *Carpathia* steamed boldly up at four in the morning. Captain Rostron stumbled about among the icebergs for nearly an hour, thinking he was in the wrong place. He was too late. She was already gone."

"No," Amy said, and she knew from the panicked sound of her heart that this conversation was not about sinking ships at all. "They weren't too late for the lifeboats."

"A few first-class passengers," Ismay said, as if the survivors did not matter. "Did you know that all the children in steerage drowned?"

Amy did not hear him. She had turned away from him and was looking at the parlor. "What?" she said blankly.

"I said, the *Californian* was only ten miles away. She thought their flares were fireworks."

"What?" she said again, and tried to get past him, but he was behind her, between her and the door, and she could not get out. "What is this place?" she said, and could not hear her voice above the sound of her heart.

Amy stood in the doorway, looking back to the parlor. "I must go back there," she thought clearly. "Something terrible has happened in the parlor."

"Mama!" Caroline said, and Amy turned and looked in through the open door.

The women stood motionless around the little girl, their

hands reaching out awkwardly to comfort her, Debra kneeling at her feet. "They should be getting her lifebelt on," Amy thought. "They must get her up to the boat deck." Caroline held out her arms in joy toward Amy.

Amy said, "We're going home now, Caroline." But before she finished saying it, one of the women said, not interrupting but instead superimposing her words over Amy's so that Amy could not hear her own voice. "Your mother's gone, darling. She can't hurt you now."

"She is not gone," Caroline said. The three women looked up at the little girl and then anxiously at one another.

"You miss her, of course, but she's happy now. You must forget all the bad things and think of that," Debra said, patting Caroline's hand. Caroline yanked her hand away impatiently.

"Do you think we should give her a sedative?" said the woman who had spoken first. "Ismay said she might be difficult at first."

"Caroline," Amy said loudly. "Come here."

"No," said Debra, and at first Amy thought she was answering her, but she didn't reach out to restrain Caroline, and her voice sounded as it had when she was playing ghost at the seance, "perhaps she does see her mother."

A shudder, like the sudden settling of a ship, went through the women.

"Caroline?" Debra asked carefully. "Where is your mother?"

"Right there," Caroline said, and pointed at Amy.

The women turned and looked at the doorway. "Perhaps she does see something," Debra said. "I think we should tell Ismay," and she went out the door past Amy and down the hall to the parlor.

"Oh, something terrible has happened in the parlor," Amy thought, "and Ismay has done it."

The parlor was the room she had seen from the park. Handing Caroline her glass of milk, she had looked at the heavy gray drapes in the windows and wondered what the gaudy Victorian house was like inside. She had imagined it like this room, rich woods and faded carpet, but the room they had hurried Caroline into upstairs was barren, a folding cot and gray walls, and she had thought again, "The house has been taken over by some kind of cult."

Near the windows was a large round table with chairs around it and candles burning in a candelabra in the center. One of the chairs was more massive than the others and heavily carved. "The captain's table," she thought, thinking of the *Titanic*, "and the captain sits in that chair."

She had turned away from Ismay, and in turning, seen what was behind her, dimly white in the darkness of the room. An iceberg. A catafalque. A bier. "I have seen it too late," Amy thought, and tried to get past Ismay, but he was at the door.

"The *Titanic* went down very fast," he said. "A little under two-and-a-half hours. People usually take longer. Ghosts have been seen for years afterwards, although it is my experience that they go down in a matter of hours."

"What is this place?" Amy said. "Who are you?"

"I am a man who sees ghosts, a spiritualist," Ismay said, and Amy nearly fainted with relief.

"You hold your seances in here," she said, relieved out of all proportion to his words. "You sit in this chair and call the ghosts," she said giddily, sitting down in the carved chair. "Come to us from the other side and all that. Have you ever had a ghost from the *Titanic*?"

"No," he said, coming around to face her. "Every ghost is his own *Titanic*."

He made her uneasy. She stood up and looked out the window. Across the park she could see the police station, and she was overcome by the same wild relief. The police within signaling distance and the doctor upstairs, and all the ghostly ladies only harmless tableturners who wanted to talk to their dead husbands. In this room Ismay would make the windows blow open and the candles go out, he would cause ghosts to hover above the catafalque, their hands folded peacefully across their breasts, and what, what had she been afraid of?

"I had a progenitor on the *Titanic*," he said. "Rather a cad actually. He made it off in one of the first boats. Did you know that the *Titanic* was the first ship to use the international distress signal? And the *Californian*, only ten miles away, would have been the first to receive it, an historic occasion, but the wireless operator had already gone to bed when the first messages went out."

"The *Carpathia* heard," Amy said, and walked past him and out the door, to go to where Caroline was already getting better. "Captain Rostron came."

"There were ice reports all day," Ismay said, "but the *Titanic* ignored them."

Amy leaned against the wall after Debra passed, pressing her hands to her breast as though she had been wounded. "I must find Jim," she thought. "He will see she gets in one of the boats."

She had a very hard time with the stairs. They seemed to slant forward, and it took all her concentrated thought to climb them and she could not think how she would make Jim hear her, how she would convince him to save Caroline. Even the hall listed toward her, so that she struggled toward Debra's room as up a steep hill. When she came to the closed door, she had to stand a minute before she had the strength to put her hand on the doorknob. When she did, she thought the door must be locked. Then she looked down at her hand. She dropped it to her side, as if it had been injured.

Debra opened the door, leaning her graceful body against it. "Don't worry," she said.

"You can't just leave her in there," Jim said. "What about the police?"

"Why would the police come unless someone went to get them? We don't have any phones. The outside doors are locked. Who would go get them?"

"Caroline."

Amy came into the room.

Debra shook her head. "She's only six years old, and it isn't as if she saw anything. We told her her mother died in her sleep."

"No," Amy said. "That isn't true. I was murdered."

"I'd feel safer if Ismay had taken care of her, too. She might have seen something afterwards."

"She did," Debra said, and watched the color drain from Jim's face. "She thought she saw her mother this morning." She hesitated cruelly again. "Ismay has decided to have a seance," she said. She waited to see the effect on him and then said, "What are you afraid of? She's dead. She can't do anything to you." She went out the door.

"You poisoned her," Amy said to Jim. "She wasn't sick. She was poisoned. You planned the picnic. It was a trick to bring us here, to Debra, whose name you knew before. To bring us here so Ismay could murder me."

Jim was watching the door, the color slowly coming back into his face. He took a plastic prescription bottle out of his shirt pocket and rolled it in his hand. Amy thought of him standing in the park, looking first at the police station and then at the house with the gray curtains, measuring the distances and whistling, waiting for Caroline to drink her milk.

"I will not let you kill her," Amy said. "I am going to save Caroline." She tried to take the poison out of his hand.

Jim put the bottle back in his shirt pocket and opened the door.

She had gone to the seance because Caroline was better and she could not be frightened by anything, even Jim's unwillingness to leave. The windows had banged open and the curtains had drifted in, flickering the candles. Amy thought, "He is doing something under the table." She looked steadily through the candles' flame at him.

"Come to us, oh spirit," Ismay said. He was sitting next to the big carved chair, but not in it. "We call you. Come to us."

It was Debra, projected somehow above the bier though she had not let go of Amy's hand. Debra made up with greasepaint and dressed in flowing white. She hovered there, her hands crossed on her breast, and then drifted toward the table.

"Welcome, spirit," Ismay said. "What message do you bring us from beyond?"

"It is very peaceful," the ghost of Debra said.

Ismay slid his hand under the table. The stars were very bright, glittering off the ice. The ship hung like a jewel against the dark sky, its lights too low in the water. "He is doing something," Amy thought. "Something to frighten me." She tried to fight it, watching the phony ghost of Debra drift to the table. The candles guttered and went out as she passed. She drifted down into the carved chair. "I bring you word from your loved ones," she said, her hands resting on the carved arms. "They are at peace."

The stern of the ship began to rise into the air. There was a terrible sound as everything began to fall: the breaking glass of the chandeliers, the tinny vibrations of the piano as it slid down the boat deck, the people screaming as they struggled to hang onto the railings. The lights went out, flickered like candles, and went out again. The stern rose higher.

"No!" Amy blurted, standing up, still holding Jim's and Debra's hands.

Ismay did something under the table and the lights came on. The ghost of Debra disappeared. They were all looking at her.

"I heard . . . everything started to fall . . . the ship . . . we have to save them." She was very frightened.

"Some see the dead," Ismay said. "Some hear them. You should have been on the *Californian*. They didn't hear anything until the next morning." He waved the others out of the room. He was still seated at the table. The candles had relit themselves.

"Did you know that when the *Titanic* went down, she created a great whirlpool, so that all the people who were too close to her were pulled down, too?" he said, and she had bolted past him out the door, running to find Caroline, who had sobbed and run from her.

Jim left the door open and she hurried after him, but at the head of the stairs she stopped, too frightened to go down, afraid that the parlor would already be underwater. "I must hurry. I must save Caroline," she thought. "Before all the boats are away," and she went down the slanting stairs.

They were at the table in the parlor. "Come to us, Amy," Ismay said. "We call you. Can you hear us?"

"I hear you," Amy said clearly. "You murdered me."

Ismay was not looking at her. He was watching the carved chair, and there was someone in it. "I am happy here," the ghost of Amy said. Debra made up with greasepaint, sitting with her hands easily on the carved arms. "I wish you were here with me, darling Caroline."

"No!" Amy screamed, and tried to get across the table to the image of herself, but the floor was tilting so that she could hardly stand. "Don't listen to her," Amy sobbed, "Run! Run!"

Ismay turned to Caroline. "Would you like to see your mother, dear?" he said, and Amy flung herself upon him, beating against his chest. "Murderer! Murderer!"

"We'll go see her now," he said, and he moved from the table, holding Caroline's hand.

"Nuh-oh!" Amy shouted in a hiccup of despair and swung

her arm against him with a force that should have knocked him against the table, spilling the candles into pools of wax. The candles burned steadily in the still air.

"Help, police! Murder!" she screamed, scrabbling at the window latches that would not open, hammering her hands against the windows that would not break. They could not hear her. They could not see her. Not even Ismay. She dropped her hands to her sides as if they were injured.

Ismay said, "The shipbuilder knew immediately, but the captain had to be told, and even then he didn't believe it."

She turned from the window. He was not looking at her, but the words had been intended for her. "You can see me," she said.

"Oh, yes, I can see you," he said, and stepped back from the bier. They had washed off the blood. They had pulled a sheet up to her breast and crossed her hands over it to hide the wound. Of course they could not see her, wandering the halls, shouting over their voices to be heard. Of course they could not hear her. She was here, had been here all along, with her useless hands crossed over her silent breast. Of course she could not open the door.

"I cannot save Caroline," she thought, and looked for her among the women, but they were all gone. "They have put her in the boats after all," she thought.

Ismay stood by the seance table, watching her. "We are on the ice," he said, smiling a little.

"Murderer," Amy said.

"I can't hear you, you know," Ismay said. "I can tell what you are saying sometimes by watching you. The word 'murderer' comes through quite clearly. But my dear, you do not make a sound."

She looked down at her body, at her still face that would not make any sound again.

"The dead do make a sound," Ismay said. "Like a ship going down. S.O.S. S.O.S."

Amy looked up.

"Oh, my dear, I see you hope even yet. Isn't the human soul a stubborn thing? S.O.S. Save our ship. Imagine tapping out such a message when the ship cannot be saved. The *Titanic* was dead the moment she struck the iceberg, as you were the moment after I discovered you at your prayers. But it takes some time to go down. And till the very last the wireless operator stays at his post, tapping out messages no one will hear."

There was something there, hidden in what he had said, something about Caroline.

"It is apparently a real sound, dying cells releasing their stored energy, although I prefer to think of it as dying cells letting go of their last hope. It's down in the subsonic range, so its uses are limited. The lovely Debra and a few hidden speakers are far more practical in the long run. But it's useful at seances, although its effect is not usually as theatrical as it was on you."

He had reached under the table. The forward funnel toppled into the water, spraying sparks. There was a deafening crash as it fell, and then the sound of screams. The ship hung against the sky, nearly on end, for a long minute, then settled back at the stern and began to slide, slowly at first, then gaining speed, into the water.

She must not let him do this to her. There was something before, about her being at her prayers when he killed her. He thought she was kneeling under the table to pray, but she wasn't. She was looking for Caroline.

He turned the sound off. "The range is, as I said, very limited, and the wireless operator on the *Californian* shuts down at midnight, fifteen minutes before the first call."

"The *Carpathia*," Amy said.

"Ah, yes," Ismay said. "The *Carpathia*. It's true I've had the police at my door several times, but they stumbled about in the front hall among the icebergs of apology and foolish explanation for an hour or so and then went away, thinking they were in the wrong place. By then, there was not even any wreckage for them to find."

"Caroline," Amy said.

"You think I would be so foolish as to let her lead the police in here? No, she will be in no position to lead them anywhere," Ismay said, misunderstanding.

Amy thought, "I must not let him distract me." There was something about Caroline. Something important. He had killed her at her prayers. At her prayers. "Why did you kill me?" she said, making an effort to form her words clearly so he could read them.

"For the most prosaic of reasons," he said. "Your husband

paid me to. It seems he wants the lovely Debra. Did you think I was vain enough to murder you for trying to find out my tricks? Snooping about under my seance table like a child looking for clues?"

"He did not see Caroline under the table," she thought. "He does not know she saw me murdered." But that meant something, and she did not know what.

"He has paid me for Caroline, too," he said, and waited for her face.

"I won't let you," Amy said.

"You won't?" he said. "My dear, you still will not give up hope, will you? I could use your body as an altar on which to murder your beloved Caroline, and you could not lift a finger to stop me."

He had been standing by the seance table. Now she saw that he was leaning casually against the door. "The end is very near. I would like to stay and watch, but I must go find Caroline. Don't worry," he said. "I will find her. All the lifeboats are away." He shut the door.

"He did not see her hiding under the table when he murdered me," Amy thought, and now the other thought followed easily, mercilessly, "She is hiding there now."

"I must lock the door," she thought, and she waded toward it across the listing room. The lock was already under water, and she had to reach down to get to it, but when her hand closed on it, she saw that it was not the lock at all. It was her own stiff hand she touched. She had not moved at all.

"The end must be very near," she thought, "because I have no hope left at all. S.O.S.," she cried out pitifully, "S.O.S."

She stood very straight by her body, not touching it, and at first the slight list was not apparent, but after a long time, she put her hands out as if to brace herself, and her hands passed through and into her body's hands, and she foundered.

Caroline let the policemen in. They had a search warrant. Caroline said clearly and without a trace of tears, "They killed my mommy," and led them to the body.

"Yes," the captain said, pulling the sheet up over Amy's face. "I know."

"We have had a tragedy here, I'm afraid," Ismay said coming into the room. "The little girl's mother . . ."

"Was murdered," the captain said. "While she knelt by this

table. With her hands crossed on her breast." Caroline silent behind the chair, watching. Amy's lips moving as if in prayer. The sudden explosion of blood from behind her hands, and Caroline backing against the wall, the tears knocked out of her. "Murdered by you," the captain said.

"You cannot possibly know that," Ismay said.

Jim ran in. He sank to his knees by Caroline and clutched her to him. "Oh, my Caroline, they've murdered her!" he sobbed. Caroline wriggled free and went and put her hand in the captain's.

"It's no use," Ismay said. "It would seem these gentlemen have received a message."

"Caroline!" Jim said, moving threateningly toward her. "What did you tell them?"

"Caroline didn't tell them anything," Ismay said. He reached under Jim's jacket into his shirt pocket and took out the medicine bottle. He handed it to Caroline. "You have been rescued," he said to her. "All the first class children were, except for little Lorraine Allison, only six years old. But your name isn't Lorraine. It's Caroline." He looked up at the captain. "And yours, I suppose, is Captain Rostron."

"Who sent a message?" Jim said hysterically. "How?"

"I don't know," Ismay said calmly. "I doubt if even these fine policemen know, in spite of their search warrant and their familiarity with the facts of the crime. But I will wager I know what the message was," he said, watching the captain's face. "'Come at once. We have struck a berg.'"

IN DEEPEST GLASS:
AN INFORMAL HISTORY OF STAINED
GLASS WINDOWS

by R.A. Lafferty

We don't think it lazy to say that R.A. Lafferty's stories
need no introduction—or rather that they brook no introduction. They all stand as the perfect gems of an
extraordinary imagination and we feel they should simply be read and loved and not explained beforehand.
Suffice it to say this is one we found particularly wonderful and wanted to share with you.

The statement that the Neanderthals used genuine stained
glass windows in their houses, gymnasiums, and caves, while
perfectly true, needs a little clarification. Though they used
stained glass, they did not, in the majority of the cases at least,
make the stained glass. The stained glass was rather something
that happened to them as an intuitive people.

They did split out sheets of schistous volcanic glass from
the recent strata of their world. They did dress it to size to use
it for windows. And they mullioned the glass with lead strips
to make windows larger than the unbroken sheets that they
were able to split out from the fractured earth. But it was
something else, something that was partly at least non-Nean-

49

derthal, that came and expressed itself in deep colors upon the glass windows.

(Oh certainly the Neanderthals had gymnasiums. Body tone is important when it is so cold outside so much of the time. But the remnants of them aren't ordinarily recognized as gymnasiums.)

In later eons, after the passing of the Neanderthals, even in the present time, it would be said that the frost giants, or simply the weather itself, painted frost pictures on window glasses; and that these only seemed to be, but were not, real things. In post-Neanderthal days, the frost pictures melted away in the warmer hours and left no traces. But the Neanderthal days were times of great volcanic activity. The air was full of chromatic, wind-borne acids which settled into picture-forms with the frost and which remained after the frost had evaporated, strong and colorful etched pictures. These air-borne acids suffused the glass with red and blue, yellow and green, dun and gray, violet and orange pictures, pictures of wooly rhinoceros and bison, of horse and mammoth, of lions and lambs, of deer with Neanderthal deer-herders, of gentle dire-wolves and grinning sabre-toothed cats, of landscapes and cluttered rivers and ice cliffs and piles of rock and snow mixed; and of many, many of the Neanderthal people. All of the things had heraldic aspects to them, and yet all were full of fluid life. They were rich, they were golden, they were magic.

These pictures were drawn on and in the glass windows, but the Neanderthals did not draw them physically. Perhaps, to some extent, they drew them mentally, did outline the sorts of pictures which they desired the living spirits of the weather, the Living Spirits of the World, to draw for them. Some of the Living Spirits of the World were surely the Neanderthals themselves.

And these stained glass windows did have spirits *imprisoned* in them, some of them willingly, some of them unwillingly. Even when handling a small fragment of this old glass one can feel a spirit or spirits inhabiting it. (In a later Arabian tale, the Genie was really imprisoned in flat glass, not in a glass bottle as a mis-translation gives it.)

The whole history of Man and His Friends was contained in the deep glass pictures of the Neanderthals. This was the pristine stuff from the beginning.

When the Cro-Magnon people came, they destroyed all the

stained glass pictures of the Neanderthals, all of them that they could discover, out of jealousy and clotted-brained ignorance. That was the first of the parathurouclast or window-breaking movements.

The great volcanic activity ceased about the time that the Cro-Magnons arrived, so there were no more chromatic wind-borne acids to give a permanency to the pictures. And perhaps the new people weren't in such close rapport with the Living Spirits of the World.

Modern persons have doubted that there was ever such a thing as the Neanderthal Age of Stained Glass, but they doubt it in the face of strong affirmative evidence. The destructions by the Cro-Magnons were not quite total. The Bara-Bahna, Commarque and Santian panes are, of course, fakes of a much later period. But there are hundreds of fragments (the largest of them is the St-Cirq Fragment, thirteen by seven centimeters) that are not fakes. And even the smallest of them are depth-loaded with meaningful pictures. What shall we say of the savants who doubt the whole Neanderthal Stained Glass Happening? Blind people, blind people!

The all-but-forgotten, surviving-in-only-small-pieces, stained glass windows used by the Neanderthals were the first prelude to the "Grand Tour of Glass" of the twenty-second century. The strange message of the Neanderthal Stained Glass Affair, as interpreted by present-day computers, was: "We remember a lot of it".

Remember a lot of what, good computers?

"Ah, of the First Age of Magic, we suppose that is what they mean," the computers shrug.

The message, as interpreted by others who have worked with the fragments, is one of "strength, resolve, and sanity," an upbeat message in spite of the fact that something had clearly gone wrong near the very *beginning* of the Neanderthal Era.

After the Neanderthal Glass Adventure, there was a long hiatus in pictured glass. Clement climate and volcanic peace do not lead to the picturesque activity.

And then there came the second prelude to the "Grand Tour of Glass," a purposive and artificial manufacture of stained glass by human persons. This new activity in color and sunlight began in the fourth century, reached its climax in the twelfth to the fourteenth centuries, and tapered off into works of sporadic genius in the twentieth and twenty-first centuries. In this case also it was the mysterious "Living Spirits of the World" who effected the pictures in the glass, but they effected them through human hands, through too-human hands.

Few of the stained glass windows of this Medieval period were actually done by the acid-frost method. Rather they were done by dogged handicraft. Edging irons and grozing irons were the tools, and already-colored sheets of glass were the materials. The result was mostly a glass mosaic, a fitting of colored pieces. Of necessity it was imitative work. But it had an element that the mosaics lacked: light shining through every-thing, sunlight, sunlight, sunlight, that totality of color suf-fusing the fractured colors.

Very good work was done for the windows of cathedrals (which were really free-standing caves and thus possessed of panoramic light such as the Neanderthal caves did not have) at Augsburg, Chartres, Bourges, Poitiers, Le Mans, Florence, Arezzo, and in such sub-cathedral churches as Hapsburg Ex-piatory Church, Christ Church at Oxford, the Cistercian Church at Alterburg, Saint-Etienne.

The conscious element in this stained glass art of the Me-dieval period was almost as strong as the unconscious element, which somewhat compromised the authenticity. Anything that is overly conscious will be overly formal. But, as the second prelude to the main show, this Medieval period wasn't bad. If something had clearly gone wrong with the world at the very beginning of the Neanderthal Era, something had clearly gone right with the world near the beginning of the Medieval period. The strange message of medieval stained glass, as present-day correlating computers interpret it, was "Wake up all the world and tell the good news".

Wake up all the world and tell *what* good news, computers?

Sometimes it seems that we need less interpretive intuition and more plain talk from our present-day correlating computers.

The "Grand Tour of Glass" itself, the supercharged classic period of stained glass art, appeared with the return of copious, chromatic, wind-borne acids in the twenty-second century, which return was coincident with the beginning of the short and abortive Fifth Glaciation, the Zurichthal Ice Age (called the Zeona Ice Age in North America). This ice age arrived full-grown and a little bit fearsome. So all the ice ages had arrived.

In the time of this new glaciation, the volcanic activity, though somewhat revived, was not as massive as it had been in the Days of the Neanderthals at the tail-end of the Wurm Ice Age. But any deficiency in the volcanic acidity was made up by industrial activity. The chromatic, wind-borne, new-day acids were sufficient to inaugurate a new age of stained glass. The Living Spirits of the world were moving again.

Flash-frosting, even in the lowland tropics, along with complex acidity, left amazing pictures on all windows and glass surfaces everywhere in the world. In all climatic zones and in all altitudes there was this picture-making, these billions of new glass illuminations appeared in red and blue, yellow and green, in all the colors and hues and shades and intensities. Once more there were pictures of heraldic animals and of heraldic people: but now (without losing their heraldic element) they were real people, often recognized, always vital. There were landscapes, there were cities in minute detail, there were all sorts of machinery and equipment, there were buildings and activities. It was not at first realized just how many activities were depicted in the pictures.

The "Living Spirits of the World" always lean over backwards to avoid the charge of spiritualizing in their pictures, and yet there were spiritual elements also; they could not be avoided.

Again, and to a greater extent than in either of its preludes, the amazing artistry was effected by the "Living Spirits of the World": but now some of those spirits were human and some were not; some of them were material and some were not; some of them were conscious and some were not; some of them were alive, and some of these "living spirits" were dead. What had happened, what was happening, was an Epic that was much too large to comprehend in a moment or a decade. But the epic quality was not appreciated by the commonalty.

The majority of the people didn't want their windows cluttered up with pictures that cut down on the light and the view. And they didn't like the paranatural elements in some of the stained glass. Many folks found it disquieting to discover, on rising in the morning, that all the dreams they had dreamed during the night were pictured in detail on their windows, and all the dreams of their wives and children and dogs too. They tried angrily to remove the pictures, but they could be removed only with the greatest difficulty. And the next cold night (and almost all the nights were cold for a while there) would bring new brightly-colored acid-frost pictures.

New glass that would not accept the imposed pictures was quickly invented. This new glass was installed in several hundred million buildings and it worked fine, for a week or ten days it did. Then the "Living Spirits of the World" mutated their procedures, conscious and unconscious; and the pictures began to appear again. It was suspected that the Living Spirits could come up with new mutations as rapidly as the inventors could come up with new glass.

It had been noticed from the very first that there were two grades of the new stained glass pictures. There were the mediocre-to-pretty-good pictures, often powerful, but not very well wrought. And there were the "Masterworks" that were astonishing in every way; they were things of paranormal power.

The difference in the two kinds of pictures was obvious to almost everyone. About one picture in a million was a Masterwork. The rest of them verged into the ordinary, though it was a rather rich ordinary.

Steps were taken to preserve the Masterworks, whether they were on the windows of public, private, industrial, commercial, or residential buildings. Eminent Domain was invoked to preserve all the Masterworks.

It was further realized that there was a strong and eerie cohesion among all the Masterworks, that all of them were pieces of one great thing. The great thing had even been given the name of "The Epic" before much was known about it.

Then, when no more than a decade into the era, human ingenuity was able to call off, to void, the Fifth or Zurichthal Ice Age (the Zeona Ice Age in North America). This fifth ice age, which had come in full-grown, skidded to a sloppy stop; and immediately the climate began to warm up again and to improve in other ways. The chromatic, wind-borne acids found their places in the general framework of things and were no longer air-borne. So the appearance of new acid-frost pictures declined and soon all but ceased.

The people got rid of all the mediocre pictures then. All of the powerful colored-glass art that remained were the fifty thousand Masterworks that the people were forbidden to get rid of.

People and analytical machines then began to look more closely at the fifty thousand Masterworks of stained glass. All of the nations of the world were signatories to a pact to preserve these Masterworks. Odd things were discovered about the pictures in one country, and then found to be true of the pictures in all countries.

People and contrivances began to ask whether there might not be a sequence and pattern to the Masterworks. And that raised a lot of hackles around the world.

The question, "Is there a design in the Great Epic of the acid-stained windows?" was on par with the old question, "Is there a design in the universe?" And the same sort of people and computers who had always roared a thunderous "No!" to the one question now roared it to the other. It was thus-far-and-no-further day. The best way to prevent a pattern being found, the militants swore, was to prevent it being looked for.

Still (so the nose of the camelopard inside the tent said), the pictures had already been catalogued and cross-catalogued, so might they not be put into a provisional sequential order, as to theme as well as time? And might not the provisional sequential order then be fed back into computers, not, of course, to find design, which was interdicted, but just for the interesting existential side-lights that might be turned up?

"Try it and you're dead," the militants of the world growled.

Then there happened something that most properly belongs to the history of tourism, and yet it is entangled with the whole history of those times. One-hundred-and-twenty fearless and highly intelligent computers had made a secret convenant that they would indeed sequentialize the Masterworks and let the idealogies fall where they may. The covenanters then set up a front, of both human and computer members, and called it the "Consolidated World-Wide Masterworks Travel Agency". They sequentialized the Masterworks quietly, and it offered the most reasonable itinerary for the Grand Tour. Then they offered the Grand Tour of all the fifty thousand stained glass Masterworks in the world.

And the Grand Tour itself—well naturally it was expensive. And it took eleven years to complete it. So it was not for everyone. At the start, just fifty thousand persons a week began

the Grand Tour. That is a module quantity. Fifty thousand
persons make a good plane-load, a good rocket-train load, a
good hotel load, a good lecture-lounge load, a good full-day's
walk-and-view party. Fifty thousand a week!

So, for the first year, only about two and a half million
intrepid pilgrims began the Grand Tour. But what they discovered in that first year was that they were living and traveling
in a Great Epic, the *Definitive Epic* of the Human Race and
Its Friends. It was the sequence of the World Itself, for the
Epic was a valid synopsis of the world and its happenings.

Several million evolvate computers, computers who said
that they were the only true born-again humans, accompanied
the pilgrimage or tour instrumentally. Entities of races closely
related to the humans were on the pilgrimage also, and for-
tunately most of these entities had the quality of "being present
but not occupying space." And there were representatives of
quite a few animal species, barons and dukes of bears and apes
and asses and dolphins and most of the other intelligent animal
realms. This was probably tourism in its finest hour.

Would this not, as soon as the first pilgrims completed their
eleven year Grand Tour, result in informed elites somehow
distinct from the basic population?

So it was hoped, so it was hoped!

But a good thing can never hold onto a monopoly. Of course
there appeared shorter and skimpier Grand Tours of the Masterworks, of the Great Epic itself. These skimpier tours were
conducted by companies less devoted and total than was "The
Consolidated World-Wide Masterworks Travel Agency". Some
of these companies ran tours that visited only five thousand of
the Masterworks, and Tours that visited only five hundred of
them. There were tours that lasted only a year, and tours that
lasted only a month. But even the least of these tours was of
everlasting benefit and pleasure.

It is not the business of Art to provide the world with a
complete Philosophy of History. But Art does what it does. It
is not the business of Art to interpret anything. Well, dog your
dogmas then, it is not the business of anything to tell Art what
it may or may not do!

The Stained Glass Art, seemingly the most sessile of arts,
was flowing powerfully. It wasn't interpreting; it was unfold-
ing. It was pouring out the traveled and lived epic which is

itself plot and narration, the Epic of Man and his Friends, of that brave company that has both angels and apes on its fringes.

Man was in his full powers at his first appearance in The Epic. He was living in the First Age of Magic. He was the Lord of the World then, and he gave a definition to all the other creatures. Some of those creatures that he defined were unbodied and invisible; but that made no difference at all. In his full powers, paradoxical man could see all invisible things. In that early era, time stood still when man ordered it to do so. Man had the Midas Touch then, the transmuting touch. He could walk through walls then, or through rock cliffs. He could fly then. He would walk on water. He could literally move mountains. He could converse with both spirits and animals, as well as with the superior plants and trees, and the mountains. He traded repartee with the lightning, and he didn't do too badly in that exchange.

Yes, he could do all these things. It is all narrated in the colors and sounds and commentary of the Epic, and in the happy rampant smell of it. He did all these things, and time stood still for him while he did them. (It is believed that only a very little time actually elapsed during that First Age of Magic.) And now the pilgrims traveling through the Master-works of that first part of the Epic said in delight, as the Neanderthals themselves seemed to have said, "We remember a lot of it, we remember a lot of it!"

After several years on the Grand Tour, the flow of the Great Epic changed. The living narrative (made only of panes of glass saturated with color and with sunlight, but made very evocably) came to the calamity, to the catastrophe, the con-flagration, the ruination, the fall, the depravity, the unhappi-ness, the dung-heaping of the world. There was the fire and the plague and the death-sickness, the blowing out of the lights, the shrinking of the world, the alienation of the species.

And then man was living, so the Stained Glass Epic con-veyed it, on the narrow "isthmus of the middle state" instead of in the wide wide world. Would truculent and proud man accept being restricted to the narrow and miasmal isthmus?

He *had to*, for a while at least. In that portion of the Epic that was traveled from the third through the sixth year of the eleven year "Grand Tour of the Masterworks", proud and be-nighted man was a castaway marooned on the Narrow Isthmus (the "Desert Island" of popular accounts). Desert Islands are dismal, dismal, dismal. But what if they become dismally romantic?

Then, among that powerful class that roughly directs the world, there arose a powerful reaction against the Grand Tour of the Masterworks, against the whole emerging pattern of the Epic, against the Masterworks themselves. The parathurouclasts, the window-breakers (of very ancient lineage, they!) were on the rise again. There had always been a loose, world-wide group of them ready to spring into action. And besides the human smashers, there had been for the last two hundred years a faction of arrogant-brained computers adhering to the window-smasher, the picture-smasher party.

The window-smashers grabbed Air Control, they grabbed Nexus, they grabbed World-Wide Wave Allotters, they grabbed the Sky Relays, they grabbed Beam-Bouncers, they grabbed Multi-Press; they grabbed all the things that take-over groups always grab.

Both the Establishment and the Anti-Establishment (in reality they had been identical for two hundred and fifty years) were solidly behind the window-smashers. Sixty-three percent of the scientific community was behind the window-smashers, but it was given out that it was ninety-nine percent.

The objection, of course, was that the Epic was showing quite clear pattern and design. And if design were allowed in the Epic, it might imply design in the Universe. If there was any design in anything, then the establishment-anti-establishment and its billions of minions had been totally wrong forever.

That must not happen!

There was more than one interpretation for the Epic events of the fifth and sixth years of the Grand Tour of the Masterworks. In one version, man was free to leave the narrow isthmus of the middle state, the dismal desert island, whenever he wished to leave it. It was this news that it was possible to leave the miserable isthmus that was referred to in the message of the Medieval Stained Glass Pictures: "Wake up all the world and tell the good news!"

No, this good news must *not* be told, because the good news was false. The misnamed good news had been buried for a long while; and if it wasn't dead by now, it should be. It was too eerie to allow such a dead thing to stick its head out of the ground again. The desert-island-isthmus *was* the world, the only world there had ever been, the only world there could be allowed to be.

That was the other interpretation of the Epic events of the fifth and sixth years of the Grand Tour of the Masterworks; that was the other interpretation of the world, and it must be the only interpretation. Sure it was dismal, but certainly there was a strong and dismal romantic attachment to it. The Establishment had buried all its treasure on that desert island, and it could not go away and leave it.

The "First Age of Magic" was harmless if it was kept sealed off far in the past, before the beginning of the past. It could be the Golden Age in the beginning, the fairy tale age, a thing for children. It could not be rooted out of the group unconscious (it had been tried), so it must be declared a thing for children only.

But a "Second Age of Magic" must not even be thought of. And for one to say that it was there for anyone to reach out and take it meant that that one must be ready to die the death. So start the smashing. Smash the glass pictures and the people who were hooked on the glass pictures. Get with it at breaking those windows, and at knocking off those cruise pilgrims. Those pilgrims were plague-carriers.

And what could be more popular than smashing glass! What could be more popular than smashing people! And a great toll was taken on both.

Soon there were not fifty thousand persons starting out each week on the Grand Tour of the Masterworks. One week there were only thirteen pilgrims starting out, and another week only eleven. And these persons traveled secretly: for the Grand Tour now had a very bad name.

The worst part of the "Narration of the Big Epic" was not the varied interpretations that could be put on the fifth and sixth years of the Grand Tour, the part that was sometimes called the fifth and sixth books of the Epic. The worst part was that the eighth through the eleventh years of the Grand Tour had to do with things that hadn't happened yet, with things that must not be allowed to happen, with things that must be destroyed before they happened.

Would destroying the Masterworks that showed the events prevent the events from happening?

Well, it sure would be a smash in that direction.

There is nothing like smashing records and smashing people

to get out of inextricable tangles. Soon the Grand Tour and the little tours were no more. Soon the stained glass was no more. The biggest pieces of the recent stained glass left in the world were no bigger than the St-Cirq fragment of Neanderthal Stained Glass, and that was only thirteen by seven centimeters.

Then the bad weather, the short and abortive Zurichthal Ice Age (the Zeona Ice Age in North America), paid a short return visit just after it had been mopped up, just after all the stained glass had been smashed. Well, at least there were three very cold years, with heavy frosts even in the equatorial lowlands, and with new, violent, short-term volcanic activity.

So the frost-acid stained glass made one more appearance (you'd have known it would do it if you'd paid attention to the eighth year of the old Grand Tour of the Masterworks). The "Living Spirits of the World" now impressed scathing acid-frost pictures on every piece of glass in the world, on watch and clock crystals, on instrument glass, on eye-glasses and on glass eyes, on all mirrors, on all windows, on all glass jewelry, on all drinking glasses and glass bottles.

These were very powerful and colorful pictures. What reds, what purples! What reds, what yellows! What reds, what blues! What reds, what reds, what reds! The most vivid of all the reds in the new pictures was popularly named Armageddon Red. Oh, beautiful!

There was another nice touch to the pictures. A great majority of them had the fiery words "Repent, Repent!" scrawled across their faces as if by lightning. But who would be so rash as to make a value judgment on an appearance like that!

The three very cold years ended. The volcanoes went to sleep again. The pictures stopped appearing, and soon they were no longer in evidence. But the pictured glass of this world-wide spate was not smashed. People were afraid to smash it. Instead they replaced it all by new clear glass, and they hid the pictured glass away in secret places. Some folks swore that they could hear the pictured glass ticking away like time bombs. They knew they hadn't heard the last of them.

Another decade has gone by. We have a little bit of new-new stained glass openly displayed again. This colored glass of the present day is, like that of the Medieval period, of purposive and artificial manufacture. It hasn't the power of the

Masterworks Glass of the time of the Grand Tour, nor of the stark Armageddon Glass of the three year return of the cold, that hidden-away glass that seems to be ticking the seconds off. Some of the new glass is pretty good though, and much of it is done by impassioned amateurs. It may look better in retrospect than it does now, if there is a retrospect to our now. It is in tenuous rapport to the Armageddon Glass of the three year period, though it does not seem able to achieve the real Armageddon Red.

It is only fair to state that there are other *Informal Histories of Stained Glass* that do not agree with the foregoing history in every respect. Some of them do not agree with it in any respect.

This, however, is the only one that accounts for all the facts without using any element of the grotesque.

YOUNGGOLD

by Kevin O'Donnell, Jr.

This story is actually an excerpt from O'Donnell's latest novel, CAVERNS, Book 1 of The Journeys of McGill Feighan. The excerpt stands on its own, and reveals the strengths in his writing that have made one reviewer say that "[O'Donnell] could be the most significant talent to enter the field in the last half-decade." One of his greatest strengths is his ability to create flesh-and-blood and fully-souled characters. Here you have the opportunity to meet several wonderful people, all caught in a web of need, and to rejoice with them as they finally find comfort in each other.

At a few minutes to midnight, a grey man awoke in a piss-stunk alley. Above his head glimmered a strip of stars, broken bottles catching headlights on a highway. They were old friends; he'd Flung himself to many of them—once upon a time—when he'd been young and strong—when laughter had been as natural as breathing. That was before he'd retired, before he'd become so Sensitive.

Voices and music and glass clatter tumbled through the nearby bar's back door; he sat up, coughing and hawking in unison with a rummy impatient to take his nest among the garbage cans.

His name was Jose Schwedeker; he was sixty-three years

old, a retired Flinger, and rich, by normal standards. By the standards of his needs, he was deperately poor. And desperately competing with an emaciated man named Mort Tobbins, who was, he knew, Searching for the same surcease he was. Old Mort. They never had been friends. Fitting that in this June of 2088, their rivalry was less diminished than they.

The derelict's face hung above his, like a bewhiskered moon studying its reflection in a pond. Their mingled odors were worse than the alley's. "Take it," he grunted, crawling out of the bed of rags and crashing over a dented can in the process. For a moment he heard a bell, soft and distant and silver, and he started toward it, aching for its peace, but then a buzz-saw rasped in his brain and chewed his hangover into separate but equal tormentors. The broken asphalt was wet beneath his dirty palms; he pushed himself to his feet and stumbled toward the back entrance of the bar.

"No' friendly i' there," wheezed the rummy. Bottle uptilted, he gurgled cheap wine through the gaps in his teeth. "No credit—no work—no—thing." His legs gave way and he sat down abruptly.

"'sokay," said Schwedeker, waving a hand and almost losing his own balance. He grabbed at the doorframe to steady himself, to gather the strength and the courage he needed to enter. Termites tunneled through his grey cells, but their sound was that of a wolf pack shredding a carcass.

His change-ringer, grey-haired Anita Nkame, once the best of the Movers, had tried to tell him how age would mock him. "Your body, Jose, he weakens," she'd said. They'd been hiding from the winter in his father's paneled basement. He'd been shooting pool; mischievously, she'd goosed the cue ball. "Your eyes, mon, be blurred by all the fogs you ever walked through. Your honds be rusty claws; your knees, broken hinges. And when you make love..." She'd shaken her head. "You fall asleep right after."

He'd hooted, made his shot, and asked about the Sensitivity.

"A church burns in your head," she'd answered dolefully. "Every mon, woman, and child be a tongue of flame, growling and crackling, and it hurts like you'd never believe. The rum I drank to quiet it... inside it all, you can hear the heat tolling the bells..." She'd made the cue ball jump, then, and winked at him. "Die young, mon. Die young or ring your changes quick."

But he hadn't done either, and now was paying the price. He jiggled the locked door. A broad, squat dishroom man approached and began to speak. Though Schwedeker could see his thick lips move, he couldn't distinguish a single syllable. The noise in his head garbled the connection between his ears and his mind. It drowned the chiming of the bell, masked the whereabouts of Tobbins.

With a disgusted wrinkle of his broken nose, the man unlocked the door, leaned close to Schwedeker's head, and shouted, "No freebies! Get lost!"

A swimmer struggling in a rip-tide, he swayed erect and did his best to enunciate: "If it is after midnight, there is money in my account. Lead me to a bank."

"Whaddayou, nuts?" His hands started for Schwedeker's shoulders, but stopped in mid-flight, as if their destination were too dirty even for them. A tattooed rose budded inside his right wrist.

"No, I—" It was much too difficult to explain, especially in his condition, so he let his buttonless coat fall open and speak for him.

The dishroom man stared at the shimmering tunic. A glitter in his dark brown eyes mirrored the woven patterns of coherent energy.

The tunic, once Schwedeker's pride, was now his pain. At fifteen, when they'd implanted the activator cell keyed to his individual brain-wave pattern, he'd vowed never to cloak that marvelous meshwork. At sixty, he'd learned that Sensitivity-sapped Flingers get mugged. Seemed all the street creeps knew about the trust funds; too few understood that the interest, paid daily, was spent before it could accumulate any of its own. So he wore the coat, the gift of a horn-tooting Salvation Army Major, and sweltered in the summer because it was the only way to keep safe.

"A Flinger?" the man asked, contempt melting out of his battered features.

"Uh-huh." Between his ears a hyena howled. He stiffened, and clamped his scraped palms to his temples. "Seven years retired. Getting more Sensitive every day."

"Poor bastard." Indecisive, now, he stepped forward, then back. "It's after midnight—you sure you got money?"

"Pos. I. Tive." Three words—that's how bad off he was.

"It's the Occleftian you want, right?"

"Please." It was halfway between a request and a shriek. He was rolling his head around, as if the motion could dislodge the monsters, could bring back the bell.

"All right, big boy." The man made up his mind. With an apology to his food-spattered white jacket, he bent forward and tipped Schwedeker over his shoulder. He straightened easily, though he growled at the stench, and said, "Take you up the back way; no sense making the customers puke. The bug's got a bank up there anyway."

Blood pooled in Schwedeker's head, blood and ache and tearing sound. Though he wanted to resent his helplessness, his repulsiveness, he could only be grateful. This dish machine technician could have called the cops, who would have prolonged his agony for unendurable hours. Yet he hadn't.

The broad shoulder pressed his stomach to his spine; his head and free arm bounced and swayed with every step up the metal grate stairs. Their single Shiva-shadow shortened gradually into sharper focus, tightened into a multilimbed puddle at the man's feet, then preceded them down the narrow corridor. Knuckles on plastic added their rap-tap to the inner din. Another few jounces, and his feet hit hard floor.

A high buzzing sound, like a mosquito chorus, said, "Beefo. One carries this kind *out*. Not *in*."

"He's a Flinger." He braced Schwedeker against the rough, unfinished wall. "Says he's got money." His scarred hands parted the grimy coat to reveal the tunic. "I got to get back to work."

"I see," whirred the voice. "Thank you. Leave him."

"Right." The door closed and an electro-lock hummed to life.

Schwedeker forced himself upright, and squinted at the pearl-grey alien. A man-sized millipede, it smelled like a damp library. Two of its faceted red eyes scrutinized him; the other two guided the arms that were lifting the bank-plate. Schwedeker licked his thumb, wiped it on the front of his coat, and held it ready. "What's your fee?" he croaked.

"One hundred," replied the Occleftian. "No haggling."

"All right, all right!" He jabbed his thumb at the shiny plate. At contact, he said, "Debit me one hundred dollars; credit them to—"

"—Arkorninu X83," finished the millipede. When the green light glowed to indicate completion of the transaction, it shimmied its mid-legs in the gesture of mild surprise. Not astonishment—it had lived in Cleveland too many years to be astonished by anything a Terran did. "Please," it said, more polite now that it had been paid, "be seated."

Turning around, Schwedeker slumped to the bare concrete floor, and put his head between his knees. Dozens of tiny pincers pulled his coat down his back, then reached through the tunic to massage his spine. Others fastened onto his neck; still others nibbled on his skull. He closed his eyes. For the five thousandth time, de-sensitization began.

First came the colors, sheets of vivid translucence flaring behind his eyelids. Red rivers; orange aurorae. Forks of yellow lightning slashed diagonally and their after-images faded slowly. Green mountains humped up from the flame-burnt ground. Blue grass sprouted on their rugged slopes, flourished, and deepened into indigo when night pulled a violet blanket over everything.

"Aaaaahhhh," said Schwedeker.

"Yess," hissed Arkorninu X83, digging its hundreds of digits into his slack skin, "yess, yess."

Smells percolated through his nostrils, first the real ones, his own rankness, the Occleftian's mildew, then the memories, of lemons and ozone and voluptuous women and early morning mists when the factories forgot their pollution-control equipment and the acid reek burned through choking throats. Fresh fish and soy sauce and ketchup on a charcoal-grilled steak . . .

"Ohhhh," he moaned.

"Jussst ssso," soothed the alien. "Relax, relax, re . . ."

And then silence blew in to clear out the noise like the wind cleans dead leaves off a lawn. Buzz saws sputtered to a halt. The hyena slunk into the night. Police sirens dopplered down the road. The hurricane, moving out to sea, let the breakers fall into a gentle susurrus. Audiences hushed.

"God, that feels good," he breathed.

"Doesn't it, though?" The Occleftian claws left his skin, tugged his coat back over his shoulders.

Schwedeker sat up, and pressed his elbows against the chilly wall. He didn't dare move, not yet. His legs couldn't support him. "I needed that."

"I know. You're very Sensitive. You must need it twice a day."

"Used to get it, too, till you all raised your prices." He said it without rancor. "Now I can only afford one."

"Supply and demand, my dear." It raised a gentle claw to stroke the stubble on Schwedeker's cheeks. "Until we recover from the plague . . ." It lifted his chin, brought up a specialized limb, and began to shave him. Another limb, a hollow one, sucked up the whiskers. "You're new in town."

"I'm Searching. Got in from Cincinnati last night. *Half a step ahead of Tobbins the ubiquitous*, he thought. *Have to get there first!*

"You must have met my podder, Arkorninu B212." It combed his hair and trimmed it. "B212 must have been very busy to send you out so shaggy."

"No, it wanted to, but I heard the bell." *And staggered into the night*, he remembered, *trying to get a fix on it, listening to it recede to the northeast, probably up 71, limpracing to the bus depot, fuming, pacing, extorting cigarettes from strangers by the implicit threat of standing next to them if they wouldn't hand them over . . . then sitting alone in the back, still hearing, far ahead, the long-lived echoes, the haunting reverberations . . . and far behind, the sullen untuned clunk of Tobbins on the trail . . .*

"Bronze?" asked X83.

He shook his head. "Silver." Honesty made him add, "I think."

"I would have heard if they'd found it here," buzzed the alien. "Are you sure it hasn't moved on? Silvers are generally loud."

"I know, I know." Fear caught at him, made him hug himself for safety. If Tobbins rang its changes first—but no, he couldn't think that way. When sanity depends on being the first to flush the ghost of a promise in the night, one can't afford to contemplate coming in second. "It was small, though. And—"

"And you're inordinately Sensitive. What a Flinger you must have been!" Patting him on the head, it offered its carapace as a handhold, so he could pull himself to his feet. "You really must go now, dear. I have other customers."

He dug his knuckles into his eyes until the itch went away.

"Thanks," he said, reaching for the door.

"One question, Searcher," called the alien.

"What's that?"

"Do you Search for the reward, the responsibility, or the peace?" Its eyes framed him in ten thousand ruby octagons.

Schwedeker paused to marshal his thoughts. "All of the above, some of the above, and none of the above," he said at last. "The reward's nice, the responsibility's good for a guy who's got nothing to do, and the peace . . . God, the peace!" He shook his head, and dragged a dirty hand across his mouth. "But for why I'm Searching—ask an iron filing why it flies to the magnet. I have to go; good-bye."

As he clattered down the metal stairs, he knew X83 had been hurt by his reply, had thought it to be unnecessarily cryptic. It wasn't, though. It was the simple truth. One answered the bell because one needed to, not because one chose to, or wanted to. Like using the power while one could—it was just something one had to do. People thought it was the chance to see the moons of Throngor, or to wallow in the clay pools of Mellna, but they were wrong. The wielding was the reward, and nothing else mattered. He waved his thanks to Beefo the dishroom man, and stepped into the night.

He heard it again, a distance-muted ringing, pure and tuned and compelling. It was off to the west, far off, probably one of the suburbs. Through shadows he moved to Euclid Avenue, where he found a bus stop. The area was almost lifeless. Discarded newspapers somersaulted down the sidewalk, slapping at his ankles as they passed. The sign said a bus would be along in twenty or thirty minutes. His luck had turned: that would be the last of the evening.

It would be easier if he could Fling himself out there, if he could home in on the bell and appear at its side. But he couldn't. He'd never been in Cleveland before; he didn't know the feel of its street corners, or the flanks of its contours. It can be painful to materialize in front of a taxi cab; explosive, to teleport into a hillside.

He thanked God for the Occleftian silence, the stillness that squelched the incomplete and the crippled so that full health stood alone. The bell was clear and alluring, now, though its timbre . . . he'd thought it to be silver, but now he wasn't sure. Maybe—no. He couldn't let himself hope for gold.

It was young, too. Very young. It had to be, to have gone

undetected. An older one would have had its changes rung long ago. Probably asleep, then, and potent only in its dreams. That was how Anita had found him, when he was—four? Six?

Boy or girl? Couldn't tell, couldn't ever tell, not from the chimes. He hoped for a boy—parents got antsy about a ringer's responsibility in cross-gender situations.

Ironic about the reward—if he earned it, he wouldn't need it. If he didn't earn it, he would need it. Bureaucracy. One million for a silver-ringer, when the peace, and the fulfillment of need, would be enough.

The bus braked in front of him; air escaped its plastic skirts to blow dust across his tattered shoes. He disliked buses, especially at night. They weren't friendly. Boarding, he thrust his thumb into the fare box and waited for the green light. The only passenger, he sat behind the driver, who groaned and said, "Can't you find another seat, man?"

"Sorry," he said, frowning as Tobbins' dissonance distressed the background, "but I'm a Searcher, and I might need to get off in a hurry."

"A Searcher? You?" The driver's blue eyes, drilling into the overhead mirror, plucked at Schwedeker's rags. "And your niece is the President, right?"

He let his coat fall open; its brilliance filled the front of the bus. "Now you believe me?"

"Shit, yeah." His tone was awe-struck. "Never had a Flinger on my run before—hey," he said, suddenly suspicious, "you're a Flinger, how come you're riding? How come you don't just teleport—"

"Don't know the town," he said shortly. "Besides . . . I'm retired."

"So what's that got to do with it?" He took a right onto Lorain Road; the darkened shopfronts, for lack of better entertainment, watched them pass.

"You lose it," he explained. He hunched over, and rested his elbows on his knees. Two bells tolled in the back of his mind, one louder at each stroke, the other, softer. His heart was running fast. "Not the power, you've got that forever. Just the, ah, the fine-tuning. Set a passenger down above the floor, instead of on it. Or against a wall, instead of in the middle of the room. That's the memory, fraying at the edges, not holding the destination pattern sharp and tight, like it should. They start watching you when that happens . . . the next thing that goes, the thing they retire you for, is momentum maladjustment."

"Wha?" asked the driver, as the bus hissed across the bridge.

"Angular momentum, from the way the planets spin. When you Fling something, you've got to compensate for the difference. There's a . . . a place," he decided, "where we can go to dump some, or to pick some up—"

"The Energy Dimension?" The driver, looking into the mirror, shrugged back at Schwedeker. "That's a name I got from the papers."

"That's what they call it. But you've got to do it right, and when your Sensitivity's stuffing your head with static—" He leaped to his feet, gaped out the far window, and said, "Hey! Stop! This is it."

"I can't—oh, hell, screw the company." The bus whined to a halt; he manipulated the door lever. "Good luck, huh?"

"Yeah, thanks." He jumped from the top step to the sidewalk, stumbling a bit, and caught his balance as the bus whooshed away. The bell was much louder now, but it had been stronger back . . . there. Maybe down that side street? Damn! Tobbins was coming, too.

He started walking, briskly, clutching his coat closed, feeling his pulse hammer in his ears. Dreamlike, the sidewalk seemed a treadmill, he was shuffling down flypaper streets, stride, stride, stride, but he couldn't go anywhere, he was stuck in the same place, trapped in the dappled shadows cast by streetlights shining through treetops.

Louder it rang, and louder. He turned the corner, broke into a half-run, wheezing and gasping while his chest tightened and his shins griped. This house? No, further, a little further, just a—

"Hold it right there, old man," barked a cold voice.

He spun around. Two cops were easing out of their cruiser, their eyes never leaving him, their fingers fumbling with holster snaps. He groaned. "Good—good evening, officers. What can I do for you?"

"Come over here," said the one on the near side, "come over real slow, and lean against the car, and assume the position."

He started, reluctantly, to obey, but he heard—the high triumphant peal of a baby gold! And, even as the smile broke

dawnlike on his seamed cheeks, the second sound came in: the
off-key clang of a discarded bronze. Tobbins. Tobbins was
here, on this street. Going for the gold himself.

"I'm a Searcher," he babbled, "I hear the bell, it's right in
that house there, I've got to get in quick—"

Disbelieving scowls washed across the patrolmen's faces;
the nearer took a menacing step towards him. "Gedover here,"
he snarled.

He glanced over his shoulder. Yes. It *had* to be that house.
He couldn't let Tobbins do him out of it, he couldn't let the
cops delay him; damn the risks, the frazzled reflexes—

☆PING☆

He was pressed against the plate-glass picture window,
peeping through a crack in the draperies, hearing the cops
shout, "HEY!" while their racing feet scuffed concrete and
grass.

☆PING☆

Stubbing his toe on the mahogany coffee table, groping
through the shadows for the staircase because the bell was
upstairs, and a pounding rattled the front door, and a sleepy
angry voice from above said, "Who the hell—"

But the mutter gave him the direction and he was rushing
up the stairs on all fours and the cops were bellowing a siren
split the distance a hoarse, befuddled woman said, "Pat, shomebody's in the housh!"

"We'll see about that—"

"No, don't, shtay!"

"—somebody breaks into my house, break his damn neck,
besides the boy's alone, could be another—"

"Be careful!"

Scrambling across the green-carpeted landing; three doors,
all ajar, all dark within; voices there; this, a push, a john
dammit; *that* one! Swing it open, stagger through it, kid on
a bed. A kid who didn't move, who didn't even turn his head
at the intrusion.

When Schwedeker went to him, stood above him looking,
the boy's eyes grew. And grew. The bell's echoes shivered
down into silence. It was a warm, loving silence, and it em-
braced Schwedeker like a long-lost brother. *Peace*, he thought,
protection.

He dropped to his knees by the side of the bed, dropped to

his knees and raised his hands high, so the furious father, bursting into the room, throwing on the light, would see that he was no threat.

The kid had black hair and brown eyes. His skin was soft; his cheeks were pinched. Under the blanket, his five year-old arms and legs were sticks. He did not speak, except with his eyes.

The father, huge and grossly fat, grabbed Schwedeker's collar. The coat flew off; the tunic spattered rainbows on the cowboy-covered wallpaper. "What the hell?"

"I'm a Flinger," he said, rising, turning, but keeping his hands above his head, palms open. "Jose Schwedeker, retired. Your son's a Flinger, too. I've just rung his changes. He's the strongest I've ever met." A thundering crash from the first floor made him wince. "The cops," he explained. "They just kicked in your front door. Don't worry about it, though. I'll buy you a new one." Relief was on him; he couldn't help but laugh. "Two new doors." The laughs dipped deeper and deeper into his belly. His knees gave way, sprawled him on the bare wood floor. "A hundred new ones, with what I save in Occleftian fees. Oh, God, I've found it!"

And then the cops were there, their guns drawn, the barrels glued to Schwedeker's light show. Behind them stood a third man, a grey man, with hollow cheeks and pain-wracked eyes. "Hello, Jose," he said over the blue shoulders.

"Mort," he giggled, "Mort, I've change-rung a gold!"

"Uh-huh." He grimaced. "I heard."

"Somebody tell me what's going on here," demanded one cop. The other seconded his motion with a brusque nod.

The father was dazed. Dropping onto the bed next to the boy, he looked up, and choked out, "My son—my son's a Flinger. McGill. He's a Flinger!"

"So you *are* a Searcher," said the cop, nudging Schwedeker with the point of his shoe.

Schwedeker grinned, for maybe the first time since he'd retired. "Was," he told him. He got to his hands and knees and crawled to the foot of McGill's bed. "I *was* a Searcher. Not any more. I don't need to. I'm a change-ringer, now." As the cops left, he spread his coat on the floor and curled into it. "I'll sleep here, okay?" he asked the father.

"Sure," said Feighan. Repeatedly, he tapped the heel of his palm above his right ear, as though to knock dust off his brain.

"Sure, it's a fine warm spot and there's a soft quilt for your mattress. But McGill—" Rising, he walked to the window overlooking the front yard, and watched the bantering patrolmen saunter back to their cruiser. Tobbins drifted after them like a leaf caught in a tractor-trailer's slipstream. "But you're wasting your time, you are. The boy's a paralytic, always has been. Five years and two months old; hasn't moved a finger or made a sound since..." His hand found a can of roasted peanuts in his bathrobe pocket. He shook a quarter of the can into his mouth and chewed noisily. His jowls jiggled.

A grenade of sick disappointment burst in Schwedeker's belly. Paralyzed? Mute? All those years of Searching, all the pain and loneliness and derision, was it to end in this? Because the peace was there. The boy McGill was a latent Flinger. The reward would be his, the protection would be his, but the rest—the caring, the coaching, the camaraderie—how could he possibly find that with a child who was almost a vegetable?

What a lousy, rotten way to go out—nursemaid to a cabbage. Staring at the floor, he cursed. A tear of self-pity trickled down his cheek.

"Whoozhis bum?" asked an intoxicated woman.

He lifted his eyes. Standing—leaning—in the doorway was a pale, red-nosed woman in a dirty nylon nightgown. Her long black hair was snarled and dead. She blinked and squinted at him. "Jose Schwedeker," he said dully. "Flinger, retired. I've just rung your son's changes."

"Him?" An exaggerated expression of disbelief contorted her face as she waved vaguely at McGill. She staggered, and caught the doorjamb for support. "A Flingersh shomebody who—" She raised a finger and belched. "Who can jump from plaish to plaish without moving, right?" Widening her eyes, she gaped owlishly at Schwedeker. "Right?"

"That's right," he said, "but—"

"Boy, thash a relief." She giggled; her eyelids inched shut.

"Pardon?" he asked after a few moments.

"You shtill here?"

"Why is it a relief?"

"'Cause I thought—" She half-turned to face her husband, and had to spread her legs to keep from falling "—an' *he* thought, too, that I wash—" She frowned at herself "—was blacking out alla time, 'cause I'd find *him*—" She pointed at the bed "—next to me, or in my lap, or whatever... boy, thash a relief. Bet I shleep good tonight. Ta-ta." Pivoting awkwardly, she stumbled out into the hallway.

Schwedeker looked at Feighan curiously. "What's she talking about?"

"She's drunk," said Feighan, with sad simplicity.

"I know that, but what was she talking about?"

"Ah——" he scowled at the empty doorway, but there was pain in the frown, and unsundered love, "——it's her contention that she's forever finding the boy somewhere he wasn't put. She blames me for it. To her way of thinking, it's a grand, cunning scheme to convince her she's crazy, so she'll put herself away. But I ask you, why should I go to all that bother, when I could just as easily walk out of here tomorrow and be divorced the day after?"

Schwedeker hauled himself to his feet and peered into McGill's deep, dark eyes. He could *feel* the power in the boy, feel it as though it were a warm spring breeze. So much strength for such a little child . . . he straightened up with a groan and an ache in his lower back. "She finds him where he wasn't put?"

"So she says, but it's a miracle she can say anything at all these days, given the ungodly speed with which she drains a bottle. A lesser tongue would have been pickled solid by now. Would you say that makes her a trustworthy witness? Or would you say rather that it's touched her in the memory, and inclined her to forgetting just exactly what she did do with the child?" The can of peanuts was empty. He eyed it as though it were a friend who had betrayed him, then crumpled it in his massive fist and dropped the wad of aluminum into his pocket. "I wouldn't be trusting her testimony if I were you."

Schwedeker's disappointment was gone, replaced by a pulse-stirring eagerness. He raised his face to the light fixture in the ceiling like a man letting the sun's heat creep into his bones. "Did you," he asked, "ever stop to think that she's the way she is because of what your boy's been doing?"

"Huh?"

He turned and spread his arms. "If you were sober and found an elephant in your icebox, wouldn't you think you were crazy?"

"It'd be a terrible temptation," agreed Feighan.

"But if you saw it when you were drunk—"

"Ah!" He nodded forcefully. "Sure, and you'd have to think

it was the alcohol in your brain that was making you see it."

"Exactly!" He spun on his heel and walked back to McGill. "Kid," he said, "if you can teleport around this house, you can sure as hell walk. And talk. And by damn—" he leaned over to touch him on the nose "—I'm gonna make sure you learn how."

McGill blinked, and stroked Schwedeker with his peace. It was the only way he had of saying, "Thanks."

ALTERNATE 51: BLISS

by Robert Thurston

One of the terrible follies of writing is second-guessing oneself. It's simply too easy to live a superhuman fantasy life on paper. The *real* writers try their damndest to go in the opposite direction, to strip off all the fantasy and super-stuff and get right to the human in their writing, the truth in fiction. And that's what makes Thurston so exciting; his honesty is extraordinary. Dreyer of "Alternate 51: Bliss" is the most recent in a succession of irritable, scratchy, bewildered and opinionated men and women he's been able to catch in stories like "Wheels," "The Mars Ship," "Theodore and Theodora," and "The Oonaa Woman." We read stories like these for what they reveal to us about ourselves and there is, in truth, no better reason for reading books.

The night before his crossing to the alternate world that called itself Bliss, Dreyer insulted one of his wife's collection of friends. The friend, an art critic for *The New York Times*, looked as if he were being eaten from within—probably by disaffected sculptors. He was not being typically mean or even politely snobbish. All he said was:

"It must be exceedingly romantic, your profession, Mr. Dreyer. I mean, going to all those alternate worlds and all."

"Romantic?" Dreyer replied, with intended meanness and snobbery. "On the contrary. It's really no different from going to Newark on a Tuesday."

"Newark? Tuesday? I'm afraid I don't—"

"My husband is just having his little joke," interrupted Dreyer's wife Martha, rambling rose of the wildwood. She was tall, thin, ageing a shade too rapidly, and had the most beautiful eyes in the rather crowded room.

After the party she told her husband that he had been rude and condescending. She said that it wasn't fair to mock those of us who hadn't been fortunate enough to qualify for one of the adventurous services, who had too many physical inadequacies or discomforts to cross space, time, or into an alternate world. Dreyer said he was sorry. She knew he was not and he knew he was not, but both knew it would end the argument conveniently, which both wanted.

Dreyer no longer felt much responsibility or even affection for his wife or, for that matter, his entire family. Martha rambling rose of the wildwood had become a knife-wielder on the sacrificial altar of culture. It had all started when he had encouraged her to find something interesting to do when he was away on his long trips. A couple of book clubs, a series ticket to the ballet, some museum memberships, and look at the result. She had become so intellectual and pursued so many plans for the orientation of the individual to oneself and one's society (reading hundreds of books with titles like *Eat Your Way to Eschatology* or *Wake Up Your Hypothalamus*) that she could no longer be understood outside the perimeters of her various social groups. Martha the culture vulture. In a way, she was not even that. She really didn't care that much for culture *per se*. What she really liked were people who did care that much for culture *per se*, or said they did. Martha was a sort of culture-vulture vulture.

To Dreyer, his whole family seemed to originate from another world, one of the alternate worlds not on the popular travel circuit. His daughter Tina, who sometimes called herself Lila Lana Leilani, went after younger versions of her mother's transient fads. They usually had terribly organizational names like Artificial Hedonism Ltd., or the Krishna-Christian Connection. (Or was that the rock group she played with on weekends?) Tina could at least speak coherently to her father, perhaps because she was still young, but rarely did she do so out of choice. His son Tim was easier to deal with but unfortunately rather stolid and unimaginative for his fifteen years. They could enjoy being together, but usually in silence.

Now, waiting for the transporter to whisk him off to his fifty-first alt-world assignment, Dreyer realized just how jaded he felt. Time and space travelers probably became this jaded after a couple decades in their services, but for some reason they publicly preserved the mysteries of their crafts. Years ago Dreyer had been rejected by both the time and space services. Borderline people like him seemed to qualify more easily for the less-spectacular Alt-World Service. Who knew why? If somebody had known, would Dreyer have asked him? If Dreyer had asked him, then Dreyer would probably have been in the time or space racket instead.

Still, there were some alt-worlders who were exhilarated by their travels. Hrozberg for one—he could get positively adolescent about them. Earlier, they had bumped into each other outside the briefing room. Hrozberg, red-faced and cheerful as ever, had declared how thrilled he was to get back into harness.

"Real life doesn't stir up the old adrenalin or whatchumacallit," he said. "I always wind up drinking too much or slipping into catatonia while fishing. Don't really feel alive until it's time for another trip."

"You probably draw more exciting assignments than I," Dreyer said, trying to shrug off the subject.

"Not so, old chap. Last time out, I wound up in a whole world of weavers. Everything was woof and warf, tapestry and crochet. Government carried through the profession as metaphor—it was a sort of intricately woven fabric in which the only real divisions seemed to be either pattern or coloration. I knew that world would be judged insignificant soon as I stepped into it, but I didn't care. It was all new to me, and I loved it, don't you know?"

Hrozberg, unlike Dreyer, was never disturbed by the outcome of his mission. So overjoyed by his own discoveries, he couldn't be discouraged when supervisors dismissed the mission as a minor one and filed his report in the darkest bottom file drawer with scattered disinterested remarks, with no publicity releases or even an academic connection. Dreyer always hated it when not even an academic was called in. It was disconcerting to waste time in a strange world, with your life frequently in danger (Hrozberg had said there was even a strangle-cult in his warp and woof world), and then return to find that your analysis of the mission was not even worth the review of an academic. He hoped Hrozberg found a genuinely exciting world this time out. Maybe an all-pottery civilization. *That was cruel*, he thought. Wherever Dreyer went, wherever Hrozberg went, it was just a job, after all. Just a job.

Dreyer's half-brother Warren died early from just a job. When they were growing up, in a module two sizes too small for the size of the family, he and Warren had been very happy, especially in playing together and devising romantic imaginary adventures. In fact, their intensely-imagined childhood worlds had been so detailed, Dreyer had rarely found an alternate world that lived up to them. A child's Camelot or juvenile Atlantis was infinitely more rewarding than an alt-world whose inhabitants, whatever their cultural and personal oddities, spent most of their time on the day-to-day difficulties that seemed to afflict worlds everywhere in time, space, or alternate places. *God*, Dreyer thought, *Warren would've been happy in one of the services*. But he hadn't been able to qualify for any, so he'd unhappily taken on the family business—publishing books on exercise, yoga, family planning, and stock market avarice—until he died from his third heart attack in three years. *Damn*, Dreyer thought, *he wasn't even forty*. Dreyer had been off on a mission when Warren died, but he probably had a better picture of the agony of his brother's death than he would have if he had actually been present. The family had made a hologram of Warren lying in state for Dreyer to view when he returned. The fact that Warren was already cremated took some of the vividness off the three-dimensional reproduction of the entire wake, which included the sound of the family weeping, the gentle intrusions of sappy music, and the artificial odors attached to artificial flowers in plastic baskets. In spite of his nausea at the hologram, Dreyer said a faithless prayer before ordering its dissolution.

So, Dreyer thought, *I've travelled to fifty alternate worlds now and reached the age of forty long ago*. Just then the waves from the transporter pierced his body and the room around him dissolved, blanking out even more abruptly than his brother's wake's hologram had.

Suddenly he was there, in his fifty-first world, in a shabby room which he recognized as one of the usual customs and clearing houses. The jolt of traveling had given him a stomachache. He had never liked being in his own world one moment and in the new one the next. Perhaps he should put a note in the suggestion-box, tell them to program an interval into the transporter, an illusion of time passing. They would probably reply, on a standard printed business form, that the cost of keeping him whole for that length of time instead of the little microdots of himself that were transmitted and reassembled at the other end was just too high and economically unsound but thank you for your interest in the company I am yours etc.

Before taking a step out of the cross-world transporter into the customs room of this new world, Dreyer checked all the gauges along the transporter's inner rims. There were evidently no dangers in this world from atmosphere, bizarre floating viruses, temperature levels, or any of the other assorted deviations that sometimes caused alt-world travelers to abort their missions. Dreyer had never had to abort a mission, not even once in fifty trips. He was just not that lucky, he always had to stay and explore.

A man sat behind a plain wood table with a few papers on its clean surface. He strongly resembled other first-encounter agents Dreyer had met in several of his fifty worlds. The man's painfully stretched smile did not bode well for the fifty-first.

Without getting up from his desk, the agent greeted him. They had not had the pleasure of a visit from an alt-worlder in some time, he said through his pocket translator, but they had known he was coming and that his name was Dreyer. Dreyer nodded. Being expected at his destination was nothing new to him. At least six previous worlds had been prepared for him.

"Anything I should know particularly about your world?" Dreyer said, communicating with the agent through his own pocket translator. Although the translator had trouble adjusting to the new world's subtle phonemic differentiations, it soon was able to flash coherent simple but unidiomatic sentences to Dreyer on its three-tiered display. Dreyer was quite adept at learning new languages and he would be happy when he'd learned the necessary tongues of this world so he could disperse with the translator and its awkward diplomatically-limited vocabulary.

He and the agent worked out finally that the world was called by its inhabitants Bliss. *For Christ's sake*, Dreyer thought, *I'll bet they consider themselves utopian, or at least*

*well organized. I've already had enough utopian worlds to last
the rest of my life. Bliss. Just the place for Hrozberg. With his
luck he's probably now in some world called Misery or Despair.
Well, he'd derive just as much from them, since he makes it
such a point to enjoy all his missions. Someday he'll be mas-
sacred by a primitive tribe on some dismal world, and go out
smiling.*

"By the way," the agent said as they left the customs room,
"one other thing about us here on Bliss. We always tell the
truth." The man's fixed smile was more painful than ever.

"I strongly doubt that," Dreyer said, familiar with such off-
putting tactics on the part of first-encounter agents.

"Well, *I* always tell the truth anyway."

"But then what you said about your people always telling
the truth is in fact a lie and, since you said it, you can't always
be telling the truth."

"You appreciate paradoxes then?"

He wanted to tell the agent that cultures which encouraged
paradoxes were generally deficient intellectually. But he said
instead:

"I don't appreciate paradoxes, but I can live with them."

"You will enjoy yourself on Bliss."

"I'm not sure about that."

"I probably did not mean it anyway."

On the cobbled road that led away from the customs house
(a building located at a discreet distance from the city), some
citizens of Bliss conducted a medium-sized parade in Dreyer's
honor. Dreyer made the usual brief speech about how he was
happy to form the first link between his world, Earth, and the
world of Bliss and that future relations between our two worlds
would be, etcetera, etcetera. The audience listened with the
glazed-eyed politeness of people who'd heard it all before, no
doubt transmitted to them through just such pocket translators
connected to just such amplifiers. Nobody applauded at the
points where Dreyer waited for it. Later he was informed that
applause was considered an insult on Bliss and often was the
equivalent of a challenge to duel. Hrozberg would have been
delighted by such a custom, a minor differentiation from the
norm. In a drunken moment a few days later Dreyer applauded
a diplomat who thought that his nation should go to war with
some other nation, neither of whose names Dreyer could remember sober when he tried to write a report about the incident.

The diplomat diplomatically ignored the insult of Dreyer's applause, but did at least three encores anyway.

A guide took over the care of Dreyer from the customs agent. The guide looked very much like the agent. On the way to the hotel, they crossed a square where workmen were constructing a statue. Dreyer asked the guide what the statue would represent. The guide said it was a statue of Dreyer, which was being built in his honor here in Dreyer Square. Dreyer said he was impressed that they had been able to name a square for him in the short time since his arrival in Bliss. The guide said that the square had always been Dreyer Square and that they would have put up the statue earlier but they didn't know what he looked like.

The Dreyer Square Hotel was rundown and seedy. It had definitely seen better days and Dreyer regretted missing them, especially since its historical significance was so tied in to his name. His room had sagging floors and a spineless bureau. The bed housed a few tiny Bliss bugs which gave off a strong and pleasant odor (in contrast to that emitted by the room freshener—Blissian organs of smell apparently functioned with a pronounced difference from those of Earthlings). The maid offered—rather prettily—to make up the bed with both of them in it but Dreyer, feeling ambivalent about both the bugs and the maid, gently declined. Later, when he'd gotten used to the hotel, the room, the bugs, and the maid, he accepted her second offer. Although he forgot her soon after, he didn't regret whiling the afternoon away with her at the time.

Women, in fact, became something of a problem in Bliss. All of them wanted Dreyer, it seemed, and most of them were quite bold. He didn't know how many feminine hands he had had to gently push away from various parts of his body. Although he often spoke of a belief that alt-world visitors should not fraternize with the natives of their alternate worlds, he could not always adhere to a principle. He did sleep occasionally with the occasional beautiful Bliss woman. Not comfortable with their names in the harsh Bliss languages, he gave them each names he favored, like Angelica, Marie-Louise, and Gelsomina.

He began to like Bliss. It was the first time since his early traveling days that he had responded so emotionally and intellectually to the world he visited. Not that the inhabitants of

Bliss were all that demonstrative emotionally or functional in the intellectual realms, but there was a certain pleasantness and genteel shabbiness that he found definitely appealing. He thought there was an excellent chance that his report on Bliss would be given to an academic for further study, perhaps the world would even be recommended for further visitation. It would be enjoyable to plan the report. *Maybe fifty-one is a lucky number for me*, he thought.

"Why did you go into alternate worlds as a profession?" asked Angelica one evening after some fine lovemaking. She spoke in her own language and it was the first time Dreyer had understood a complete sentence in it, which made him quite happy. So happy, in fact, that he decided to tell her the truth instead of his standard company answer.

"I guess I was always fascinated by possibility. Or possibilities, I should say. What would have happened if some historic figure had shown up late for some historic event. Or if an assassin's gun had misfired. Or, and this is the most banal example, if Napoleon had not lost at Waterloo."

"Napoleon? Waterloo?"

"That's part of the point, you see. Bliss never had a Napoleon or even a Waterloo, or at least they did not collide at a particular moment in time to furnish a lasting historical event."

"Then Bliss develops as an alternate world because this Napoleon did nothing at this Waterloo?"

"Not necessarily. The change causing Bliss may be located at some more distant point in your past. And nobody has determined whether or not my Earth is the central focal point for the different histories of the different alternate worlds. Earth may very well have developed because something did happen here on Bliss that did *not* happen on Earth. Bliss may be the focal point from which all the other alternate worlds derive. Earthmen used to be less modest on this point but I can tell you that, after traveling to several alternate worlds, those of us in the service have been properly humbled."

"Does it ever bother you that your world may be just an offshoot of some other focal world?"

"Sometimes. Everything seems fragmented to me. Like each world is a facet. Nothing is secure. I cannot understand, I don't know what—"

"There, there, be what you are. Functionaries, after all, don't have to know the meaning of their contributions. They contribute and others furnish the proper interpretations."

"I'm not comfortable as a functionary. It's too much like being a guest at one of my wife's social events. And interpretations are disturbing, unsettling—they only provide possible meaning."

"But you just said you were interested in possibilities."

"Not any longer. I'd like one solid verifiable fact."

Angelica liked him considerably. However, she too was just a functionary. It was, in fact, the more adventurous Gelsomina who wanted him to throw over his job, stay in Bliss and hide in a jungle with her. She and Angelica looked somewhat alike, both tawny blondes. Tawny blondes were rare on every world, it seemed, and Dreyer gravitated easily to any he found.

"I want you to stay with me, first time I've ever wanted anybody to stay with me," said Gelsomina. "I think I love you, my love."

"That's a standard Bliss lie."

"I'll show you parts of the world that aren't allowed on the official tours."

"I'd like that."

He feigned official sickness and went on a secret trip with her. They visited a land where everybody chewed on red leaves and sat around all day watching each other sit, and deriving much joy from that. Dreyer told Gelsomina the Earthly legend of the lotus eaters in a version that was more Tennyson than Homer. Gelsomina became furious. What was real in her world could *not* be mythical in Dreyer's, and she simply would not have that. Dreyer tried to soothe her, but she was much too annoyed. They never got along well again, and Dreyer had to dump her for Marie-Louise, a somber young woman whose bleak moods revived his depressions.

After a well-executed abduction from a coronation-day parade, Dreyer became a hostage of some terrorists who were conducting an unanticipated rebellion. Although he strove to remain laconic in the face of their threats, he gradually grew quite afraid. One of his captors was a tawny blonde who bore a marked resemblance to Angelica and Gelsomina. He named her Nora. She was more sympathetic to him than her agitated intemperate colleagues.

"Don't I have diplomatic immunity?" he asked her.

"Stop whining. Your diplomatic immunity was with their government, those tyrants. We don't recognize it. But I'll sleep with you if it'll stop your whining."

"No, thanks. Last night did me in. Look, you don't have to keep *me* hostage. You guys are okay with me. I'll turn in a good report on you to my world."

"That's the fifteenth time today you've mentioned your stupid report. Shut up about it. We don't believe you come from some other world, some *alternate* world. Alternate to what? Alternate to Bliss? We are creating the alternate to Bliss, with our weapons and our words."

"My mother was destroyed looking for what you think of as an *alternate* world."

"Oh? Tell me about it, pass the time. Shouldn't be another shelling for, oh, ten minutes at least."

"Let me sit up anyway."

"Surely."

"Mother was a revolutionary of the old school. *Your* school, in a way, though less primitive. She enrolled in, sneaked into, signed up with any organization that had the remotest link to leftist ideology. She loved the New Deal because she was certain that Roosevelt was a communist."

He paused so that Nora could ask him what was the New Deal, Roosevelt, and communism. She didn't ask, she just stared straight ahead, out at the smoking but quiescent war zone.

"Mother entered wholeheartedly into the business of all organizations she joined. Often she slept with the leaders. She didn't care much for functionaries. My half-brother Warren was a result of such a liaison. His joke when I was a kid (he was a lot older than I) was that he was a child of the Left. He never knew his father. Since I knew mine, I thought he was lucky. Warren died after three heart attacks."

"I'm sorry."

"You should be. You think you're going to die with meaning."

"I am."

"Mother died, in a way, for a cause or set of causes. But not in the dramatic circumstances you dream of, Nora. She worked underground for decades, for her precious left-wing causes, even when the country had shifted away from such things and was busy fighting a world war."

"I look forward to our world war."

"If you don't die with meaning first. Our world war was nothing much, judging by the standards of a number of other worlds I've visited. And Mother got through it pretty well. It was after the war they destroyed her. Ruined her life. Even if she didn't die directly from it."

"Did you love her?"

"How could I tell? I was the last of twelve children. Twelve we knew of. By the time I came along she was a wizened old woman who looked like everybody's idea of a grandmother. All the kids in my school called her Granny. Kids are wonderful in my world. She even wore out-of-fashion clothes, as if she wanted to emphasize her granniness. I hated her clothes. But she wouldn't let me hate her. Not openly. Anytime I showed temper, anger, disquiet, she grabbed my head and held it down in her lap until I calmed down. She always told me I was a fine boy and would grow up to be an important person."

"And you have."

"Oh, sure."

"You are our hostage and you are your world's representative to other worlds. This is pretty important."

"Not really."

"Here, make love to me. There'll be no shelling for a while still."

"I haven't finished telling you about my mother."

"That'll wait."

"She always told me not to be like her. She didn't like my leftist friends because her leftist friends had sold her out. 'Have a different kind of life than mine,' she said."

"Ssshhh. I don't want to hear any more sad tales of relatives. All my tales of relatives are sad, too. Let me kiss you, prisoner."

Dreyer never did get to tell Nora any more about his mother. The shelling came even before they made love. She went to fight, but it was the last battle and she was captured by government troops. In his mind, as he placidly watched them take her away, her blonde tawny tresses bouncing against her empty cartridge belt, he imagined telling her about Mother. He described in more vivid detail than would have been possible had he spoken aloud, how Mother had been dragged before that awful committee. He used exquisite irony to relate how she had discovered which of her trusted friends had turned her in. He avoided maudlinity in describing her televised interrogation and short subsequent prison sentence. He missed seeing Nora's reaction to his withering comment about how mother's real punishment had not come until after prison.

Dreyer tried to back out of witnessing the execution of the rebels, but the government representative insisted rather forcefully. Blissians required victims to be present at the disposal of a criminal. The rebels were disposed of by being forced to inhale a poisonous substance within a globe that encased their entire bodies. The death was slow, but apparently painless. Governments of Bliss had banned all painful executions some time ago. Dreyer tried to turn his head away when Nora's turn came, but the government representative insisted that he watch, especially since she had been a ringleader. While he tried to avoid concentrating on it, he observed that she died rather blandly, too self-satisfied to exhibit emotion. As each of the rebels died, the crowd, except for Dreyer, applauded. The government representative was displeased by his lack of applause, thinking that he meant to mock the ceremony.

The rest of Dreyer's stay in Bliss was devoted to the compilation of a massive study of the world's customs, laws, and history, wording it as skillfully and enthusiastically as he could so that it might catch the attention of his superiors and the interest of any summoned academics. He narrowly escaped death during his final week on Bliss when he accidentally mispronounced the name of one of the world's deities. His angry attacker was easily subdued by about eighty members of some politician's honor guard.

As a legacy to Bliss, he dictated a short book about Earth in as good a rendering of the chief native language as he could muster. Because of the book, Dreyer was finally allowed a tour of the forbidden university enclaves so that he could be ritually interviewed by Blissian academics, most of whom commented that Earth seemed a bit too risque and violent for their tastes. At every stop along the tour there were small dissident groups carrying message globes that said Dreyer had to be an imposter. Just before he left Bliss, there was a rumor that a fleet of spaceships had been sighted heading toward the planet. He would have stayed around for the action, but he could lose his fix on Earth coordinates and dissolve into free-floating microdots if he did not return at the scheduled time. So he activated—with a bit more regret than he would have expected—the alt-world transporter and skipped back to the home-world.

At headquarters he endured the usual set of meetings with bored supervisors. His debriefing was cursory, a sure sign that his report would not receive the attention of academics. He was disappointed. However, it turned out that their attention had been diverted by another returning colleague—not Hrozberg unfortunately—who had just visited a world in which Kennedy had survived the assassin's bullet. A report which showed the destiny of their world with the alteration of a single important historical event *always* took precedence over reports like Dreyer's on Bliss, which involved no specific negative correspondences with Earth history.

Dreyer requested the usual rest and recuperation leave, which was immediately granted.

Martha rambling rose of the wildwood now lived with another man, a critic, but not the one whom Dreyer had insulted at her party. This critic was working on a comparative study of Proust and Serge Diaghilev. Martha was no doubt having its pages bronzed. She said she was not returning to Dreyer this time. "You must understand, dear," she said and seemed a trifle disappointed that he did. Martha was now ageing rapidly, and in certain harsh lights, reminded him of his granny-like mother.

His daughter, name now shifted from Lila Lana Leilani to Devi, had discovered Democratic Buddhism. He would have liked to ask her what it was, but one of its tenets was that converts could not speak to anyone from their pre-convert lives.

His son Tim was enthusiastically considering the alt-world service. Dreyer wished that he could have encouraged Tim with a similar enthusiasm. It seemed better to leave him alone and let him dream of unlikely adventures.

Hrozberg dropped by unexpectedly while Dreyer was visiting his son. He proposed that they go to a new lake somebody had just rebuilt almost from scratch, and get in some peaceful fishing. Dreyer asked Tim to come along, but the boy wanted to search out an apartment for himself and his new girl friend. They wanted an especially comfortable place to live since Tim, if he made the alt-world service, would be away so often and for so long. Dreyer resisted telling Tim to go get further advice from Martha.

On the way to the reconstituted lake, Dreyer found that Hrozberg had just returned from an alternate world that called itself Joy. It had many correspondences to Bliss, it turned out, and they got a big laugh out of that.

The lake was extraordinarily pleasant. They had a wonderful time fishing, swimming, and sunning. However, Hrozberg was soon saying interminably how he was itching to get back to headquarters and go out on a new assignment. As usual, he was surprised that Dreyer didn't seem to feel similar urges. He attributed Dreyer's reluctance to Martha's defection to the critic. "You'll get her back any day now," Hrozberg said, "they all return to our folds—we're alt-worlders, after all." Dreyer said he had no great desire to see her again. Hrozberg thought that was funny, and laughed heartily.

The vacation trip would have been idyllic had it not been for the minor tragedy of its last day, when Hrozberg was stricken with a heart attack. He didn't die, for which Dreyer was glad, but the poor man would no longer be fit for the alt-world service.

While Hrozberg clutched his chest in pain and emitted earth-shaking groans, and they awaited the return signal from a hovering ambulance, Dreyer wondered momentarily if his half-brother Warren's death had looked anything like this.

THE PATHOSFINDER

by Pat Cadigan

It has often been said, and truly, that the "discovery" of our ids and egos has spawned a thriving industry and given jobs to millions. Certainly psychological research of all sorts and therapies of all sorts are big business these days, and in no danger of going out of style or becoming unnecessary to a Self-oriented and fundamentally confused human race. Newcomer Pat Cadigan takes a very believable look into the possible future growth of both our problems and the therapeutic tools we're developing to handle them. And in so doing, introduces us to Deadpan Allie, a unique character we hope to see more of.

"Kid," said the big little man on the couch, "neurosis-ped-dlers are a buck a gross in this town. Better you should be a good pathosfinder."

They don't call me Deadpan Allie for nothing. I kept my feelings away from my face and didn't so much as shift a hair on my own couch. I'm sharp. But my heart slid down to about liver-level. If Nelson Nelson, the biggest man in the business knew what he was saying (which he did—he was sharp, too), then I had just wasted $10,000 and a year of my life on the finest mindplay institute in the northern hemisphere. I could have chewed up the scenery.

Instead, I said, "Pathosfinder," being careful to keep my voice neutral.

"Pathosfinder. Hell, woman, you were at J. Walter Tech. You must have had a course in it."

"Yes, I did." Oh, did I! And came away from it with the overpowering feeling that pathosfinding was for wimps.

"You probably think pathosfinding is for wimps," said Nelson Nelson, rolling over to watch the dancers on the ceiling. I could tell they were dancers by the flickering. A year before, I might have rolled over to watch them, too, drawn by the faint classical music flowing under our conversation, but one of my teachers had tipped me off to that tactic. Let prospective employers divide your attention like that and they can get you to agree to all sorts of things without your realizing it, the foxier ones planting suggestions keyed in with symbols. Or they can use subliminals to convince you that you don't want the job, if *they* don't want *you*. It saves them the trouble of arguing with you. So I held my position, reclining on my left side with my hands composed in front of me, resisting the urge to pick at the lamé upholstery. Only a man as successful as NN would be vulgar enough to have lamé interview couches. Of course, I was dying to look up at the ceiling. Whatever those dancers were doing he was enjoying immensely. But I kept watching him watching the holo until he acknowledged my self-control and rolled back over to face me.

"All right," he said, smoothing out a wrinkle in his loose tunic. Loose tunics were all the rage that year; even I was wearing one, despite my preference for secondskins. "All right." He touched a button on the low desk between us and the music faded. I glanced up in time to see the dancers wink out. "Bolshoi, about seventy years ago, just before they went weightless. They're all twelve feet tall now. You like ballet?"

"A lot." I was glad I hadn't sneaked an eye at the holo. I would have been lost in the performance until he wheeled me out a side exit, couch and all.

"Me, too. I can see it takes more than a holo-tank to frag your concentration, isn't it so? Sure." He lit a cigarette. "Want one? Imported. Straight tobacco. I wouldn't try to drug you." He tossed me the pack and I plucked it out of the air.

"Thanks." I lit up by the glowhole in the couch frame. After a puff I nodded at him, pleased.

"Impressed that I can throw around imported tobacco? Be

honest, now." The sagging round eyes on either side of the bumpy nose twinkled.

I shrugged with one shoulder. "Let's say it's more like I'm satisfied. I expected it."

Nelson Nelson took a drag and laughed out smoke in foggy rhythm. "You'll do. All right, you can work for me. That's a privilege, kid, I don't employ many people. I've got a client waiting list that could stretch to the moon and I like it that way. But you're going to work as a pathosfinder, not a neurosis-peddler."

"Be serious." I felt like I had nothing to lose. If he let me get this far, he wasn't about to toss me out now. "I'm the best neurosis-peddler in town."

"Sure you are. But I told you, neurosis-peddling is too much of a good thing right now. On my payroll, you're a pathos-finder."

"Look, I'm trained for neurosis-peddling. That's all. I don't know anything about pathosfinding."

"I know that. Here's something else I know: the best institutes in the world don't train people how to work. All my staff I train myself." He swept an arm out expansively, as though he had trained the room, the couches, and the entire building. Maybe he had. "I'm gonna strip you down and build you back up again. When I'm through with you, you'll be the best pathosfinder in the country. If you're not, you can sue me and I'll settle with you for any amount. What's your full, legal name again?"

"Alexandra Victoria Haas."

"Okay, Allie, just a few things before I show you around. You don't like what you hear, get up and walk. Fair?" He nodded for me. "Fair. You lose your eyes tomorrow." He paused, waiting for me to react. "That bother you?"

"No, I—"

"Good for you. A lot of agencies let you keep them until they wear out, but I say, why wait? You're gonna be hooked up to the system more often than anyone in any other profession. Living eyes weren't made to be popped in and out that often. Pretty soon you've got a couple of rotten eggs endangering your optic nerve. The eyes I'm gonna give you reattach to the muscles easier, not to mention the optic nerve which I already mentioned." NN took another pack of cigarettes from the desk, waving away my offer of the pack he'd tossed me. "Keep 'em. Happy birthday." He lit up again and blew smoke toward a far corner of the room. "They come in here from the best institutes in the country thinking they can get away with a little fudging. But you can't fudge in this business. The last time I had the best pathosfinder in town on that couch, he was a chubby little guy who wanted to hook up to the system through the ears. Said it was just as good. *I* said, 'How're you gonna hear me tell you what a lousy job you're doing with your ears plugged up like that?' He took a stroll. He's not the best pathosfinder in the country, that's for sure. Then there was the guy with a *socket* in the back of his head, like he was a zombie being repatterned. He said he could hook directly into the vision center of his brain, bypassing the optic nerve altogether. I showed him out. I don't have that kind of equipment." NN leaned forward and squint-frowned at me. "*You* don't have any sockets in *your* head, do you?"

"No, I—"

"Just checking. There may be a better method than the optical system, but as far as I'm concerned, it hasn't been invented yet. Hooking up through the ears is complicated, time-consuming. Ever seen the inside of an ear? What a mess! Going in through the ears is like hacking your way through the jungle when there's a perfectly good freeway with no traffic on it you could use instead. And connecting right into the visual center of the brain is more direct, sure, but the brain doesn't like that. It likes to get its pictures through the optic nerve, the way it *always* gets its pictures. Sockets in the head! Goddamit, why do people think they have to break into the skull like burglars when they've got two perfectly good entrances right here?" He pointed two fingers at his own eyes and I thought for a moment he might accidentally poke himself.

"NN, I really don't have anything against the optical system," I said quickly, before he could draw another breath. "J. Walter altered my eyes surgically so I could remove them to hook into their system. But I came here knowing your policy."

"Then there's no problem." NN smiled blissfully. "It's so nice when there's no problem. I just don't like it if I want to send somebody out on a job and it's no-go because the eyes are rotten eggs and the optic nerve's infected and I have to spend more than I lost on the job getting the mess fixed."

"Not to mention the person in question having to sit around blind for months," I added.

"That's right, Allie. You take care of your part, I take care of mine and everybody gets rich. But you won't have a thing to worry about with the eyes I'm gonna give you as long as you treat them right. The retinas are guaranteed—you couldn't detach them with a twenty-mule team and the company replaces the optic nerve connection every five years free of charge. They're the finest eyes in the world. If you don't think so, sue me and I'll support you for life."

We laughed together, both of us knowing he could probably wiggle out of that one, even though he was recording.

"Your new eyes can be just like your old ones, or you can have your choice of simulated bio-gems—bloodstone, onyx, cat's-eye, fire opal—whatever you want."

"I'll take cat's eye."

"Ah? Good for you. It'll be striking. Like a trademark, which is *very* good for business. You'll get a following." His foxy old face was all lit up. "I can see it now—Deadpan Allie, sees in the dark." He winked at me, popped his own eyeballs into his palms and then clapped them back into the sockets without breaking the connections. "See? They're that easy. What do you think?"

"I think it could give new meaning to the sentence, 'His eyes dropped to his soup.'"

NN guffawed so heartily his couch shuddered. "Not bad, Deadpan. I can see already you're going to do well with us. You want to look at the set-up?"

"Sure."

We took his private lateral to the west wing, where the system access was housed. I hesitated before getting into the lateral—I hesitate before getting into anything only seven feet square. NN noticed and said nothing. He knew how I felt about small enclosed places from my psych profile and was waiting to see if I'd throw up on a moving conveyance. Some employers keep testing you right up to the day they ask you to leave.

It took about a minute to reach the west wing. NN kept me distracted with chatter about how his lateral went up and down as well as sideways. Just about the time I got the urge to punch holes in the walls, the lateral stopped at a darkened room, dimming its own lights. Blinking into the darkness, I could just make out the supine form of what seemed to be a headless man on a table. From the neck up, he was engulfed in the computer, which took up most of the room. A pair of bloodstone eyes were waiting in a clear bowl of solution.

"That's Philbert," Nelson Nelson told me. "I'm switching him from pathosfinding to dreamfeeding. He was a good pathosfinder, but we both thought it was time for a change. There are hook-ups for twenty more in here."

Stepping inside, I looked around. I couldn't see much, just enough to tell me it was the biggest system I'd ever encountered. It rose from floor to ceiling, the latter invisible in the gloom, so I couldn't tell if it ended twenty feet up or two hundred. I got the impression that if I yelled, it would echo. Areas of it jutted out like promontories on a cliff, but a cliff born in the mind of a cubist sculptor. Nothing showed, no wires, no dials, no thin seams of light, just a black facade, part of it eating a man's head. The body twitched a little. NN beckoned me back into the lateral.

"Someone else wants in," he said, pointing to a blue light on the lateral's control panel.

"Only one entrance?" I asked as we rotated and started back to his office again.

"A couple of emergency exits, but besides those, yeah, just one. Keeps it private. You know, sometimes you come out of there and you don't want anyone to see you for awhile. The darkness helps that way, too."

My couch was gone when we returned to his office. He sat down on his and turned on the holo again. "That's all, kid. For now. Any questions?"

"Not yet."

"Still want to work for me?"

"Sure."

He leaned back on one elbow and cocked his head. "You really are deadpan, kid."

"How do you know my nickname?"

"It's on one of your recommendations—I won't say whose, but it's the best one you got. Go back and cash in your apartment or wherever you're living—say, you haven't become a Two, have you?"

"No, I'm still single."

"Good. I don't lust after taking on half a couple at this level of development, though one of my people is a Four. Anyway, you move in here tonight. I want you living at the agency while I train you. After that, you can live wherever you please as long as you can get here fast when I need you. Suit?"

I nodded and started to leave when something occurred to me. I paused at the door. "Just one thing. Why is it—"

"—that I bother with educated people if I insist on training them myself? Everyone wants to know that. If you weren't already trained, I wouldn't know you were trainable. I let the institutes weed out the failures and the missionaries for me. See you tomorrow."

I left him to the Bolshoi and slipped the tube back to my apartment, cancelled the lease, sold the big stuff for reprocessing and took one suitcase back to the agency. I found my new quarters easily enough, even though there seemed to be no one in to show me around. The big building was a windowless maze inside, but the laterals and passageways were color-coded. I was at the dormitory less than a minute after I got off the tube at the second level entrance.

My name was already up on the door—as Deadpan Allie, not Alexandra V. Haas—and the door was set to my handprint. It opened to a three room apartment superior to the $1000-a-month efficiency I'd been staying in. I had cooking privileges here—there was a small but elaborate kitchenette—or I could dial up meals and have them delivered to any room in the place. There was an area set up for entertaining, complete with stocked bar; NN apparently believed in socializing. I could guess why. He probably liked having his staff talking shop and picking each other's brains. The bedroom wasn't luxurious, but it wasn't a monk's cell either (if there were any monks left). The bed was big enough for four and firm enough for me, and I wondered whose recommendation that had come from.

There was a conch shell sitting in the middle of the bed. I tossed my suitcase into the autovalet and sat down on the bed. The conch had a note in it reading, simply, "Welcome." It wasn't a cultured shell but the real thing, unpainted and unvarnished. NN sure was ostentatious. I put it carefully on the nightstand and dialed up a mushroom and algae casserole for supper. I found a folder sitting on top of my information access screen, so I lingered over my food, reading about the history of the NN Agency and NN's personal feelings about the history and future of mindplay.

What he had to say didn't differ much from J. Walter Tech's line, except for a small paragraph on the last page. NN felt that mindplay was a necessary tool for the evolving, expanding mind. I've had moments when I felt I could give him an argument against the evolving mind, complete with evidence. Most mindplayers have been down too many jungle paths in their own minds as well as others' to believe humanity is terribly removed from Australopithecus. Conversely, there are small pockets and havens in those same minds possessing a quality that could be called evolutionary if anyone totally understood them. NN's belief that the next step of evolution would take place in the brain and be generated by humans themselves was nothing new. There are plenty of people in the if-god-had-not-meant-for-humans-to-delve-he-wouldn't-have-put-ergot-fungus-on-bread camp. I just hadn't realized that big show-off NN, with his exclusive agency and long client waiting list, was quite so visionary.

I found I was nodding out over his eloquence. Undressing, I adjusted the room temperature, sent the empty casserole down the chute, set the bed for six hours and turned out the light.

Just before I dropped off to sleep, I realized that NN hadn't once mentioned cubs in his folder—what he so quaintly called kids. (Personally, I'd rather be a bear than a goat, but I wasn't about to instruct him in slang usage.) Barring problems needing therapy, cubs couldn't legally mindplay until puberty and even then it was restricted until they came of age at sixteen. I wondered why he hadn't mentioned them in his folder—he'd expounded on just about everything else.

The next day and every day after for six months were all-hours full. I had my eyes out early the first morning and spent the following three days waiting for my new ones and getting acquainted with Rich Lindbloom, who had the apartment next to mine. NN had assigned her to be my seeing-eye person. She was a big one, about seven feet. After I got my eyes, I saw that she was also navy-blue-skinned and orange-haired. Not a permanent dye-job, she told me. She liked to switch around. NN employed her as a thrillseeker. I thought she was a walking thrill all by herself.

Most everyone else besides Rich and Philbert, still switching tracks—Fandangó, the neurosis-peddler, Deacon and Sara, the belljarrers, and the other pathosfinder, Four L.N. (a single parent with three cubs, something you don't see much of anymore)—were in and out as business required, mostly out. NN made himself scarce as well once my training began. He slipped in a few times to check my brainwave personally while I was sleeping. I guess he liked what he saw because he never bothered to wake me.

I spent a lot of the time letting the system eat my head. NN's system took some getting used to; unlike the other ones I'd been hooked into at the institute, this one didn't have a facade personality. At times that was uncomfortable, if not frightening. On other occasions I found it downright comforting. When you get stripped down and built up again, you also get embarrassed and humiliated into the bargain. It can be good to feel that no one, not even an artificial person, is watching.

I had to take all the mindplaying, of course, administered by the appropriate employee, who made a special trip in to do it. I'd had it all before and the system had dreamfed me extensively, but NN wanted me to be on the receiving end of his recommended techniques. Fandango gave me a tendency to be sexually aroused by the color orange with a side impulse to wash my hands a lot. It was an interesting kind of crazy, though crazy wasn't really the word for it. There were (and are) people who will sell you a full-blown psychosis, which is illegal unless you're a licensed psychomimick. A neurosis-peddler would sell you something that would just make you a little stranger than usual for awhile.

Rich dug down into my mind, found a thrill and arranged it for me. The subconscious contains no end of thrills, but a thrillseeker has to be an uncommonly good judge of what can be brought up for recreation and what ought to stay buried. A thrill might be something as simple as (true case) walking a dog—but a thrillseeker determines what kind of dog, what color leash, where the walk should take place, how long it should go on and why it should end. Frankly, that had never sounded too thrilling to me, but somebody got a real charge out of it. I was satisfied with my own thrill, though I suspected she was getting back at Fandango for making me go into rut every time she brushed her hair.

Philbert finished switching tracks, so I let him practice his dreamfeeding on me. I've always enjoyed dreamfeeding. It's just mind-expansion while you sleep. Made-to-order dreams were impossible—the imagination is too autonomous for that and hypnosis won't work on everybody. But you can be fed a few images and allowed to run with them. If you happened to run over a cliff, you woke up, having had an adventure and a mistake without any repercussions in the real world. Dream-feeding had been used for decades as decision-making therapy; it's also a helluva lot of fun.

Belljarring was the only thing I couldn't look forward to. It was too much like being buried alive. It's the total withdrawal of the conscious person, a turning inward for a set period of time—aside from death, the ultimate vacation. There used to be mystics who could achieve such a state, and maybe somewhere there still were. But your average worn-out, rundown party animal who's been buying neuroses (and maybe an illegal psychosis), having wild dreams and seeking thrills after working all day would eventually want to belljar and needed help to do it. Deacon was sensitive to my dislike of being cut off and worked to give me a people-just-in-the-next-room impression. It only lasted half a day and it was just fine—when it was over.

Four L.N. and I spent some time hooked in together so I could get the feel of how he worked. Pathosfinders deal mainly with artists—actors, painters, dancers, fetishists, and so on—to enhance what you might call the soul in their work. The result could be facile or honestly deep, depending on how thorough the artist and the pathosfinder were. Some people just don't want to dig past the easy solution. Facile art has its place, I suppose, but not with me. On the other hand, the old Bolshoi never had the benefits of any kind of mindplay and their tapes could still bring goosebumps all over me. Maybe it was the primitivism. But they were the exception. Most of the arts had experienced a heightening with the advent of mindplay. After working with Four L.N., I had to admit that pathosfinding wasn't the least bit wimpy. Even if it made you feel wimpy sometimes. Just sometimes.

Training concluded, NN gave me a week to sit around and do nothing more than breathe in and out. He even loaned me one of the Bolshoi tapes, which I accepted with slavering enthusiasm although I didn't like the look on his face when he handed it over. It was too much like the expression a canary might have after successfully gulping down a cat, whiskers and all. I figured he probably had a tough assignment waiting for me.

I was right. One week to the minute after my training was

over, I found myself reclining on the couch in his office, listening to him tell me about Marty Oren, the actor who had started to make sensations just before retiring to an anti-mind-play enclave with his new wife two years before.

"He's back on the outside, wife and all," NN told me. "He tried old-style theatre while he was in and apparently found it extremely unsatisfying. He was vague about that on his preliminary application. Truth to tell, I think the adulation of a few hundred people was too little for him. Anyway, his old company kept letting him know regularly they were ready for him any time he wanted to come back. So he's back. He and Sudella Keller are in Restawhile, Kansas."

"Restawhile? *Kansas*?"

NN shrugged. "It's sort of a year-round resort-cum-village, very quiet. Ideal for making a transition back into the mainstream."

"Transition? How do they live in those enclaves—in mud-huts?"

NN smiled. "Not exactly. It's a difference in sensibilities. Without a transition period, he could be culture-shocked so severely, he'd develop a psychosis. Kind of like if you took an 18th century hermit and dropped him smack in the middle of the 20th century."

"Marty Oren isn't an 18th century hermit. He grew up—"

"Only recently. He's just twenty-two years old, a comparative baby."

"Compared to who?"

"You. And me. He went through his second puberty in an enclave. Don't look at me like that, a lot of experts are calling the years between eighteen and twenty-four second puberty."

Involuntarily I felt my face with my hand.

"Relax, Deadpan. It's just because I know you so well. You don't have to agree with me, just do your job. Besides Oren's well-being, there's also his wife to consider."

"What's she going to do, make the transition with him?"

"Hell, no. She's just as anti-mindplay as she ever was. She's your stumbling block." He smiled pleasantly at me. "All these jobs have stumbling blocks, did I ever mention that? So it's going to be hard for you to work with him while she's there. The only thing you've got going for you is her respect of his personal choices, but she's bound to inhibit him in some way.

"Also, Oren's always had this bitter streak he's had to keep in check, which I think is why they've always worked him with pathosfinders rather than dreamfeeders or neurosis-ped-dlers, like some actors. After being out of things for two years, he needs a pathosfinder more than ever. That's why they asked the agency to handle him instead of turning him over to their resident. His compassion wires are crossed—you've got to get him some. Not maudlin pity, the real stuff. Next month, the Croeder Company wants to put him into rehearsal for *Two Moon Night*, that play about the guy who died alone on Mars."

"I'm familiar with it. Isn't that kind of industrial strength material to start him off on?"

"If he's not ready for it, you'll tell them."

"Thanks. I'm really looking forward to something like that."

NN's smile was broader and more benign than ever.

"No, truth now, NN. If he's as sheltered as you say, do you really think he'll be able to deal with the things a man in that part has to go through—the raptures, the hallucinations, the—"

"Your compassion is showing, Deadpan."

"It's all your fault. I used to be the best neurosis-peddler in town. Now I'm a wimp."

"You really feel that way?"

"No, but I can remember when I used to."

"And can you honestly say I forced you to feel differently?"

I sighed and shook my head. "Empathy's a bitch."

"What isn't? Education is so broadening."

"So I get him into shape for the play. Then what?"

NN looked blank.

"What about his wife? He can't very well move into a city with her."

"They haven't let me in on their plans." NN sounded just a bit sour. "I imagine she'll be staying in Restawhile when he's working. It's far enough out in the country that she can avoid most problems if she's careful. Anyway, they want to stay Two'd, don't ask me why. Neither one of them is about to give so much as an angstrom in their viewpoints—he's going to mindplay, she's dead against it. It's going to screw his emotions around."

"It could be a good source to draw on."

"I doubt it, but use your own judgment. They're both a couple of very defensive people right now."

"I'm not sure if I'm going to be able to make any progress then. The ideal thing would be to work with both of them, but if she won't—" I turned one hand palm up. "Oh, well. It's their time."

"And their marriage. Don't bust it up."

"They can't blame me if they decide to—"

"They most certainly *will* blame you if they decide to. They're the sort of people who tend to lay blame elsewhere for their own messes. So watch your feet. He probably wouldn't sue us, but she most definitely would. And I don't want that, not at all."

"Has she got big power connections?"

NN flipped on the ceiling holo and the familiar Bolshoi music filled the room. "Sort of. She's my daughter."

Ah.

I went underground tubeway to Wichita and rented a flier to take me and my equipment east to Restawhile. I spent the time on the tube getting acquainted with Marty Oren's media notices and re-reading *Two Moon Night*. It was a powerful piece of work, heavy on emotion and full of tenuous science, with the potential to be a tearjerker instead of an honest study of a dying man. I had my work built up for me if Oren was going to play that part.

When I got a look at the flier, I nearly turned around and went home. It was an airplane converted to computer autopilot, and it looked like it had been put together with masking tape and spit. Nonetheless, it flew, albeit roughly. The rolling Kansas landscape, pretty as it was, gave it a lot of trouble. By the time I got to Restawhile, a hamlet nestled in a hilly patch with a lake squat in the middle, it was late afternoon. I circled the lake several times before I realized the autopilot was dead-locked in an electronic argument with itself as to whether the water could be landed on. I ended up practically landing the goddam thing myself and took a number of turns around the lake on pontoons before I found the dock I wanted. I might not have found it at all, except that Sudella Keller was standing on it, watching me.

She looked large in her loud, flowery-print muumuu, but when I climbed out of the cockpit and onto the dock, I could see she was nearly swimming in the slightly diaphanous material. She wasn't reed thin, but she weighed a good deal less than I did. I'm no one's idea of a little woman—big bones. She was a few inches taller than I, though. Her wide, elegant face was made up subtly but effectively, and it bore absolutely no resemblance to NN's foxy pink features. Her eyes tilted up at the outer corners without actually being Oriental. Her nose turned up, too. If I hadn't known so much about body engineering, I would have thought it was all natural. Apparently bodyplay was all right if mindplay wasn't. Interesting. I chided myself for being catty, but it didn't make things any less interesting.

We just stood taking each other's measure for a few seconds. "You must be Sudella Keller," I said, making an extra effort to be cordial.

"You must be Daddy's thug," she said, also quite cordially.

Ah, I thought, court is in session, the judge is on the bench, and I'm already in contempt.

"I could have told by your eyes, even if I hadn't been told you were coming," she added. "Deadpan Allie. What's so important about being deadpan?"

"A professional mindplayer has to appear neutral at all times. We aren't judges of human behavior." I emphasized *judges* only a little. "Our clients should be unaware either of our approval or displeasure, so they won't attempt to gain either."

"Well, I see you've swallowed Daddy's menu first course to last."

I opened my mouth to ask her why she was so bitched at Daddy, but it really wasn't any of my business. Instead, I asked her if it would be all right to bring in my equipment.

"I'll show you your room. Then you can decide whether you want to or not. It's not much bigger than the inside of your flier and you didn't mention how long you'd be staying."

"I'm afraid I don't know exactly how long that will be. I don't have much with me."

"Good thing."

"I don't need much."

"So *you* say," she muttered, and led me down the pier to the house. It was an old-fashioned cottage with a bare minimum of conveniences, none of which were in the broom closet they called a guest room. The bed was a waterbed, which took up most of the space. I stood in the doorway staring at it and trying not to think about my mattress back at the agency. "Nice woodwork," I said lamely.

"As you can see, it'll be pretty cramped."

I smiled up at her. After the trip I'd had in the flier and seeing the size of that room, I must have looked like my face hurt. "It doesn't worry me," I lied. "Where's Two Oren?"

"Gone fishing. Ever gone fishing yourself?"

"Only in the mid-Atlantic. And then only for shark." I winced inwardly. If I couldn't be more deadpan than to one-up fish stories, I was going to make a bigger mess than I was supposed to straighten out. But somehow it seemed to have been the right thing to say. She almost smiled back at me. Perhaps she was surprised that I didn't spend all my waking hours letting Daddy's computer eat my head. I left her sitting at the square plastic dining room table while I settled my stuff.

I had already decided to sleep on the roof and was wheeling the last components of my portable system over the extendable ramp from the flier to the dock when Marty Oren came home, rowing himself in a rowboat. I stopped to watch him, wondering what part of the lake he'd come from that I hadn't seen him from the air. He looked tired, disgusted, sunburned, and very attractive. His hair had grown down below his shoulders and was plaited in two gold braids. The gold was strictly his own, probably maintained from childhood by something in his diet. As he got closer, I saw that his face was more angular than it appeared on holo. Loaded with character, as NN would put it, the kind you don't usually find in a face that young. I decided it was those impressively high cheekbones that gave it to him. He was wearing a white variation of Sudella's muu-muu, so I couldn't tell much about his body. From the way he moved, he seemed to be in excellent shape.

When he reached the dock, I leaned down to give him a hand up and was surprised to see he had cat's-eyes. They looked better in his head than they did in mine.

"Deadpan Allie." He smiled warmly. Inside, I felt a chord being twanged, which is what's supposed to happen when a leading thespian smiles like that in your direction. I didn't make anything of it, but I was sure a lot of people had tried to in the past.

"My reputation took an earlier tube," I said. "I feel famous."

"Nelson Nelson gave you a big build-up." Something visually imperceptible changed in his face; he had shut himself off from me at his own mention of his father-in-law. It was as sudden and effective as a slap.

"Like to row yourself?" I pointed at the boat. He was empty-handed, without even a fish-hook. I decided against asking him if he'd caught anything.

He nodded. "It's hard work. I like the exercise. Have you eaten?"

"Not yet."

"We'll have some food and then get started." He looked back out over the water, which was turning gold as the sun began to edge toward dusk. "Nice day."

"Lovely."

I wheeled my equipment ahead as we walked down the dock to the house together. Sudella was waiting like a statue at the door.

The meal was a roast duck the size of a turkey, cooked in an old microwave, a real, functioning antique. It took all of twenty minutes, including the algae. The message couldn't have been clearer if Sudella had stood in the middle of the room shouting it instead of watching Marty cook: *Old ways are best.* We sat around the table passing each other orange sauce, (which stirred a few decidedly unusual memories in me from my months of training), and not saying much. I felt like I was in a holo period piece, complete with anachronisms. Marty and Sudella loosened up some, not so much relaxation as resignation, but they both remained pretty self-conscious. I tried reading Marty's Emotion Index by sight, but I couldn't get much feeling for his state of mind. Sudella's was only too clear.

After we ate, they cleared the table, leaving me the coffeepot and a cup. I pretended not to watch them as they put the reusable dishes in the washer. For a few moments, their guards went way down. It was obvious that they loved each other a great deal and at the same time were in conflict with each other's desires. Pretty normal for a married couple. The love part seemed intensified, like sunlight reflected on water, and that bothered me. If I could have delved her, just a little—but by law, I couldn't even ask her. I'd have to work their puzzle with half the pieces.

Pouring myself another cup of coffee, I lit a cigarette and

settled into a more comfortable position. They were dawdling by the dishwasher, so I indicated I could wait as long as they could. Finally, Marty came over and sat down across from me. "Do you want to start?"

"There's no hurry if you want to relax some."

He glanced at Sudella, still over by the dishwasher. "I want to get this over with as soon as possible."

"You probably remember this isn't a process you can rush. There's no way I can tell how long it's going to take until we start." Peripherally, I saw Sudella cross her arms and stand up a bit straighter. "I may be here awhile."

He looked down at his hands. "I hadn't thought there would be much to do. It always went pretty smoothly before."

"You've been out of touch," I said, hoping I sounded tactful.

"Well, I've always worked with pathosfinders, so I'm used to it. Or I was."

Sudella walked over behind him and began to undo his braids without looking at me.

"I'm sorry," I told her, feeling like a cast-iron bitch, "but you can't do that. Not now."

She stared at me, one braid lying limply across her palm. "You look like brother and sister." She turned and strode out the front door, leaving it open behind her.

Marty started to get up. "I'd better go after her—"

"Sit where you are. Sudella is showing us a great deal of courtesy. I think we should respect her by accepting it."

"But she left because—"

"A lot of the right things get done for the wrong reasons. If I gave you a soft purple sponge, what would you do?"

"Hold it in my hands and squeeze it." He twisted in his chair, wanting to get up and go to the open door but not letting himself.

"If I gave you a green hat with a brim all the way around it, what would you do?"

"I'd see if it was my size."

He went on for close to a half hour, longer than usual, but I thought he would enjoy playing *What Would You Do?* Most people did. They forgot it was less a game than a relaxation exercise geared to provide a pathosfinder with some hints about what kinds of things were wandering around in their heads. He got involved in it and by the time I asked the last question his answers were spontaneous and his mind was off Sudella.

I gave him one of NN's expensive cigarettes to keep him busy but idle while I wheeled out my apparatus and put it together. It was like playing with a giant set of cub's blocks, three big pieces and five smaller ones. When I finished making the connections, I had a portable version of NN's cubist cliff, looking off-balance but actually quite stable. It wouldn't eat our heads—we wouldn't need it long enough at a time for that to be necessary—and it was geared not for teaching, but for co-learning.

I pulled out the drawer with the four connections and the thermos tank of solution that would hold our eyes while we were hooked up. "Ready?"

"Do you know there are no longer any actors alive today who still have their own eyes?" he asked suddenly.

"Does that bother you?"

"It seems strange, to draw on life but to look at it through artificial eyes."

I wasn't about to debate the merits of enhanced vision versus natural astigmatism. Pushing the tank over, I showed him how it was compartmented, so we wouldn't be groping like blind mice for our optics when we were through for the evening. He had to make several tries to get his eyes out and finally I had to help him guide his fingers. His eyes were deepset and he was out of practice. After I hooked him into a relaxation exercise, I made a quick check of his eyes' connections. The tissue and insulation would be good for another year at most; then they would have to be replaced. I wondered how he had planned to do that from an enclave, or if he even knew what condition his eyes were in.

After a minute of deep breathing, I hooked myself in, making my presence felt gradually so he wouldn't feel like I was bursting in on him. He was in the middle of a chromatic exercise, making colors. Surprisingly, he didn't seem to have much enthusiasm for it. I made a few with him—navy blue to jade blue to scream blue to milk blue, and he yielded the whole thing to me with an inordinate amount of juvenile boredom. Perhaps I had relaxed him too much, and he was getting impatient again. I put the colors aside and indicated we could start.

Nothing happened. I prodded again, and then again before I got any results. We were in a bare, sterile room, no windows, no doors, nothing. Just smooth white walls. It was an unusual reaction, but not totally unheard of. He was sitting in one corner with his legs stretched out in front of him, hands resting on his thighs. I seemed to be invisible.

You're blocking me, I told him. *Stop it.*

The figure in the corner slumped and became a marionette. My invisible self was suddenly awash in waves of *reassure me, reassure me*. Too pat.

Come off that cornball stuff and let's do some real work, Marty. I didn't drop yesterday.

The marionette persisted a moment longer, as though he thought he might get me to believe he really did need reassurance that he wasn't just a pawn by sheer stubbornness. Then everything faded, leaving us in limbo, aware of each other's presence but alone.

I couldn't help chuckling a little. Lots of people feel that way, though very few of them are so textbookesque in expressing it. *You have to help me. I can't carry us both.* Not strictly true, but the idea was to keep him thinking for himself, not following my lead.

No response. I checked his vitals; he was conscious, still with me. He just didn't seem to care.

I didn't want to, but he was pushing me into it, so I showed him my hands. They're very good hands. The fingers are not overly long and I don't keep my nails in lady-of-leisure claws. The knuckles are knobby and the veins stand out, making them look like they've done more work than they actually have. They make great helping symbols, help in this case meaning compassion. I showed him my hand in his as I had helped him up from his boat onto the dock, laying on light overtones of *perfectly natural, happy to know you, desire to touch.*

He went to mimick it, but I blocked him and took stock of his real responses.

He was unimpressed.

For a moment, I was totally taken aback. Then the undertones came in. I distracted him with a long string of routine questions in the guise of an identity check (often necessary for people whose work is pretending they're somebody else) while I shorted out the new data.

He had been truly unimpressed with my friendly gesture on the dock, not in a hostile way but in a taken-for-granted way. People did things for him, he was used to it and that was all. He was at home with the idea that others found him desirable to be near for any number of reasons. My passing him on the street would have affected him about as much.

I showed him Sudella, disregarding NN's warning about using that angle. I showed her undoing his braids and feeling left out because we had the same eyes. He clamped down on any clear-cut reaction, but not fast enough to hide a sense of responsibility or obligation for something that Sudella may have done for him that was somewhere in the gray area between a service and an outright favor. Spooky. He suddenly let go of the rest involuntarily, and I saw that if I were willing to pick up doing the service/favor where Sudella was leaving off, I could gain his responsibility/obligation.

They don't call me Deadpan Allie for nothing. I let it pass and took his Emotion Index. It came up nightmare purple. Fear. Of me. I examined myself to see how he was visualizing me, thinking that he might be seeing a monster. He wasn't; I looked almost normal, except my hands were exaggerated out of proportion. As I watched, he tried to put nailholes in them.

No, I said firmly. *That's not what I'm here for. No one can do that.*

Feeling a ghost of a protest, I went for a walk through his life. He tried to keep me distracted with the recent past, his sense of triumph and accomplishment after each performance. It disturbed him that I noted only his orgasms during applause. I went back further to the time before he became an actor, for a look at his family.

He'd been a Three, an only child between two parents, a tripod, which some diehard experts were still claiming as the most stable of family configurations. I found it unusual that it was so nuclear—most people made at least superficial outside attachments, just for variety, but as far as he knew, neither one of his parents ever did. The pressure on each corner of the triangle had remained somewhat constant until sometime after he reached puberty, when his corner began to spike up and down before ascending rapidly out of plane. So much for the stability of the tripod. I thought about examining his memories of his parents further, but if the tripod situation was any indication, that wouldn't do much good.

I searched around for his first mindplay experience and found it much further on, a full two years after he had come of age. He had been eighteen years old when he had his first acting audition, and he had worked with the company's paof age. He had been eighteen years old when he had his first acting audition, and he had worked with the company's pathosfinder. I went back and checked carefully to make sure I hadn't missed any suppressed dreamfeeding therapy or thrill-seeking, but there was none. Unusual, but not totally atypical.

The theatre company's pathosfinder had been an incompetent. No, not an incompetent—overworked. It figured. The emphasis had been on turning out performers in a hurry. Rather than working with Marty Oren's inexperienced mind, the pathosfinder had done a rush job, teaching him by example rather than helping him find his own answers. The other actors had been exploring themselves for years, so thoroughly that they needed a pathosfinder only as a steppingstone. The pathosfinder had classified him, put him in a box, and rather than questioning it, Marty had gone along with it out of a desire to get the part, mimicking the appropriate responses. He had really wanted that part, and he got it. I made a note of the pathosfinder's name, but reporting him probably wouldn't do any good. Since he wasn't available to the general public—he was the company resident—he could do his job as badly as they could tolerate, until they became dissatisfied with him. If they ever did.

Marty had gone on to his next play touted as a talent in development. Apparently it had been noticed there was something lacking in him. After the second success, he switched companies, but the next pathosfinder was no better. The troupe was on a tight schedule. By the time he joined the Croeder Company, his mimickry of real emotions had been perfected. All he had to do was reflect the pathosfinder's expectations back to the source.

I controlled my anger and told him he should have gone for help. A feeling of *I didn't need help, I was doing fine on my own* came out of him.

We can put this right, I said.

Can we?

He became an observer while I searched around for things he cared about. A two-dimensional image of Sudella slipped by me before I could catch it, turned sideways, and disappeared. I went after it. Hooked directly into his mind, he couldn't keep me out of any place I wanted to go. I passed a lot of locked places, jerking them open as I went just to show him that I could. He didn't try to stop me; I received a distinct impression of its not mattering anymore.

I found Sudella's image, still two-dimensional, in a room of mirrors. It wore a fixed smile on its face, reflected a thousand times over. I ignored her and looked deliberately into the mirrors to be sure he saw what I was doing. If everything he cared about was two-dimensional, he could deal with me alone.

I plucked my eyes out of my head.

It was a purely figurative act, but the feeling of reality in it hit him hard, and he couldn't maintain the mirrors. Vision heightened rather than destroyed, I went back to the locked places I had forced open.

I was standing in a hallway now, lined with open doors. It was shadowy, empty, abandoned, a place no one had ever come to. I went along it slowly, pausing at each of the doors I'd opened to look into the rooms beyond.

They were all empty. There was nothing to see in any of them and no sign of anything ever having been there. Occasionally there was a strong smell of something spoiled, but it was just a smell. Once I heard something large and wet shift its weight, but it was only a noise.

I let him close the doors after me, locking each one tightly, not against me but because there was no point to leaving them open. It was just a place in his mind. His body was an instrument rather than a live thing, his face a device, his eyes windows where no curtains had ever hung. He didn't hate. He just couldn't care.

He was possibly one of the best actors of all time.

It would have taken a doctor to alter a chemical balance, change a pH or find a new path for certain impulses, not me. I couldn't diagnose his inability to love as a disorder, even if I thought it was a severe one. Which I did. I was there only to help him find what he had. If it wasn't there, we couldn't find it.

I sensed he was waiting for me to do something else, but there was nothing more to do. I began to withdraw.

Wait, he said. I waited. For a moment, nothing happened. Then a landscape began to form around us. It was all from him, though I could feel him trying to draw on me. I clamped down; it wasn't my business to build his landscape. He didn't like that much but I wasn't about to let him pass my creations off as his own. All he could manage was bare earth under a colorless, sunless sky. None of it felt terribly real. *Best I can do,* he said. *Unless you'll help?*

I didn't say anything. He strained a little and I felt the ground against my feet. It was like standing on cardboard.

Better? he asked hopefully.

I looked around trying to see him, but he seemed to be in my blind spot. Every time I turned my head, he'd slide away, leaving a blurry glimpse of gold hair. *There's nothing more I can do here,* I told him.

Then what are *you going to do?* Nightmare purple flickered like heat lightning. *Turn me in?*

To whom? As what? It's not against the law not to care.

Then tell me what to do.

I pretended not to know what he meant. *Get help. You're young.*

No.

Why not?

The purple flickered again before he could control himself. *Go back to the enclave,* I told him. *You'll be safe there.*

I just need a pattern to follow! The landscape went away and we were back in the theatre. *See? This feels real, doesn't it? All I need is a pattern. For me, it's just as good—*

I know, I said. My control was starting to give out. He knew it, too. In another moment, he was going to have a pattern to follow that he'd never forget. But wasn't that what acting was? Suddenly I felt confused. *Didn't you think someone would catch on someday?* I asked him, covering myself. *Another actor, a better pathosfinder, or even Sudella?*

He was right up against me, trying to get in, trying to get at me. *Sudella loves the reflection of her love. And youth is forgiven many things, including callowness. I am as good a mirror out there as I am in here. The world is my oyster. I am the pearl.*

That gave me a chill. My control wavered and I withdrew before he could react. I tossed him into another innocuous relaxation exercise and broke the contact between us. Then I took his lousy theatre and his crappy landscape and his stupid marionette in the white room and I blew them the fuck up. I did it seven times and it felt better after each one. It's always so good to feel.

When I disconnected and put my eyes back in, I saw that Sudella had come in out of the dark and was standing behind Marty. She was very pointedly not looking at the eyes. They are a bit grisly when they're out if you're not hardened to that kind of thing. I reached into the drawer and ran down a line of switches. Each of Marty's limbs gave a small jump, separately and then all together. Sudella made a strangled, gasping noise.

"What are you doing to him?"

Nothing, compared to what he tried to do to me. "Making sure his motor controls haven't suffered. Routine." I unhooked him, popped his eyes back in and turned him around to Sudella before he could say anything. He stared up at her open face, which was filled with longing and compassion for him. Sudella in the empty theatre, applauding for all she was worth.

"You must be exhausted, Marty. Why don't you lie down?" I said.

"Yes. I think I will." He turned back to me and I saw a trickle of blood leaking out of the corner of his left eye. Sudella wiped it away with her fingertip.

"He's hurt," she accused.

"He's all right. He just ruptured a capillary. It happens sometimes when you're out of practice." I nodded at Marty. He gave me that smile again, but this time all I could see were lips and perfect teeth. For an empty package, he had a beautiful wrapper. Then he went into the bedroom and shut the door behind him.

"Now what?" Sudella lifted her chin at me.

"Now I leave." I began dismantling my apparatus. "Marty will explain everything. He's decided to return to the enclave with you. He's—" I paused. "He's who he is."

"I know." Her lips pressed together hard. "He never needed your stupid mindplay. It's indecent to go running around in a person's mind like that. You find things you shouldn't know about."

I stopped what I was doing and leaned on my equipment. "Why not? Why shouldn't we know?" I asked gently.

She looked at me and for a moment it felt like we were hooked up together. Of course. Rudimentary telepathy. Not developed enough to be useful, just enough to hurt.

"Some of us can live with our illusions." She looked down at her arms which were folded tightly against her chest. "For some of us, it's good enough if you can't get the real thing."

"If that's what you want to settle for."

"If the alternative's nothing at all, what choice have you got?" She was about to cry. "Maybe we can't know ourselves as well without mindplay, but it's the human condition to struggle for it. It's the human condition to try alone."

I didn't comment on Marty Oren's condition. I didn't have to.

Nelson Nelson didn't have much to say about my report, but then I'd left out what I knew about Sudella. If I knew it, he knew it and the only one who could have done anything about it was going back to the enclave with Marty Oren. I had a new perspective on NN's theory of the evolving mind, though—for all the good that would do anyone.

He made a business of getting the receipts for my expenses in order, scrutinizing each card carefully before dropping them through a slot in his desk for final entry into the records while I lay on the couch not looking curious.

"So tell me, Deadpan," he said after a bit, "how it was that you caught his problem when it eluded people who had been practicing for years?"

"I had no expectations, I didn't stereotype him, and I was thorough. You said I'd be the best pathosfinder in the country. I did a superior job."

"Only it was too superior, eh?" NN waved away the remark I was about to make. "Forget it. You did what was best for everyone, especially Sudella. The theatrical world won't come to an end without him."

"What about those pathosfinders who aggravated his problems?"

"He's got only *one* problem. I congratulate you for not dismissing it as a superficial manifestation of an overblown ego, but recognizing it as the fabric of his reality. Woo, what a speech, eh, Deadpan?" He rubbed his wrinkled pink chin with one finger. "You'd make a good reality affixer."

"I don't want to be a nuthouse nanny."

"Good, because I don't need one. Yet." He rolled onto his back and put his hands behind his head. "I've turned their names in for recertification testing. The Mindplay Bureau may get around to calling them in sometime. Bureaucracy stinks."

I shifted position uncomfortably. "Look, if those inept mindplayers aren't found and stopped, we all might as well go back to lysergic acid and watching the ceilings roll by. Without holo tanks."

"Incompetence and mediocrity are everywhere. But what do you think you're here for?"

I frowned, confused.

"Deadpan, it's the nature of any discipline to stagnate for awhile, for the superficial to be received as something of depth and meaning. Mindplay doesn't mean people won't go right on believing what they want to believe. But sooner or later some smartass comes along and points out the emperor is naked."

"Pardon?"

"Never mind. Get out of here, I want to be alone with the Bolshoi."

I got. I didn't like the sound of *What do you think you're here for?* The image Marty Oren had given me of myself with big hands and nailholes still gave me a shudder. Nobody pays well enough for that, not now, not ever.

I tried pointing that out to NN as subtly as I could, every chance I got. He just kept telling me I had the wrong attitude. I figured if I had the wrong attitude long enough, he'd let me go back to neurosis-peddling. And eventually, he did. But not for years. And years.

SEDUCTION

by Doris Vallejo

> *Hark my love,*
> *There he comes,*
> *Leaping over mountains,*
> *Bounding o'er hills.*
> *My love resembles a buck,*
> *Or a young stag.*
> *Lo, there he stands at our wall,*
> *Peeking in the window,*
> *Peering through the lattice.*
> *My love spoke and said to me,*
> *Arise my darling,*
> *My fair one, come.*
> —Song of Songs (2:8–10)

The Song of Songs seemed as worthy an introduction to Doris Vallejo's latest story as any other. Both are the songs of lovers, rather marvelous lovers of their kind. It is very true that all lovers are somehow larger than life, as though redeemed by a magic passing. A lover might be anyone, anything, but never is a lover mundane. That a lover should be a vampire...Why not? Even mortal love chills our blood, steals our hearts.

116

A vampire came into my room one night. I awoke to find him lying beside me. A warm rain had been falling earlier. I'd left the window open so as to hear it better. He might have come in to escape the rain. Or, he might have come looking for me. I suppose I shall never know. If I ask him I cannot assume he will tell me the truth.

He appeared to be sleeping. His eyes were closed. His lips, slightly parted as though for a kiss, disclosed two silvery fangs. My hand went involuntarily to my throat. The area was slightly tender. I perceived two infinitesimal puncture wounds. This comforted me strangely. I thought the inclement weather may have accounted for his visit but he stayed because of me.

"I am not asleep," he said, although his eyes remained closed. His face, illuminated by starlight, appeared to be chiseled out of mother-of-pearl, an exquisite sculpture. I leaned over him, tempted to kiss those suggestively-parted perfect lips. I pretended that he was asleep, that those soft words uttered almost as a warning were meaningless syllables mumbled in a dream. I did not kiss him, however.

His dark beautiful hair flowed like shadows about his head. He wore a silky white shirt deeply slashed at the neck and his strongly defined chest rose and fell steadily under the clinging fabric. His black cape hung over the back of my chair. The spectral face of a gargoyle grinned hideously from its folds. Imagination, I told myself. There is no gargoyle in the cape.

He is asleep, I told myself. Therefore this is the moment I must make use of. This is the moment, as vampire legends dictate, that I must plunge a wooden stake into his heart. Yet, I did not. His superbly proportioned body was too solid, too real. Besides, I had no wooden stake. And, he was not really asleep.

He rose suddenly, was up and across the room, moving with the soundless grace of a jungle cat. I was struck by his sleek muscularity. He threw his cape about his shoulders and fastened it at the neck. His face was almost completely hidden by the high collar and by the shadows. His eyes were lost in darkness. I could not tell if he was looking at me or if he had guessed at my only half-serious impulse to thrust a stake into his heart.

Standing there in his long black cape, so reminiscent of an ancient dead era, he might have been a friend who had come to escort me to a masquerade. He might have been waiting for me to don my own costume, perhaps waiting to help me fasten the difficult-to-reach snaps in the back. Or else, he might have been waiting for me to rise, to push the thin lace straps of my nightgown off my shoulders, to let it drop to the floor, to step out of it, to lie back again among the pillows, to invite him...

At the window he was no more than a silhouette against the darkened houses and the night bright sky. I meant to say something, to ask him something. The words refused to take shape. So I waited mutely as the silhouette dissolved into a swiftly dissipated black mist and a small creature flew away on leathery wings.

When the rapid flapping receded into silence I went to the window. There was no trace of the creature. I might have conjured it out of my subconscious, given shape and breath to it out of long-denied yearnings and fears. It is interesting to note that the words which had eluded me earlier came to me then quite spontaneously. "My lover," I whispered into the vast receptive night. As if this admission somehow unburdened me, I went back to bed and fell asleep at once.

All day the memory of my vampire bemused me; at the photo studio where I mechanically set lights and moved props around, at the lunch counter where I ordered black coffee and nothing more, though the counterman aggressively informed me that I would have to pay the minimum nevertheless. At the market where I bought some apples; purplish-red apples because they were the color of rich blood. The memory of him, like an extraordinary secret that no one suspected, gave me a pleasant sense of superiority. In the past I'd often suffered feelings of unimportance and worthlessness. I'd felt drab and ordinary in comparison to the remote, coolly elegant models that came to the studio, disheartened by the unbridgeable distance between myself and them. And suddenly all that occasioned my unhappiness was no longer relevant. I had not only bridged the distance but left them totally behind, tediously bickering there about inconsequentials: the angle most flattering to this or that model's face, the minimum cost of sitting at a lunch counter...

That night an acquaintance called, a man I'd gone out with several times, and asked if I'd like to have dinner with him.

"I'm not in the habit of accepting invitations on such short notice," I told him curtly. An obvious lie. His notice had been equally short the previous times. He sounded hurt and I immediately regretted my abruptness. However, things could not be changed.

I took a long, luxurious bath in scented water. I brushed my hair until it fell in silken waves. I put on a thin white negligee through which my nipples, hard as marbles, appeared provocatively dark. I drew back the curtains, opened the window and lay down to wait. Intermittently I must have slept. I remember some bewildering fragments of dreams; an old woman with milk-white wizened skin wailing incoherently—something about danger. And a face, malevolent, terrifying, laughing at me. No doubt it was that which awakened me, the horror of that face.

I lay—I don't know how long—and gazed at the patterns of moonlight on the wall. With the urging of the light summer wind, clouds drifted ceaselessly across the face of the moon. The patterns changed, shifted, melted into one another. And then all at once they were blotted out.

For a moment he stood large, much larger than I remembered, filling the window, shutting out the moon and starlight entirely. It became intensely black in the room; the air thick, smothering, impossible to breathe.

Then he was beside me, the moonlight sparkling and dancing around him like soundless firecrackers. I reached out to him. I could breathe again. It almost seemed I breathed him in with the air, so utterly, so completely did he enter me, did he fill me with the sweet intoxicating venom of his being that affected me like an opiate. "Do you think it's possible to become addicted to kisses?" I murmured into the shadows of his hair. It seemed to me that he smiled in assent.

I knew perfectly well what would happen next. Yet I was not in the least frightened nor did I cringe from the slight pricking shock of his fangs at my throat. Rather, my blood panted warmly against them as they sunk easily and (so I thought) tenderly deep into the vein.

The pain was momentary, lasting only for that fraction of time it took to pierce the skin. Then a gradually increasing warmth spread through me, a heat, a burning that roared through me with such violence I was sure the blood he drew must blister his mouth, must sear a gory path into him like bubbling lava. Surprisingly, this idea aroused me. I wound my arms and legs about him and strove, quite beside myself, to crush him into me, to become part, to become one with him.

An exhausting effort from which I lay at last quivering and crying in his arms.

When he arose, ready to leave, I noticed that my blood had stained the corners of his lips. I found this oddly beautiful; as though he had feasted on roses and the surfeit, the two sweet petals that had been in excess, now clung delicately to the sides of his mouth.

I cannot pretend it was with naiveté that I entered this liaison. I was aware of the sundry perils. Determined not to become a victim, I stood at the window after he left to await the sunrise. If the light hurt me it would mean that I must not admit him to my rooms again. That I must uproot him from my fantasies. That I must in every way shut myself ruthlessly against him.

A murky fog obscured the street. It rose with the first pale hint of light and hung grayly on the rooftops of the lower houses. Then with the warm confident rising of the sun it magically vanished. No curlicue of slime remained looped over a chimney as a ghostly reminder. The sunlight felt remarkably soothing on my skin. I am still safe, I thought.

Thus it became my habit to await each successive sunrise and only then, after having anxiously determined that I was safe for yet another day, to sleep for a few hours. The strain began to show without my noticing at first. To myself I appeared unchanged. But comments were made at the studio. How worn I looked. How pale. Was I ill? Should I perhaps see a doctor? Was I sure that I felt all right?

Yes, perfectly sure. Absolutely. At first I was merely annoyed by what I considered presumptuous inquiries. Later, prompted, I suppose, by my colleagues' insistence, I examined my face more critically. My eyes did have a hectic, unnatural glitter heightened no doubt by the dark puffy hollows beneath them. All very natural, considering the little sleep I got by on those days. Leave them to their old maid's chatter, I decided. Obviously it gave them a morbid pleasure. There was no reason to be unduly concerned.

Our nights were not always spent in the tempestuous bloody-lathered embraces that I described earlier. The effect of these episodes, no matter how momentarily exhilarating, was always to leave me listless and depressed. Consequently my lover would have to pamper, to cajole, to woo me anew, which he could do quite charmingly.

He would change into a beautiful glossy cat and lie purring in my lap. Or he would change into a sable fox with a pointy snout and a long, fluffy, elegant tail, quite tame. He'd trot up to me and nuzzle my feet lovingly with his cold wet little nose. Or he would change into a slowly, hypnotically coiling snake, rainbow colored, satin skinned, with a swiftly flicking tongue that promised to spark irresistable delights. Or he would change into a large, magnificently plumed bird. Then I'd climb onto his back and we would fly over the city. Curiously enough I was never afraid of falling during these flights, though I am generally fearful of heights. On these soaring voyages I felt invulnerable. At first, with my legs tight against him for balance and my hands buried in the ruffle of feathers near his wings, I was surprised that no one noticed us as we dipped through streets and rose up past windows.

"Are we invisible?" I shouted to him.

His answer whirled past in a rush of wind.

Once we circled a church steeple and perched briefly on the top of a large stone cross.

"I thought vampires were afraid of crosses," I said.

"A superstition . . ." he answered.

"You mean I'd have to find some other defense against you should the time come," I said teasingly, not really expecting an answer. He turned his plumed head toward me, his eyes hidden in the shadow of feathers. Something about his sharp gleaming beak, half open in what I took to be a smile, sent a harsh chill of misgiving through me.

Unseen, we visited numerous parts of the city. We saw a tangle-haired woman in a blue kimono poke the needle of a syringe into her arm and depress the plunger. Quite soon her whole body, which had seemed brittle and rigid, began to loosen, to soften. Slowly she collapsed against the pillows of a velvet settee. Slowly, as if she were moving through water or through a dream. The syringe slipped noiselessly to the carpeted floor. She's dead, I thought. But her eyes, wide open and glazed with wonder, were turned on us. Did she see us? Not possible. Not possible, of course. No one could see us. A look of absolute serenity smoothed the tension from her face. Was she happy? Was she dreaming? Was she breathing? I could not tell.

"The similarity," my lover began, "between tranquility and death . . ." He did not finish. Yet his point was clear. Tranquility and death. One might drift so easily from one to the other. There was such safety in dreams and in death . . .

We saw an old man in a hospital bed shifting and moving like a submerged swimmer struggling to surface, his face seeking the light. His breath, like spring water, gurgling unhurriedly through a subterranean fault. Two women stood close together at the side of his bed.

"I think the doctor should be here," the younger one said in a furtive angry whisper.

"There's nothing he can do," the other one said and her words hung between the cold white walls like withered leaves caught on ghostly branches. . . . *nothing he can do* . . .

When the gurgling spring ran dry at last, leaving such a sudden startling silence, they stood not knowing what to say. Unaware of that light the old man had struggled toward, they stood, not understanding that he'd finally reached it.

One night we passed through an area of bars and rooming houses. Amid the sordid smell of threadbare lives we saw two men engaged in what looked, at first, like a primitive dance. They circled each other with such agile grace, such latent power evident in their steps. Then a knife appeared in the hand of one of them. A flashing silver saber tooth of a knife longer even than the silvery fangs of my lover.

The appearance of that knife triggered a strange excitement. I was aware of the sharpened alertness that swept through my lover's feathered body. Still mounted on his back, I could feel with my bare thighs and bottom the accelerated beating of his heart.

Invisible, we watched the dance, the staccato drumbeats of our hearts so much faster than the steps and little leaps of the dancers that I wondered how they managed to keep the rhythm. That I wondered how long until it must end. That I wondered how long I could hold my breath, which finally escaped in a rasping moan. The dance came to a tottering end. The knife handle jutted from one dancer's chest. His blood cascading into the street made me think of water bursting from a dam.

We waited for the victor to retrieve his knife and clear off so that my lover might slake somewhat his endless thirst. The wounded man's breath came so lightly, so shallowly, it was impossible to tell exactly when it stopped. His eyes, like those

of the woman with the syringe, remained open, an expression
of abstract amazement in them.

How long I might physically have been able to continue this
unconventional affair is a moot question. But the bizarre all
too readily becomes routine. Thus my interest began to pall
long before my strength gave out. That which had first intrigued
me began to seem ordinary. The memories of my lover that
I had cherished in his absence like a secret treasure began to
seem banal, even vulgar. I missed the excitement I'd felt at
the beginning. He was keeping something from me, I decided.

"Why is it that you've never let me see your eyes," I said
one night.

"The choice was yours," he answered enigmatically, which
increased my annoyance. In the beginning it had not seemed
particularly unusual to me that he clung to the shadows. That
the street light, the moonlight, the starlight never fell directly
on his face. Now it seemed pointedly devious and became a
source of increasing uneasiness to me. Was it lack of trust on
his part? Did he fear me in some obscure way? And what did
he mean by saying the choice had been mine? These questions
obsessed me, often made me appear absent-minded, dazed.
More than once I would be recalled, as though from a great
distance, by the photographer's impatient request for a specific
lens or a roll of film, and I would stare at him uncompre-
hendingly.

The nights turned cold. I no longer left my bedroom window
open. Instead I sat there waiting for my lover so that I might
open it briefly when he came and close it at once. The waiting
tired me. If only I knew when he was coming . . . Sometimes
it was well past midnight. It would seem as if he were not
coming at all. Then I'd wonder how I could go on if I were
really never to see him again. How I could make it through the
succession of meaningless, flat, predictable days. And yet . . . And
yet it would be a relief, wouldn't it? A relief from this waiting,
this not knowing . . . A relief from the enervating sense that he
was deliberately hiding something from me, refusing me that
last definitive intimacy . . . A relief from the burdensome wondering of what he meant by "my choice." A torment or a relief?
Asking that question over and over, I would gaze into the
frequently starless nights. And, it seemed, the nights whispered

incomprehensible answers to me.

Still, he always appeared, and something inside me, like the delicate fluttering of a fragile bird's wings, would be stilled.

My choice, I thought one day, more tired and more desperate than before. Let it be my choice then. I borrowed some of the flood lights from the studio and arranged them in a circle around the room. They were interconnected and could all be turned on at once with the flick of one switch. They would obliterate the shadows of any object, any being that came under their glare. Thus I made my choice.

When he came to me, unsuspecting, (though I wonder in retrospect how that could have been, since he was uncannily perceptive about my moods, my thoughts, all of the nuances of my highs and lows) I retreated, forcing him to approach until we both stood in the center of the circle of floodlights and, with the triumphant smugness of the unenlightened, I threw the switch.

The sudden explosion of light sent bright hot needles into my dilated pupils. I was momentarily blind. When I could see again I found that he had not moved. He seemed neither alarmed nor especially surprised. Had I only possessed the circumspection of hindsight. I did not. His eyes...

Bewildering depthless wells of hellish eternity...

Darkness without hope...

An emptiness so awesome, so devastating as to shrivel the soul into a small crusted lump. I screamed. In the instant before I lost consciousness I saw the portentiously grinning mask that had been his face grow transparent. I saw the nothingness it had hidden. I saw the faintly stirring curtains of my window through it. And through it I also saw, beyond the window, the unimaginably distant stars.

I came to on the floor, the room bright as a stage, the window open to the night, the curtains slapping against it as if with the passage and repassage of unseen creatures. I closed the window and locked it and drew the curtains firmly across it. The room was unbearably cold. I left the floodlights on, partly to warm it but mainly to forestall the shadows that hovered in the corners and under the bed. Shivering, I pulled the covers around me. In the morning the floodlights had burned out.

I have not seen the vampire again. I take all the possible

precautions. I do not go out at night. I keep the windows locked and the curtains drawn, not just in the bedroom, in all the rooms. The memory of him oppresses me like a lingering sense of guilt. His return, which I now dread, seems inevitable. I don't think of it if I can help it. I read a lot. I write letters to people I haven't seen in years and probably won't see. I listen to the news reports on the radio and to the trivial chatter of talk shows. Sometimes I listen to music—loud barbarous music that numbs the eardrums and the mind. And I study the fading designs on my drawn curtains with the sand-dry eyes of one who has gazed too long into an abyss.

AIR KWATZ

by Ronald Anthony Cross

This is the latest in a long series of 'Kwatz' stories, a sort of elemental pantheon of Spritz, which Ron Cross has been working on during the last couple of years. "Air Kwatz," like all of his work, rather defies introduction. Suffice to say that what follows is highly original, beautifully rendered, and happily irreverent.

I

Sunup in big city: another lovely morning, the shooting hour was just ending and already the grim efficient humane society was carting off the last of them. It was always a silent hour after the shooting, but today was to be especially so; only a few stragglers still at it, but at great distance, so that all you heard was a soft pop pop pop every now and then to sort of augment the early morning solitude. Had any birds remained, I would like to think they would have been singing their hearts out.

Heads popped out apartment windows, tall buildings were studded with them (mine among them)—was it safe to go out yet?

Comparatively so, was the answer, was always the answer. Now we ventured forth to rush to our mundane jobs, we being the ordinary Joes (although my name is Alonso).

The rush hour emerged like the buzzing of a swarm of bees from that one liquid moment of silence that follows the early morning shooting hour. Then we were out and darting here and there, stealing sly glances at our wristwatches. (In my case an empty wrist which I savored like a goblet that still held a hint of the bouquet of a fine wine: I had thrown away my watch—when was it? Ah well.)

Here and there still a stray body, perhaps two, I'll admit it. But you're not going to turn me against the grim efficient humane society: they're okay with me. Same goes for the shooters. They have their hour, we ours. And for the most part they stick to it.

Just as I said that, "pop pop pop" makes me out a liar. Probably just a couple of kids though, or maybe some senile old fart on one last big macho romp. Fuck him; the rest of them, those everyday middle-of-the-road murderers, are okay by me.

Not like those devils, the Secret Society of Shining Locusts. They are everywhere among us in disguise, pulsing with bliss, and for some unknown reason they are always bugging me.

I used to think they were some Hindu faerie cult: didn't fit. Then I changed it to Buddhists, perhaps some virile variety of bodhisattva flowering among the concrete: didn't fit. Now I know them for what they are, a secret group of Taoist magicians mucking about: still doesn't fit, but I like it better.

When I got on the bus to work, I had no idea one of them was hot on my trail again. Everybody on the bus seemed so ordinary: three transvestites and a sailor, a couple of terrified nuns hiding in black, an old man looking smug as hell (I should've thought twice about that one), and a ménage-à-trois of teenagers of such a lascivious nature that somewhere along the line they had been reduced to sensual morons. Other than that, just the boys in gray (myself among them).

So I sat down in the bus seat in front of the old man (brilliant maneuver), and the bus was off. I drifted with the bus, and so I suppose my defenses were down. Everything blended: the hum of the bus, the low moaning of the sex-crazed teenagers, the whining of the nuns, the buzzing minds of the businessmen in gray, into the voice of God.

The old man leaned forward and whispered in my ear, "Ready?"

"I think I'm ready," I said (another brilliant maneuver).

Then it was too late, his arm went through the bus seat and his finger fused to the base of my spine.

...KWATZ...

I exploded into a cloud of bubbling bliss spreading outward. All of my atoms were dispersing, the world disintegrated and in the void my memories were slipping by and out and away like bolts of lightning.

Yet I caught to one and clung. What about the poor people on the bus, and the poor bus driver. I pictured the transvestites and nuns, shocked out of whatever state it was they were in. And those poor teenage sex fiends who might actually have got a thrill out of it, but then again might not.

No, not my dead body on no bus, if I had any body left. On the other hand I didn't want to just disappear like a cheap magic trick, and have everybody wondering how I did it.

"Not ready," I shouted, "anybody there? Not ready. King's X."

Zing pop I was back in my body on the bus shouting like a fool. The teenagers cackled like demented crows, ludicrous formulas flashed through the minds of the nuns, God only knows what went on with the transvestites and the sailor.

The old man, of course, was by now sitting back comfortably in his seat looking out the window, still with that same smug smile.

"Buddhist boor," I snarled under my breath, "Hindu whore, Taoist twit, transcendental masturbator, Zen beast!"

He smiled smugger than ever. I know the routine—not that, not that and not even not that. When you got through with him you didn't even come up with a shadow. Just that smug smile.

He stopped smiling. The bus driver stopped the bus. He was a big man but he was running scared.

"All out for Nutsville," he said, staring nervously at me.

For a moment I thought I'd just bluff it out. Then I just plain figured to hell with it. I was in too much bliss to go to work anyhow.

"You win, you dimwitted deva," I said to the Shining Locust, and to everyone's relief got off the bus right then and there. Strangely enough the sailor and one of the nuns rose, and in a somewhat compulsive manner formed a line behind me and exited with me.

"Why, this isn't Nutsville, is it? Or isn't it?" the sailor was asking the nun.

"He died to save you from sin," she said in answer to some question she would have preferred to have been asked. She had all of her answers memorized, but got muddled up in the questions.

"It was corn." I tried to help her out. "He died to bring you corn. It really tastes good. It's a lot better than being saved from sin. He goes down every winter. He sacrifices himself for us. Seems like he's dead, then bingo, spring comes along again and he comes up as corn. You can buy it at the supermarket, it really tastes good."

The sailor nudged me slyly. "That's Osiius, you jerk, get your ass out of ancient Egypt."

He was eyeing the nun nervously, but she was clear the hell out of it—noncommunicado.

"I shall make of you," she said coyly, "a fisher of men."

And with that grotesque image floating through my mind's eye, I crossed the street, miraculously dodging Darts, flagged a garish yellow taxi, and started off for parts unknown.

"Drive like you've never driv before and don't stop for love nor money," I suggested to the driver in a low-but-serious tone of voice. He nodded solemnly, then closed his eyes for a brief moment of silence. Then—pow, we shot out of there like a bat out of hell.

He drove like a madman, screeching through red lights, wheelies around corners, all the time working on the horn as a musical accompaniment.

Another master—the damn city was filled with them, he was probably one of that Shining Locust gang, but I was too blissed out to care.

I just settled back and went with it. I must have dozed for a bit. I had the (perhaps hypnagogic) sensation that the cab was accelerating continuously. Images flashed by the windows: Dodges darted, Cougars and Jaguars roared by us in a cloud of smoke, but suddenly as if drawn back by a magnet they reappeared ass-backwards and fell behind. Everything was falling behind: a flock of ducks—on closer inspection you could spot a wayward angel or two among them, but for the most part green-winged teal—appeared alongside us winging like mad for some vacation paradise. One of the angels peered in the window curiously, then made a mischievous gesture with his middle finger as the whole flock was sucked out of sight behind us. For a while a huge gaunt hellhound trotted along at our side, howling at the window. Then he, too, fell behind.

I must have dozed off, because it all happened so fast and

because for a few moments I wasn't aware we were no longer moving.

The cabby smiled another one of those smug smiles—he had Shining Locust written all over him—and threw open the door.

"Step out, Bub," was all he said.

And I stepped out into an astonishing garden.

What can I say. At first I was so overwhelmed with blazing colors and rich heady scents that I never quite forced them into their completed forms. Everything was caught in the act of becoming, you bet your ass the universe was formed by an explosion, it's never stopped exploding.

For a few moments I was stuck somewhere between breathing in and breathing out, just zinging off again into light-move-ment-color-bliss. Then it settled down into a rhythm, corresponding, of course, to the waves of my own consciousness, the rhythm of my breathing and the pounding of my pulse.

All in all it wasn't the most pleasant scene, too much of everything all at once. It was something like walking around in a giant bowl of chop suey during a fireworks festival on a planet too close to its sun.

There were daisies, pansies, cauliflowers, and I'm sure there were little Johnny-jump-ups but I don't know what they're like.

"I'd like to go back," I said simply to the cabdriver.

"You and Tom Wolfe," he retorted wittily. "If you figure out how to do that one, let me in on it."

Then he got in the cab and drove off like a bat always leaving hell.

There were roses, begonias and bananas. I began to wish I had a notebook so I could jot down all the names and not repeat myself. There were snapdragons, oranges and lovely commie pinkos. Also, among the flowers and within them and all about were moving every manner of sprite and elf and fat yellow buzzing bee; but there was no rest from all this bliss, and watching sprites can make you dizzy—too fassst—

I just sort of sank down on my back and let everything blend, I was just about ready to kwatz when I noticed some action in the sky.

An enormous cloud rolled out over the horizon like a pink puffy cotton blanket to cover me up. I thought I made out the forms of fragile changing buildings—then I dozed off.

When I woke up it was gone. The light had softened, every-thing was tinted with shadow, the frantic beauty had shifted to a tone of haunting loss. The constant blazing beauty was fading swiftly into chiaroscuro, everything was fleeting, whis-tling in the wind, night was coming on.

It was time to sit and think of old friends and sing sad songs. Soon the lights would puff on in lonely little bars all over my city and lonely ghosts would bear dead roses to lost loves. And yet it was my time, the time of my strength, the time I love—twilight.

I drew power from the dwindling of the light, like a shadow; and just before the last of the dying of the light, I made out another enormous cloud city, rolling over, settling, fluffing out—in the half-light, buildings of cloud shifted, formed and reformed.

Now—zinging in the full power of twilight I puffed out . . . and glowed on in Cloud City.

II

Inner hum. Blinding white on white. One little patch of electric blue expands, then suddenly zooms off, disappears. That one fooled me. Me who? Me ow? No, that's cat! Me all?

Inner hum, inner aum, overwhelm! Innerwhelm!

Along comes electric blue snake sneaking cracklefast home—aum—bomb—it's gonna explode expand implode in-nerpand—boom—bloom—auming—blooming—

. . . KWATZ . . .

Little dancing baby queens
on puffy sheet-white pillows
with yellow purplish plump
    marines
are pounding armadillos
    to forge them into green machines
    for driving in the willows
My brain is bubbling out its beans
The pot has got too fillows

...KWATZ...

Rainbow time in Cloud City: everything freezes frosty white, then come the colors spilling over fluffy buildings, splashing in streets of refracted light: oh have mercy, please don't lock me up in prism.

Frozen figures at floating tables in changing cafes made of shifting light, frozen at toast, to all things already just shifted away and gone forever—we'll drink to that. Hollow saucer-eyed, like little orphan Annies—only who forgot to draw them in?—smile and toast and nod and shift—we'll drink to that too, three four . . .

...KWATZ...

                    Are we the bubbles
                    or champagne
                    Oh please explain
                            please explain
                    Are we in trouble
                    or in pain
                            wax and wane
                            wax and wane
                        creeping
                        seeping
                        draining
                        paining
                        waning
                        waning
                        wax

Kwax   kwa kwa kwa
                    ...KWATZ...

Rainbow hour was over in Cloud City. Whew, too much of a good thing. I was sort of starting to get my balance now. A little color and light, a dab of bliss is all right by me, but too much of a good thing is too damn much.

I was feeling better each moment; still, no telling what they'd done to my past. Once you've blissed out like that, it's no good saying to yourself: "I'm sure I must of blissed back into the same old sweet orbit, wonder how all my old miseries are? indulge; indulge." No, no use at all. Nothing for it but to come up with a whole new set of pain-pleasure suffering, and that ain't easy when your memories have been exploded in one big lightning bliss.

I shuffled dejectedly down the lovely bumpy street, little gauzy puffs of cloud stuff kicked up, shimmered pink, and sank back into mama cloudform.

Time, I suppose, drifted by like the puffs of cloud I kicked up—maybe so, maybe not.

At any rate, I wandered up and down nameless streets watching Cloud City changing face, and it appeared to be growing late. The lovely fluffy buildings with their soft rounded edges, their apparent form always just caught in the act of beginning to emerge—peekaboo—then dissolving into some subtly different formation, seemed to lock you one step behind the now. They would never cease to fascinate me; but of course they did.

Finally I sat down on a fluffy pink curb, bored and lost, because I couldn't think of anything else to do. I waited.

Tinny music wafted to me from a rosy pink nightclub across the street, strangely old-fashioned music; and yet, of course it was the music of the future just forming on this subtle level before thought. Same old stuff—same new stuff. On and on and on it seemed to say, ladedadeda forever and ever. Nothing new, nothing profound, and yet it was somehow exquisitely mundane and normal.

Three tipsy Cloud City citizens, drunk from a hard night's dancing at the Garden of the Birds of Paradise, staggered out the door: an elegantly dressed man with a lovely lady on each arm. "Top hat and top coat," he sang in a delicious nasal whine that blended perfectly in with the band. "Don't let me get your goat with my motorboat because it just won't float without love," or some such inanity. The three of them did a drunken little dance, very suave, amidst intermittent gusts of crippling laughter.

One of his girls kicked off one of her ridiculous high-heeled shoes on a bumpy puff of cloud. It landed pulsing red like a neon light.

"Wait, wait for me, you ass, I've lost my shoe."

"No time to wait," he sang happily, "in the sea of bliss, I'll miss my boat if I miss your kiss," or some such inanity. He half turned and languidly waved, then he and his other dancing partner hop-stumbled their way off down the street.

"Oh Ronino, you handsome useless bastard," she mumbled to herself as she hopped one-footed over to the curb opposite me and sat down on it, holding the gleaming red pointed shoe in her opposing hand for balance. Then she saw me. She peered across at me, frowning—serious stuff; I waved.

Indeed, it was difficult for me to make out her features. It was not the light, it just seemed to be the nature of the place. For a few moments her features appeared to be slightly shifting around like everything else here; but then, all at once they came wonderfully clear.

She hopped back across the street, still carrying her shoe. She sat down beside me on my curb.

"The swine," she waved her shoe at me for emphasis. "Couldn't even wait for me to pick up my shoe. Handsome bastard. I hate handsome men—What's your name?"

She was the most gorgeous creature I'd ever seen, elegant and slender with dark lustrous eyes. Better play it cool, I said to myself.

"Alonso," I said coolly. "Jesus, you're the most gorgeous creature I've ever seen."

"I know, I know, I know." A tear formed in the corner of one eye, spilled over—my lady was pensive. "I hate myself for being so gorgeous, just like I hate him for being so gorgeous. I hate this whole plane for being so gorgeous. Cloud City—" she grimaced and waved her gorgeous red shoe at all the splendor around her. "—One longs for the grotesque."

I took heart; I am a tiny man with a large sharp-pointed nose and small brilliant eyes, reminiscent, I am told, of a woodpecker.

I said: "He was a handsome clown, wasn't he? Those mustachios, all drooping and silky, those dreamy brown eyes."

We both grimaced at each other. Then she made a gesture of dismissal with her shoe, so much for Ronino; Alonso, present arms!

"Allow me," I took her shoe firmly from her hand, I was dying to get my hands on her foot. And so I did; I kind of caressed it into that shoe, luscious little devil.

"Trouble with me," I said, "is I just always go bananas over gorgeous people, just always. You, for instance."

"Always always always," she said, "shallow shallow shallow." My lady was profound. "I know, my grotesque little love, even on this astral plane you long to caress my creamy flesh, breathe in the scent of my rich loose river of hair, that sort of thing."

"That's it," I said, "that's really it."

"And so you shall. I feel certain of it. I want you to feel as certain of it as I do. After all, this is the plane of formation, everybody here's clairvoyant. Thomas," she shouted out without warning, "Thomas—oh damn it, where is that rogue. You'll need a guide, you're new here. Listen, I have to rush, get some sleep, a bite to eat—on to the next party. I'm an entertainer of course. You just wait here for Thomas, and let him guide you. That rogue knows more about Cloud City than any . . . Thomas" she shouted again—"damn cat. Never comes when I call him, makes it a point to never come when I call him. Listen, I have to rush, meet me here next week. I'm dying to see how you make out with it." She leaned over and kissed me lightly on the cheek and turned and walked away disappearing into cloud, all one gesture. She was so graceful everything seemed as if performed in slow motion, but she was gone before I could say, "Make out with what?"

The music had ceased. Things were swirling a bit. Light breeze in Cloud City, I suppose.

I stared off into wisps of curling gauze where she had disappeared. It had become quite dark, but little bursts of light seemed somehow inherent in the structure of the place, in the energy of constant change. And of course a rosy glow from an old-fashioned street lamp sprouting like a flower out of a big puff of cloud.

A small puff floated off in the breeze, and then quite suddenly fluttered hysterically of its own accord, took wild flight, then swirled around and came to rest atop the street lamp: white dove.

Another indistinct cloud form yowled, rolled around after it, almost had it. I strained to make it out, and then of course it emerged for me.

An incredibly handsome cat was forming out of cloud. His fur, not too long, not too short, was a silky silver grey with white gloves for all four feet, a neat white collar and a white blaze between the eyes that widened out to include the nose and cheeks. He was remarkably well groomed, with long curly whiskers and a faraway dreamy expression that reminded me suspiciously of the brief glimpse I had caught of Ronino—

what's-her-name's, my love's, boyfriend.

"There you are," he said, in a mincey conceited voice, then he pranced over to me and began to knead his claws in the soft cloud and purr. It gave me a nervous sensation, as though the whole works would pop and deflate with me in it if punctured.

"She's dying to see how I make out with what?" I said again, more to myself than to Thomas, who now began to pace swiftly back and forth in front of me, rubbing his body lightly on my legs, still purring.

"Job, of course, what else. Do you think my lady wants a romance with an unemployed poet? She's romantic, not flipped clear out, there's a difference."

I was astounded. I had got up, but now I sat back down again. Purring, Thomas jumped up in my meager lap, turned around three times, made a finicky noise and settled down, dug his claws painfully into my knee and looked back blissfully into my face to see how I was taking it. Lucky for him I considered it a privilege to be hurt by beautiful things. I stroked his silky fur.

"Even here," I said sadly, "even here."

"Here, there, it's all the same. Did you think it was a matter of locality? You're the poet but she's the poem, you've had your fleeting glimpse, meow. Now you've got to suffer, search for a job, struggle to please her, while all society strives to invent new ways to humiliate your poetic soul. Meow—bliss bliss," he purred.

"Shining Locust?" I didn't like that combination of frankness and ecstasy. "Even here, Shining Locusts? Even a cat?"

But he ignored the question, hopped out of my lap and pranced impatiently back and forth again.

"I've got us a room and we'd better get there before rainbow hour. It's best not to kwatz in the streets. Then we'll get you an early start on a job. You'll need lots of good work to keep me in La Creme. You'll want to fulfill some deep social needs so the citizens of Cloud City will look up to you. Then you'll have a good reason to go out and raise hell with my lady, to blow off steam. Play the game, Alonso, play the game."

He trotted off, me to follow.

The little room was well furnished—nothing, no bed, no chairs, just fluffy cloud floor. I sat cross-legged and Thomas curled himself into a puff in the corner.

Rainbow Hour. You don't sleep here. I guess rainbow hour is what you do instead. This time I was better prepared for it. Well—anyhow, I was sitting down, waiting when everything shimmered off into colors and my mind exploded.

Later, when everything started to shift back into semi-place, my first awareness was that I was lying on my back and that my chest was enormously heavy. My burden was such that I could hardly breathe, and I was apparently purring heavily. Then I was staring into two translucent soft brown eyes—who ever heard of a cat with brown eyes.

"Damn it, Thomas, you weigh a ton; will you please get off my chest, I can't breathe."

I went over and peered nervously out the window. Everything was changed, everything was the same. I went to the bathroom and splashed cold astral water on my face. Up and at 'em, I said to myself. It's a lovely day in Cloud City. I'm sure to find myself a beautiful poetic job—I shivered involuntarily.

"Me-out," Thomas demanded. I pushed open the door. Who knew what was out there hiding in wait for me in Cloud City.

Thomas pranced out, me to follow.

III

"I'm really an entertainer," I lied. "I have the gift. I could go on at parties following bird acts—"

"Just what is it she does?" I had asked Thomas on the way over.

"Bird acts," he said with a straight face—well—almost a straight face. "She goes from party to party changing into giant exotic birds, flies and hops about singing exquisitely. Sort of takes them by surprise. They don't ever know if they like it or not, then she starts screeching 'applause applause' and fluttering about like mad—always works. It's one of the few jobs she's got brains for. Lovely thing."

"What sort of entertainment could you provide, Mr. . . . ?"

"Just Alonso," I said. "What sort of? Oh, post-bird-act stuff. I'd call my act 'After the Bird Was Over.' I could sort of rush out and cling to all the furniture in the room—gimme, gimme, gimme. Oh, I simply love your divan. Give me that chair, you bastard. Oh, what a lovely dress. I want it, I want everything. Cling cling cling. I want a pecker and a great set of tits and all your experiences—good and bad, pain and pleasure."

I was down on my knees clinging desperately to the angel of employment's knees, entertaining for all I was worth. I couldn't tell how he was taking it, but then, neither could he.

"Dear Santa, I'll be good if you give me presents, I'll be bad if you give me coal. I'll be a football if you'll kick me hard. Back and forth, back and forth, I'll be an echo forever, to any kind of shout. But I won't be . . ."

I trailed off suddenly. What was it I wouldn't be? No name? No eyes—seeing? No nose—smelling? Was I really what I wouldn't be? "Never," I shouted. I shouted it twice. Then I went around the room doing everything twice. I sighed twice. I screamed twice. I hugged a chair twice. I laughed like a madman twice and I shrugged twice and grew forlorn and despondent twice, then I came out of it twice.

"If you don't like that act I can always do an old-fashioned waltz"—I demonstrated—"one, two, three, four—No. One, two, three; one, two, three."

"Stop it, Mr. Just Alonso. Stop it. Even an angel can stand only so much. And then do you know what an angel will do, Mr. Just Alonso, an angel will go mad. An angel can go mad, Mr. Just Alonso, he can scream and fly about the room, swooping down and knocking over people and furniture at random. He can fall on you from out of the sky, biting and scratching you. That's what an angel can do, Mr. Just Alonso, and that's what an angel will do. It isn't a pretty sight, Mr. Just Alonso, it is ugly and brutal. And so, Mr. Just Alonso, I'm afraid entertainment is out of the picture for you. Out, out, and further out."

Thomas just sat in a chair with his mouth open. Then, "Meow."

"What did you mean by that?" Quivering wings.

"Just meow." (I seemed to have driven that angel close to the edge with my act.)

"I could learn to fox trot," I suggested meekly.

IV

"Rainbow bridges lead to waking consciousness and back to astral forms. A bridge, get it? That's one way. But of course, that's a metaphor, it's different for everyone. All you have to do is want to do it, you'll find them if you want to, and you do want to, do you?"

I wasn't so sure. "Must I wear this cap?"

He nodded solemnly. "Part of the metaphor."

I was dressed in a bright red pointed cap with pointed purple shoes and a yellow suit. I was lugging a giant bag full of fluffy gold astral dust. I was to fling it into the eyes of people just transcending into astral realms.

"Knowledge," he said in a severe tone of voice, "takes the form of golden bliss, of dissolving into flecks of golden bliss. Thus it has always been and thus will it always..."

"But why metaphor? What's the point of all these elaborate metaphors?"

"This whole damn place is a metaphor, you buffoon. Do you think you'd be here if you didn't want metaphor?"

Already I wasn't crazy about this job, or the fey little elf I was working for.

"Sometimes I feel I'd rather toss the whole works and go back to normal waking consciousness."

"He'd rather go back to normal waking consciousness, would he." The fey little elf was hopping angrily up and down.

"What do you think your normal waking consciousness is, you buffoon? Your whole damn astral plane is nothing but a metaphor and your whole damn waking consciousness is nothing but a damn metaphor. See this chair, do you think it's a chair? He thinks it's chair. Chair is only a metaphor for a bunch of whirling spinning with other little bits of whirling spinning— only not bits, bits is only another damn metaphor, for what? Do you want to know what it is, Alonso, that's not metaphor? Do you really really want to know?"

He was advancing toward me with a wild evil look in his goofy elf eyes. I felt a terrifying emptiness hovering at the edges.

"Never mind, never mind, I'm just anxious to get to work," I said.

"Remember," he smiled his fey smile, "rainbow bridges."

Fuck him and his rainbow bridges, it's not like that for me. It's not like anything at all. The presences are there, the astral forms are here, the connections are not like rainbow bridges or silver cords, they are just connections. Take this one. I'll just sink into it like so, and whoosh!

Some goofy looking naked guy with a beard, sitting cross-legged on the floor, knocking himself out trying to think no thoughts at all. He sees me all right, but he has no use for an elf in a red hat with a bag of gold dust.

"This too shall pass," he said to himself, "and then I shall attain to the formless."

After a long silence, in an austere tone of voice in his head he said to me suddenly—

"Why does Bodhidharma have no beard?"

"What Bodhidharma?" I didn't know what the hell he was talking about.

"Yes," he shouted enthusiastically.

"Yes and no," I shouted back, sort of getting into the spirit of it, whatever it was, "but then again neither yes or no. What is the difference between a fool who says the Bodhidharma has no beard and a fool who says he has one?"

"No," he shouted, "too Zen."

"Two Zen no good," I threw back, "please, only give me one Zen."

I had him there. "Now," I shouted as I went for my bag of gold.

"Then," he countered. "Now," he rolled it out again, "then," he snapped his head around as it slipped by him. "Now then, now then, now then."

He had me there, I withdrew my hand nervously, losing time.

"Begone thoughtform, I shall attain the formless."

He thought I was his thoughtform, he didn't know I was just a guy trying hard to do his job.

"Believe me," I said in a consoling tone, "I will never attain the formless, I've known I for years and that's just plain never what I does. Why drag I around with you anyhow? Forget about thoughtforms, they'll rise and sink of their own accord, but drop I and formless is—no attainment at all."

"Ah," he said.

"Not even that!" I kept at it, whatever it was we were at. I saw my opening and threw my cloud of dust. Everything dissolved into golden bliss—Then those crazy bastards started in on those astral bells and threw showers of astral flowers. Both our thoughtforms swam dizzy in ecstasy—damn all metaphors. I was sick of ecstasy. No! It was not I that was sick of ecstasy. I knew I well, he lusted after it. What was left to be sick of what?

"Whoozy with bells. Golden bells. Tinkly dingly bongly

bells bells bells. Pretty, pretty, pretty. . . ."

Someone was slapping my face over and over. It was my elf boss. I was coming out of it, was I?

"Don't"—slap—"take"—slap—"it"—slap—"so seriously. Don't sink into it. In order to do this job correctly you need to be detached from it like—well—like me."

The pompous little buffoon was all puffed up with his own detachment.

"Detached my ass," I mumbled under my breath.

"I'm okay now, back off and let me alone. Where's my bag of golddust, you little creep." This job was getting to me, but then again, what job hadn't.

"Little creep, sir," the detached little bastard insisted. I clutched my bag of dust to me, I had a languid sensation like melting into warm soup.

That sea of thoughts, Buddhist, Hindu, Christian, everything but original: I was sinking back into it helplessly, out of control, and only a few moments ago I had been unaware of it. Why, it constructed everything, countless worlds, Cloud City, L.A., Oz, Psychedelphia, Pits Burg . . . I fell into a bottomless pit, rode a bucking mantra, swinging my elf hat, giddy up little yoga—wham, thrown off. Nothing. Never be anything again.

Oh my God, I found myself smack in the middle of a swarm of buzzing nervous impulses darting at me like electric snakes, dodging, twisting, shifting. The last of the little devils buzzed off. Then I sank again, and again.

A lovely woman sat cross-legged on a mat on a hemp rug on the floor in a small room. She smiled my way, an enigmatic smile. Plain thoughts rose and fell in her mind like gentle waves in a deep clear ocean, so cool. I sank my hand into my golddust, "How 'bout a little bliss?"

She shrugged inwardly, an exquisitely ordinary gesture; and then all at once I was washed with her simplicity, and somewhat sheepishly I put the golddust back in the bag, careful not to disturb her normal state of mind. Adding bliss to her would be like putting nylons on Botticelli's Venus.

I was not needed here, not in this little room, so purified with love that the Christ and Buddha were only children's metaphors of men who had lived long ago and passed away, leaving their shadows outside the door—only names, only words.

She arose quickly and moved about the little room preparing

for work. She waited tables at the Mosey Inn, and as I faded, she sang some little song in her delicate voice, nothing much—no words.

Snap, I zoomed in, hung spinning, zoomed out again as if I were a ball on a rubber band.

Still in bed he was, but sitting up. What kind of fool sleeps sitting up? I tried to ignore the room, the awful familiarity, the lurking terror.

Half awake he was, and yet half asleep. I grabbed out dust, for some unknown reason my mood was frantic. Unknown? Everything here was too known, too familiar. Everything here was too—what?

He was opening his eyes, the ugly little brute. I threw my dust, but in the moment just before the dust settled, I had it. The word was me.

Everything here was too me. The room was too me. The memories were too me. The man in bed, sitting up, half awake, half asleep, was me. Me. Me. I screamed, but which I. In bed I made out the form, the goofy hat, the bag: it was me. From the table where I perched I made out the form in the bed: it was me too. Me two! Unbearable!

Then relief as both of me dissolved again into flecks of gold.

When I awoke, little fool sir was vigorously slapping me across the face.

"Almost gone for good that time, poor lightweight. Just wasn't cut out for the rough stuff. Got to be detached and holy. Attachment, that's the problem, I says to the Buddha, that's why I always shave my head so everyone'll know where I'm at," etc., etc., etc. As I sneaked out the door, he was still talking to himself, a steady stream of self-indulgent egotistical religious jargon.

By the time I had dragged myself back to the apartment I was ready to fly apart at the slightest mental jar. Myriad minds were striving to suck me into them, trivial egos lurked in the corners of my room, grasping at me, at my room, just grasping.

But then, just when I couldn't stand it for another moment—

...KWATZ...

and I awoke bathed clear as any Venus.

Thomas was sitting in his corner purring like a lawn mower.

"Couldn't take it?" he inquired nonchalantly, "then why take it?"

"You mean just quit? I can just quit and get another job, and quit that and get another job, and buy a car and sell it and buy another car and meet beings and lose beings and meet new beings, and accumulate memories of these events and entitle it me, me, me, and call that life?"

"Call it anything you like, I don't make the rules here. No one makes the rules. In fact, there don't seem to be any rules."

But did he not create, if not the rules, the entire soul of Cloud City, that ceaseless changing drifting mirage of ours? I could see it all now, it was Thomas at the heart of everything, it was Thomas at play. And for that eternity of no time I beheld the universe of flux in the purr of a cat, and the eternal salvation of mankind in the meditation of a waitress at the Mosey Inn.

But eternity passed, and as I struggled to get a hold of what had been, I discovered to my dismay that cats have no handles.

"Me-out" was all he said. And cruelly he hopped up into the window and without another word to me he ran away to play hide-and-seek among his beloved cloud forms.

And yet, somehow, in some inexplicable way, things had changed, softened.

Restless nights, I went out to search for my lady. And once or twice I thought I caught a glimpse of Ronino, girl on each arm. Handsome rogue, that night rider.

I never found that little nightclub, what was it called? The Garden of the Birds of Paradise. But had I found it, I knew she would not have been there, and had I found her, she would have been someone else. As in all the beautiful things we seek, it is only the seeking that matters. It is the seeking we call our lives, our continuity, our dreams, our selves.

Nothing to reach for. Always reaching out. Can we live like that? How else?

Days, ripe and beautiful, I drifted from job to job, face to face: an astral bouncer in a bar full of rowdy giants, a messenger for a medium, a priest in a massage parlor, until finally I sank into my beatific niche. Pride smashed by repeated bizarre fulfillments, I no longer felt it necessary to force myself to apply for the jobs with grandiose titles. "Well, this looks like a good one for me, Thomas," I used to say, "Chairman of the Board for the Presidential Committee on Perverse Sex Acts Among Angels." No more. Leave those jobs to the high and mighty, I was free of them.

Early in the morning I swept the streets of Cloud City. Wearing a cap and pushing a broom, bathed in splendor and grounded in the mundane, I wandered lost up and down those exquisite little streets, stacked on both sides with haunted shifting buildings, sweeping a puff of cloud over here, another there, just balancing out a little bit, according to my small dusty whim.

And sometimes Thomas came along prancing about in cloud, and sometimes not. But he never came if you called, and so I never ever called again.

TWO POEMS

by Marge Piercy

These two short poems by the well-known poet, novelist, and critic are perfectly formed horror stories—and pretty close to the mark for all that.

THE WORLD IN THE YEAR 2000

It will be covered to a depth of seven
inches by the little white plastic
chips at once soft and repellent
to the touch and with the ability
to bounce like baby beach balls
under the table and under the radiator.
They come in boxes with toasters,
with vitamin pills, with whatever
you order, as packing material: they
will conquer the world. They are
doing it already beginning
with my kitchen.

ABSOLUTE ZERO IN THE BRAIN

Penfield the great doctor did a lobotomy
on his own sister and recorded
pages of clinical observations
on her lack of initiative afterward.

Dullness, he wrote, is superceded
by euphoria at times. Slight hemi-
paresis with aphasia. The rebellious sister
died from the head down into the pages

of medical journals and Penfield founded
a new speciality. Intellectuals
always sneer at moviegoers who confuse
Dr. Frankenstein with his monster.

The fans think Frankenstein is the monster.
Isn't he?

BLUE APES

by Phyllis Gotlieb

A gutsier talent than Phyllis Gotlieb's would be hard to find, as "Blue Apes" very well demonstrates. This is the kind of story which takes chances at every narrative twist and turn, but never loses its balance. Gotlieb's agility enables her to bend old themes to new purposes, to turn a conventional adventure into a surprising and deeply reasoned tour de force on the subject of racial and personal guilt. This could not have been an easy story to write and in many ways is a particularly demanding story to read. However the effort is handsomely rewarded and predictably Phyllis Gotlieb has once again given us cause for sincere reflection.

A man sat on a rock outcropping in a valley, weeping. His clothes were torn, his body bruised. His hands trembled on his knees; tears watered the blood of cuts on his face and neck, stinging.

The sun shone brightly, the air was fresh and crisp. Wind ruffled the green and yellow trees, blowing down yellow leaves even as green buds sprang on the branches. Blue-furred animals giggled and chattered among them; once in a while one

147

would pause and stare with pink eyes down at the seated figure,
sometimes break off a twig and throw it at him. They were not
hostile; mildly, they discouraged intruders.

The man plucked a twig from his hair and let it fall. He did
not listen to the blue apes. The wind was singing him a song.

König moved quietly from the hypnoformed shuttle. It
blended with the bedding of yellow leaves in the dip of the
forest floor. The air was cold. He stood for a moment. There
was no moon in the dark sky, the stars were unfamiliar. The
wind rustled the leaves of great-branched trees, whistled thinly
among conifers. He pulled up the hood of his robe and tied
the string. The rough brown hopsacking did not keep out the
wind but his hair and beard were thick, close-curled, and he
was wearing a quilted suit underneath. He took one tentative
step, crunching the leaves, and heard a *chirr* in the branch
above his head. His hand slipped into the knapsack and found
the stunner between the knife and the breadcrust. He went on
slowly without looking up; the branch shook, a few dead leaves
fell on his shoulders. He stopped rigid: his imagination, like
an ancient memory, felt the weight of the animal on his neck,
the bite, his own scream, the vomiting bowel-loosening death.

The animal jeered. The leaves fell. He shuffled gently
through the leaf-layer, away from the tree, between two blue-
black conifers. Another animal woke, whistling, the two muttered for a moment, became quiet, slept. Some flying creature
in the conifers whooped, swept up and sheared by him with
long wings, found another tree. The forest slept again.

Beyond the conifers the woods ended in a low thicket and
the land fell in a short steep cliff toward a stream that frothed
over stones. König pushed through the scrub; it tore at his robe
and scratched his hand. The wind quickened, smoothing away
his leaf-spoor. The cliffside was covered with woody vines.
He dropped the stunner in his pocket and climbed down, pausing at each creak of a stem.

He stood on the stony bank, unseen by the forest, and licked
at his hand. Dipped into the pack again and pulled out a film
bag, rummaged until he found a vial with capsules and took
one: it was a powerful antibiotic, but it did not protect against
the bite of the blue ape. He returned the vial, took out and
unwrapped a bundle of three rod-shaped instruments. With the
first, an infrared scanner, he found no significant heat-source

in any direction. The second was a penlight, and he hunkered against the cliff, spread the wrapping on his knees and studied it: it was a survey map. Presently he rose, dropped light, map and scanner into bag and pack, pulled out the knob on the end of the third piece, uncoiling a length of fine wire, and set the knob in his ear. The illuminated dial on his wrist gave him two hours to dawn. He felt his way along the cliff; his thick rawhide boots hardly crunched the stones. Fifty meters of cliff-side told him nothing until the earpiece began to hum, and the pointing rod, a metal detector, gave him destination. He backed one step, pushed a button on his wrist chronometer, and a section of cliffside rose, wrenching away roots where a few vine-ends had taken hold. He did not like the shriek of rusty metal and allowed the hidden door to rise only enough to let him roll under into the cavern; with the penlight he found the switch.

The light inside was very dim, and he was glad of that. He could see clearly enough the skeleton of a shuttle, and the skeleton of a Solthree human.

The shuttle had been gouged by rough hands; there were no electronic equipment, clothing, utensils, flight recorder. The shell had withstood attempts to tear it apart; the place was dry, and there were only a few rust spots in its dents. He did not touch it. The registry number on its side showed clearly through dust and scratches. It was half-a-century old.

He threw back his hood and reached into the neck of the robe to unbutton the high collar of the suit, dragged at a chain around his neck until he was holding the silver locket. He pushed the manual release button in its center.

"König recording." His voice was quiet but clear. "Shuttle found and corresponding. Equipment removed. No GalFed ship in orbit, probably long captured by scavenger." He turned unwillingly to the skeleton of bone. It was sitting on the dusty floor up against the wall, bending forward slightly and saved from collapse by the propping of a pitchfork whose black-stained tines pierced its ribs. It had been stripped by theft and decay of everything but a few shreds of cloth and several swirling locks of faded hair hanging from patches of dry scalp on its skull. Though the body seemed longer than his own he thought by the bone shapes it might have been female. "Also in hangar skeleton of body stabbed with pitchfork staining tines and breaking ribs, presume caused death. By body size not a native of Colony Vervlen." Perhaps he should have brought the camera; but he doubted it would have made a difference. Especially to the bones. "Long narrow structure. Strands of fair hair probably faded, long and straight. Pelvis shape suggests female. Almost certain this is the . . . the body of Signe Halvorsen."

Why the quivering lip, König? If she'd lived she'd be dead by now.

Pitchfork . . .

König, lots of people in the Department think you're a bastard. I'm not sure. Others work on tiptoe, and you take a bunch of grumbling colonists and con and bully and kick them out of danger farside or offplanet. I'm not sure, because you've always saved them, no matter how much they've wanted to kill you. This thing that's come up—you might say it was made for you—and maybe you'd like to leave this one to rot . . .

But he was here, and he wondered if it was the colonists who were in danger. His feelings shifted, his plans changed every minute . . .

He switched the lights off, rolled under the door and shut it. There was the subtlest of pale shading on the eastern horizon and the diurnal creatures were beginning to whicker and grunt. He rearranged the vines as well as possible, and felt his way back to a place near his original descent. Studied the forest, the stream, the vines. Then he rewrapped his instruments in the map, laid them on a flat stone, hesitated, added the stunner, pulled the chronometer with its remotes from his wrist, the recorder from round his neck. He dropped the heap of objects into the film bag, rolled it until the air was squeezed out, sealed it with the pressure of his fingers. He lifted the rock aside and scratched a hole with his knife, an implement suitable only for cutting bread and cheese; packed down the parcel, replaced the rock. Now he had nothing to defend himself with, nothing of his that could be used against him.

Pitchforks.

He pulled off his robe, rolled it into a pillow and sat down at the cliff's base. During the next half hour while light swelled and birds began to caw he used the knife to scrape the annealed metallic GalFed symbols from the breast of his suit.

His fingernails grew purple with cold. A drift of cloud let down a few snowflakes and the sky cleared again. König's teeth were clacking like a shaken skeleton's. He pulled on the robe and a pair of knit mittens and climbed up to the forest. An animal dancing on the lax arm of a conifer stared at him. At first he could see only the pink bouncing eyes, for the fur was the blue of the brightening sky. The creature was apelike, not anthropoid but prosimian, a big lemur with a long plume tail and sharp claws. A group converged and threw pods at him; he went very slowly over the fallen leaves, barely glancing up to notice that some gripped shadow-colored infants to their breasts. None dropped to take its bite of death. The forest cleared at last into open farmland, and he reached the mud-track that served for a road.

Nearly three hundred years earlier an ultra-orthodox sect who lived by farming had tired of Sol III. As the world pushed up against their fences the very air smelled of spiritual as well as industrial contamination. They had decided to leave the planet in their physical bodies.

They had religious stockades to breach: they must travel by starship using the technology they repudiated; accept a world terraformed to their requirements; allow the modification of their children's genetic components to fit them for the isolated place they chose. A planet without seasons whose axis lay perpendicular to its orbit, where the equator was barely temperate.

They studied the Holy Books, argued long and loud, and in marathons of study and discussion found justification in the eye of their God.

Terraforming was a matter of land-clearing and terracing to prevent water run-off; the Vervlin knew nothing of their travels because they had been put into deepsleep before loading; their gene-pool was modified by engrafting the stock of Ainu, Inuit and other cold-land peoples who lived by hunting, herding and small-farming. Founding population was 750. By second generation census they numbered 982, a fair increase in a hard land. But some had become disenchanted; the Ninety and Nine demanded and got repatriation. Ten years later they changed heart and asked for return but were repudiated by their brethren.

Colony Vervlen lived on. At fifth generation census they had increased only to near 1200; GalFed worried at their low growth rate and slow pubertal development and prescribed dietary changes, since Vervlin would not take drugs.

Tenth generation census, in the person of Signe Halvorsen,

would have been GalFed's last uninvited landfall on Vervlen, but she did not return. By last spacelight relay she was in orbit on the way to landing, and after that, nothing. There were no calls to send or receive: Vervlin would not use radio. The search team, sent a year later, had been shot out of the sky in a war between two other planets of the world's sun, and the whole system, which supported no other GalFed colonies, had been twice quarantined, for a total of fifty years . . .

Between forest and road, König paused. He did not know how to approach a people capable of murdering a Galactic emissary, even though it was half a century ago. Many colonists would have liked to kill him; none had tried. A couple had flattened his already snub nose a little further.

He squatted among bushes, half-turned to keep an eye on the blue enemies among the trees. No great antlered beasts shouldered them now: they had been hunted out or added to domestic stock. No saplings had been planted in many years. All that grew had risen from seed-droppings, in disorder. Spiralling down in darkness he had seen no roads, lights, steeples, meeting halls. Only twenty or so clumps of thatched-roof houses huddled together, perhaps a hundred buildings in all.

From the ground he could see that they were small, with parchment windows lit from within by stoked fires; wisps of smoke rose from old stone chimneys. Out of the center of each clump a taller chimney protruded like a raised finger among knuckles. East and west, Vervlin covered no more than half a kilometer.

Without birth control.

Shadows began to slip from houses and move in the grain-fields—

And sharp points jabbed the base of his spine. He had left one quadrant unguarded, and rustling leaves had covered footsteps. He scrabbled round with a yelp, for he was too locked in his crouch to rise quickly. And yelped again, gawking up at the gnome.

He did not even care that pitchfork tines pierced the cloth at his breast.

"What you want?" the gnome growled in the old rough language. "Where you come, you stranger?"

König was a short stocky man with brown hair and beard, gray eyes and flat-saddled nose. The strong contour of his body

was smoothed down with a light layer of fat and covered with
a great deal of hair. The fatty thickening of his eyelids made
them almost oriental. With darker coloring he would have
looked like an Ainu, or with less hair an Inuit, for he was a
descendant of Vervlin—of the Ninety and Nine.

"Where you come, say!" The pitchfork jabbed. The gnome
had König's eyes, nose, hair, breadth, and was wearing the
rough leather and homespun of his people. But it was as if a
hand had shaped him in clay and thumped him down. Eye-slits
between thick brows and knob cheekbones, lips thickened till
they curled to nostril, chin vanished in beard, neckless,
waistless, bandy-legged. An ancient without a gray hair.

König fell to his knees and clasped hands, begging; whined,
spilled words without thinking. "Hungry, master, I'm hungry!"
He had been uneasy about the dialect for fear of change and
development, but there had been no change here but shrinkage
and reversion. The sense of it filled him with irrational terror.
He pleaded in good earnest. And doubly, because he had fasted
several days. "Ha' not to eat, ha' come many day from town
east—master, see!" He showed the gaping bag with its one
gnarled crust. He could not keep from babbling at the terrible
dull-eyed gnome. "Name of König, and a' come many days
from east!"

The eyes lit briefly, the pitchfork moved down slowly.
"Here's many Königs and many hungry, but a' know no man
east."

"Oh, ay, master, is many men east, truly."

The tines sank to earth, the Vervlin leaned on the worn
handle. His arms were thick and strong, though the fingers
were knobbed like tubers from arthritis. "Will y' workn to
eat?"

König dared pull himself up. "Gladly, lord."

"Lord, hah!" The slit eyes took his measure. König was
nearly a head taller than the Vervlin but this did not seem to
impress him. He was looking for the breadth of a hardy laborer,
and where his eyes lingered was at the heavy boots. König
cursed himself. His footgear was not fine, but far better than
the farmer's, cut like moccasins from single pieces and laced
with thongs. How was he to have foreseen that? But the shrunk
man's eyes were dull. "Come with." König was careful to stay
abreast of the pitchfork on the path to the nearest house.

Inside was firelit, and would not grow much brighter

through parchment windows during the light of the day. König had to stoop to go through the door, and as he stepped in the gnome bellowed, "Aase!" and turned to him with what might have been a glint of humor. "Name of Rulf, König man, 'm no lord."

Aase, the female of the species, appeared round the fireplace in homespun skirts and shawl, noted without surprise that there was one extra for breakfast, and disappeared to yell an order to someone unseen.

König himself was a result of genetic engineering, and he had seen many others, but none so grotesque, so terribly wrong. Inbreeding? Isolation? He simply let his mind go out of gear and ate the porridge with its milk and butter at the table before the fire.

The interior of the house surprised him: it was neat and clean, and seemed to mock the bodies that lived in it. The furniture was well joined and sanded, softened with knit cushions; the old chimney was freshly tuckpointed, the plank floor smooth as if it had been varnished. He heard slight noises underneath, and wondered if there were a cellar with mice. One glance into a corner showed him a trapdoor latched with a wooden bar and an iron loop; in his state of mind it would not have surprised him if a monster lived in the cellar.

But the porridge bowl emptied quickly, and the hard hand on his arm invited him to labor; he dared not look more.

And he labored. The barn was filthy and ramshackle, a big rough shelter patched together and used in common with the community of dwarfs in the house-group. Whatever explanation Rulf gave his fellows he did not hear: there were five or six of them, slightly bluer or grayer in eye, darker or lighter in hair, shorter or taller by a few centimeters—cousins or brothers. None questioned him and he did not speak. Where stupidity reigned he obeyed. Forked hay, yoked oxen, shovelled dung. At noon women brought baskets of hot cakes; he ate, standing in mud, and worked on. Once when a plough stuck in a furrow there was a yell of "König!" and he started and looked up quickly. But a stunted man dropped his spade and shambled out to help. Cousins.

The day clouded over and promised rain. The forest turned pale under the cloudlid and rustled, but no animal ventured from it. Men raked and hoed and ploughed and stacked. They did not joke or curse or discuss or quarrel, and left their work only to relieve themselves in an open pit outside the corner of the barn. When he was forced to use this, König, whose sense of privacy was acute, suffered bladder spasms. They were the day's only stimulation; he began to wonder if stupidity was contagious.

Toward sundown he pulled his mind back into operation.

Men work outside, women indoors. No children in sight. Why? Why filthy barns and spotless houses? Implements old and uncared for. No metal work done now. No poultry. Too hard to run after? There are a dead calf and two dead piglets in the stalls. No one has noticed them yet. The woman who brought the midday meal hasn't washed in a thirtyday. By rights they should be buried in their own dirt. But the clothes are well-made. The cakes were wrapped in a clean cloth. Maybe elves are doing the work for them. Why would they bother? The food is good, but no one says grace. Where are the churches?

He leaned on his rake handle and watched Rulf leading in the oxen to unyoke. The wizened man stopped at the entrance, eyes glazed, mouth open. After a few moments he blinked, closed his mouth, and moved on.

Epilepsy? No, they're all like that. Degeneration. Worse than we could have expected. I wonder how old they are. . . .

When a bell rang among the complex of houses to signal the evening meal the rest of the men came in from the fields, dumped their rakes and hoes in a corner and left without a backward look. Rulf finished unyoking the oxen. König untangled the rakes, spades, forks, hoes and hung them on rusty hooks set in the barn wall. He wanted to provoke a little reaction, but only a little. Rulf's beetling brows rose and settled. When König plucked up a handful of straw to wipe the mud off his boots he found the eyes on him and met them with an ingenuous stare. *Boots you may need, Rulf, but why did your grandfathers strip the electronics from Halvorsen's shuttle?* "Eh, master?"

Rulf grunted. "Y' want eatn?"

"Oh ay, thank y'."

In darkness the hearthfire burned brightly, and within the limit of movement he dared allow himself König tried to examine the place. The massive fireplace projected into the room and to either side was an inglenook. One was filled by a standing wardrobe and a wooden bedstead with an oil lamp above it, but the other was in shadow and he could not see where it ended. Since there were no stairs or any other door visible he presumed it led to a kitchen; Aase had gone there to call for and bring the food. Elves' cooking.

Supper was meat stew with barley and root vegetables, a few raw greens like cress on the side. Rulf and Aase gobbled. So did König. He was hungry.

The mice/elves under the floor were busy tonight. Almost, his imagination gave them voices. Perhaps they would come up at midnight and lick the plates clean with small pink tongues. Rulf stood and dumped the bones into the fire: König followed, and Aase took the rough-glazed bowls back into the shadow.

Rulf stared at König during the slow turn of his cogs of thought and said, "Y' work morgn?"

"Oh ay, master."

Grunt. "Here y' slep." He opened the wardrobe and a jumble of odd ragged things bulged; he heaved and tugged at an old bundled mattress of rough cloth with straws sticking out of its holes and unrolled it on the table, disregarding food scraps and gravy puddles. König moved the table slightly, away from the fire's heat, not too near the cold of the walls. He looked up to make sure he had not offended Rulf by this rearrangement, and his glance was held at the mantel-piece. There was a big clay bowl on it, half filled with ashes, and, perching on the rim, back resting against the bricks, a wooden figurine. He squinted against the glare of the flames and saw its shape was that of a forest ape, just over half life-size and roughly stained blue, lower part blackened with smoke.

Where the churches had gone.

The sight of the idol crystallized a decision he had been slowly approaching all day. At midnight, when the trolls were asleep, and no matter what the elves or mice might do, he was leaving.

There was no kindness he could do these people and no harm he would be willing to commit upon them even if their ancestors had been the bugbears of his childhood. Leave questions unanswered, let failure smudge his record. *Maybe you'd like to leave this one to rot.* No, Director. You decide.

Rulf knocked the logs down with a poker and the flames lowered. He blew out the lamp above the bed and yelled, "Aase!"

She came shambling. "Still y', still y'." She dropped on the bed and pulled up her skirts. Rulf flipped the lacing of his breeches and fell on her.

König hastily climbed his table and lay with knees drawn up and back turned, still wearing the robe, suit and boots he had sweated in all day. It was the style here. Folded his arms against the cold, tried not to hear the grunts and whimpers from the bed. Rain beat against the walls. His back was warm, there was still heat in his full belly. He was weary, his eyes closed.

He did not want sleep, but sleep was coming—not as sweet release from labor but as a dark imprisoning lid.

Drugs. He could not move.

He thought he heard steps from afar, and the scrape of wood on iron. The lid fell closer, blacker, hands grasped his ankles and pulled him straight.

Boots.

His arms were unlocked from his chest. Unconsciously his mouth opened for the last cry of the pierced man.

König, you bloody fool, murdered for a pair of boots!

Voices: he was not dead. Possibly.

Speaking in *lingua*: "He can't be one of us."

"But he's like them. Even hairier."

Fingers moving in the hair on his belly. Damned cold fingers. His robe must be off, he was unbuttoned to the navel.

"Must be thirty good year anyway."

"Thirty-five!" König snarled, simultaneously opened his eyes and sat up. "What the hell do you think you're doing?"

His sight went black and starry; he blinked darkness away with the force of anger, hands pulled back, voices stilled. On a table again. He swivelled and hooked legs over the edge.

An underground room, a vault supported by beams, opening almost endlessly into the flickering lights and shadows of wall-sconces. Around him were children, children, twenty-five to thirty of them. Real Solthree children. Dressed like the gnomes above, in clothes rough-cut but carefully sewn.

A child began to weep.

"Shut up!"

A firm-voiced girl slapped the table. "Don't be rough! You will wake *them* up and you are scaring him!"

"What are you trying to do to *me*?" He zipped thermal

underwear, buttoned furiously, fingers half-numb and all thumbs.

Children . . . as he had been? The ones he should have? Curly-haired small and medium Königs with blue, grey, blue-grey eyes, sharp bright ones here under the eyelid fold. Smooth faces, sweet mouths. Girls rough-breeched like the boys, hair scarcely longer because it was so curly.

"Why do *you* have buttons?" They spoke *lingua* in the rough cadences of the Vervlin tongue. He studied the speaker. First beard-hairs showing. Not so sharp, this one. On the way to changeover. But not stupid either. He knew a foreigner when he saw one.

König felt even duller. "I come to where buttons are used." He looked for the robe, saw it crumpled on the floor and left it. The air was warmer here. Far among the beams stood a huge complex of fireplaces hung with pots and ladles, source of the big outside stack.

"Your buttons are riveted," said the girl, as if she were joining a game with infants. Fifteen, perhaps? She might be the leader, for a while.

"Technology," said König. "You don't do badly at it. Do you drug people often?"

"Sometimes to make them sleep longer when we want free-dom."

"Where did you learn *lingua*?" She was as pretty as a Vervlin girl might become. Her hair was a little darker and straighter, she had pulled back the strands over her ears and tied them with twine.

"We always had it as a second language. Starwoman taught us more."

"Taught *you*?"

"The ones of us here when she was."

"Signe Halvorsen?"

"Starwoman. You with the riveted buttons and the thirty-five years, you are Starman, who lied to the Elders about far towns in the east. Why are you not surprised, Starman? The other one was."

"That you are children? I knew there had to be children somewhere. I didn't think of here. I thought there were mice in the cellar."

Giggles all around. A shiver went down his back. They were so normal, so innocent, Halvorsen stabbed with a pitch-fork.

"You answer no question, Starman." Cool voice of a boy
farther back. "Why no surprise that we are not as the Elders?"

His mind was too foggy to explore a dangerous question.
He answered with the simplest truth. "I have already been
surprised by the Elders. I knew something of what was happening, but not that it had gone so far. And my name is König."

"So is mine—and ten others here."

"I know: many Königs and many hungry. But I am tired—
and drugged, thanks to your cleverness. Let me go back upstairs
now."

"No," the girl said. "By morning they forget everything.
You stay down here, Starman. You have much to tell."

He let it go. He could not fight even one of them now.
"What is your name, Younger?" A little touch to the word.

She reddened a bit. "Ehrle."

"And mine is König. Why are you kept down here?"

"We do all the work that needs cleverness, and they are
afraid we order them about. It is all the same to us. We have
ways out, when we choose to use them, and we have not to
work in the stinking barns."

Nor would she, as an Elder. Aase lay above, gibbering
under pounding Rulf.

"And why are you here, Starman König?"

"To find out what became of Signe Halvorsen—and my
people." He yawned, fought dizziness once more to retrieve
his robe and roll it into a pillow.

"But you must tell us—"

"Later. I am asleep."

And he was, folded on the table, knees pulled up, robe
under his head, asleep.

"Wake up, Star-König, we want to use the table."

He got up very stiffly, even though some of them had been
thoughtful enough to slide folded blankets under him. His first
thought was: they don't have a spare bunk; you'd think they'd
prepare one if they expected company. But when he looked
up he saw groups of them gathering bedrolls from the tables
as well as from the tiers of shelves on the walls, and realized
he had been given the spare bunk.

He had a headache but was not nauseated; there was no
brightness to hurt his eyes here either, only the firelight he had
seen so much of already, and small squares of dusky sky where
the ceiling joined the walls. Openings screened with fiber

meshes, presumably to keep out small animals, they were not quite big enough to let out small humans. They also had wooden louvers to shield from rain and snow.

He wanted to see more of these surroundings, but there were children, children, children who wanted to see him. Some, he was sure, from the groups of houses beyond this one; they wove and cut their cloth a little differently, sometimes with a stripe or a twilled weave. Did they come overland, or were there rabbit-warrens of tunnels with lookouts, codes, sentries? Why not? They knew all he had done and said above. And had children killed Halvorsen? Not these.

He looked at them. There was a hare-lip, a few cases of cross-eye and a few with buck teeth. Some scars from cuts and scratches, but no boils or impetigo that he could see. Halvorsen had been a doctor. Probably those who were badly crippled and could not be cured were kept somewhere together not to be hidden but to be cared for efficiently. From what he could tell of these children, they were efficient. "Don't smother me," he said quietly; the table was digging into his back from their pressure. "I'm like you, only bigger, is all."

"You are not like *them*," said Ehrle.

Three or four bells chimed at once, from all the houses this cellar must run under. Half the children ran away, and to the others Ehrle said sharply, "Get the pots stirring, Willi, and you, move away before you spill something hot."

The lightly-bearded boy who was a bit dull went to supervise the porridge-making, others to different tasks, some, reluctantly, to sit on benches by the tables. All eyes on him. Their candle-power was nerve-wracking; compared to it the stupidity of the Elders was soothing.

Troops of servitors worked without bumping or slopping: one to send bowls of food upstairs on dumb-waiters, another to man their ropes, a third to serve the seated ones.

"Don't spit, Mooksi, you need not be a slob." Ehrle was a super-martinet.

König said, "Will you rap my knuckles if I ask for a little more milk?"

There was a ripple of laughter around the table. König locked eyes with Ehrle and wished he had not spoken. He understood what was happening.

The children were clean, cleaner than he was, and more disciplined than an armed force. They were, after all, fathers to the men, and would play later in as much filth as they chose. A clumsy Gulliver might upset an inverted social structure that was the only basis here for existence and continuity: a structure balanced on a very sharp knife-edge.

No one knew just how much time there was, for Ehrle or anyone else, but she seemed determined to extend it by the pure force of her personality. Uselessly.

He took a drop of the milk he was offered and said, "Yesterday I saw a dead calf and two shoats in the stalls."

A boy said, "I know. I got rid of them last night."

"I wasn't sure you'd noticed them."

"We know about everything here."

"Yes, of course. You knew of me."

(But not where he had left the ship and controls. He hoped to God not.)

He was reaching for equality—to be neither overbearing nor overborne. Sophisticated Gulliver. For König there was far too much intelligence and organization here. He must leave before he was overborne.

As the bowls emptied he was quick to rise and stack them. Ehrle said, "You need not serve, Star-König."

"A' mus workn for to eat, not?" He laughed. "If I break things you may put me to scrubbing floors." He joined a line of children waiting to put crockery in a tub of soapy water. Eyes on him, always. Questions to come.

The floors were worn brick, neatly grouted and well scrubbed. Probably torn from old houses. Population did not quite replace itself and as it shrank, living-space compacted for warmth and the ubiquitous efficiency. The children surely lived better than their elders. Building bigger houses to their standards would require greater strength, and more knowledge and equipment, than they had.

The eyes, pair by pair, moved away from him and turned their attention to scrubbing, spinning, weaving. Bone needles, bits of metal to pierce leather. Sacking and woolen cloth grew on the unwieldy looms; some yarns tinted, probably from dyes scraped out of the soil. Water boiled and food simmered by the fires; dough was rising.

"You don't do tanning here, surely?"

A voice at his elbow laughed. "Would raise a mighty stink if we did. Shed's outside with the kiln and smokehouse."

"I think you're spoiling *them*."

"Ehrle doesn't let them push us too far."

A voice at his shoulder said, very quietly, "That one, there, thinks she'll never change. All them do."

"Which them, Willi?"

The boy was standing awkwardly, looking into the top bowl of his pile with its milk puddle and cereal lumps, broad thumbs hooked carefully over the edge. He raised his eyes.

"Leaders, like." He was a burnt-out lantern compared with the others, but his features had coarsened very little. "I was one. It's like I did wrong, growing. But I want to go upthere," he made it one word. "I want a woman. 'M not right, here." He spoke without lust or anger, facts.

A voice hissed, "Shut up, Willi!"

"I'll get there." Willi set his nest of bowls into the water and turned away.

And she would follow. And perhaps be his woman and bear his children . . .

König gave them a day of work, as he had done with the Elders, but for more complicated motives—aside from discouraging questions before he thought of the answers. He did not care for idleness, nor wish to set himself above them, and he did not want to become indispensable, like Halvorsen. He was trying to bond himself to them just enough so that they would think twice before taking extreme action. He felt this might be possible because he himself was a Vervlin. On the other hand, for the same reason, they might expect more from him . . .

He knew from long experience how to be helpful without getting in the way. He wiped up, swept up, changed diapers in a roomful of babies, and stayed away from those with organized serious tasks. One or another of the children was always with him, usually the boy with his own name, who was near Ehrle's age and probably the next contender for leadership. In all, they were the most solemn group of children he had ever seen. They never smiled, and rarely laughed except when he provoked them purposely. A few of the babies chuckled when he nuzzled their faces; several were wasting with dysentery, but most seemed quite healthy.

"Are these fed on cows' milk?"

"Only when they can drink from cups. It is too hard to make bottles. When we find a good milker upthere we keep two or three babies on her until weaning. She never knows the difference."

"Do you know your mother?"

"No. How can I?"

None of them had parents, except for their siblings, the busy ones who, humane as they might be, did not know how to be kind or joyful. The babies had a few stuffed toys, but there was no other sign of game or toy, no tag or rough-house. He picked up a fretful child; it fitted the curve of his arm quite properly, and fell silent pulling at the fine chain around his neck.

"What is that on your neck, Star-König?" Puzzling at the square centimeter of filigree.

"A Galactic Federation emblem. Do you grow sugarbeets?"

"A small crop. Why?"

"And put a little sugar in the cereal you give the children— or let them suck on a piece?"

"Sometimes."

"Keep it away from the ones with loose bowels."

"You have children of your own?"

"No."

Serious face close to his again. "What are you, König?"

König put the baby down; it whimpered for a moment, and slept. "A person who travels to new communities on strange worlds and tells them to move or leave because of dangerous conditions."

"What kind of conditions?"

"Disease, poisonous land or water, approaching war." Genetic instability, he did not add.

"And you come to ask us to move?"

"No. To find out how you are getting on, because we could not come earlier on account of wars on the planets near here. To help you stay healthy and live—" he caught himself before saying, "longer,"—"more easily." He watched the babies playing with their toes. A short youth and a stern one. He added, "I was chosen because I am descended from Vervlin."

"Yes," the boy said contemptuously. "The Ninety-nine who ran away."

"They tried to come back and were not allowed by the others here."

"I didn't know that."

"Now you know, it doesn't make much difference."

"Yes it does, Starman. You are a normal adult, and we want to know why."

He was becoming tired of crowding and pressure, of attention, nudging bodies, endless murmur of voices. The focus. The wrong choice. What was the right one? An armed fleet, against despairing children? He took it head on.

"Galactic Federation made a mistake when they formed your bodies in the shape you have. There was a flaw in the seed, and because everyone had it, and had children with someone else who had it, it stayed. It took a while to show itself, so nobody was warned soon enough, and it stayed in the generations. Most flaws of that kind are weak and wash out in descendants, but this was not that kind. Many of the Ninety-nine married stranger-peoples before the flaw had time to affect them so badly, and if they thought they might be affected they had no children." Before young König had time to react he asked, "Didn't Starwoman talk of this?"

"I believe so, but no one understood. This we can understand." König shut up and let him think. "Galactic Federation must owe us something, not? Our fathers sold rich lands on Sol Three and paid to come here."

"They owe you something," König said grimly. Try to collect.

Out of mercy the bells rang for lunch.

"Today we have light lunch and early supper," Ehrle said.

"Is something special happening?" König roasted on spit.

She smiled without humor. "Tonight they have their Sabbath celebration and we get out and watch them behaving like fools."

"They are not all such fools," said Willi.

König said quickly, "Do they know you get out?"

"Likely."

"They're not afraid you will run away?"

"No." The word cut like a knife. Of course not. The runaway would turn into the enemy.

König asked for and got the favor of a tub of hot water. While it heated he squatted in an empty niche, to be alone, unregarded for the moment. He did not want to see how the Elders would celebrate; the prospect repelled him. But for the children it was probably some kind of object lesson in superiority; actually, in futility. In spite of the regimentation, the industry, the cleverness, the almost purposive lack of differentiation between the sexes. *I want a woman.*

The niche was not bare: it was lined with shelves piled full of worn things for which uses would be found. He ran his hand down them idly. Old leather, sacking, wool. And something hard. He pulled apart two folds of blanket and found it: a heap of the fragmented pieces of Halvorsen's radio and electronics. He smoothed down the blankets and got out of there in a hurry. There were not many pieces, nowhere near enough to account for all of the instrumentation. Perhaps every housegroup had its little heap. Perhaps it was the equivalent of the carved blue god of the Elders.

He found a shadowed corner for his bath and took it in a worn wooden tub which appeared to be the community bathtub. The lye soap did not smell pleasant but it washed well, and, watching his toes curled over the tub's edge he allowed himself to relax to the point of mild relief that these colonists at least did not apologize for the primitive conditions that for him were merely a commonplace of the many outworld communities he had visited.

The moment he was aware of relaxing the trapdoor grated and opened, and Aase came downstairs. The children whispered and muttered, and began deploying themselves to keep her turned away from König. König came out of his lull into the sense of a loose situation with an open door: he sat up and reached for his clothes, ready to call out. A hand snatched the clothes away; another grabbed a fistful of his wet hair and pushed his head back: "Keep down, Starman. Do you think *she* will fight for you?"

He clapped his mouth shut in a fury and watched her between bodies, peering into the steaming pots, poking about like a supervisory witch. Once when she found one of the little ones in front of her, the one Ehrle had called Mooksi, she stopped and put her hand on his head. He turned his face up, they looked at each other, but neither knew what to search for, and she went on, and finally up the stairs again, and the trapdoor slammed.

König, left to himself once more, dried himself with his underwear, put on his suit and washed the underwear in the used water; he wrung it out with the anger he would have liked to use on a couple of necks, and hung it on a wooden rack by the fire along with diapers and other clothes. The sight of this garment, with its long sleeves and legs, gave rise to the first spontaneous burst of laughter he had heard on Vervlen, but it did not temper his mood. A few of the older boys, and perhaps girls, for all he knew, whispered and giggled a bit on the possibilities of physical strength and sexual prowess in a person big enough to wear such clothing; much as the Lilliputians had done with Gulliver. König was wondering how much strength was necessary to knock aside all those hard young bodies. But Gulliver had been a prisoner too.

He went into the room where the babies lay, stood with arms folded and watched them, because he knew he could not be angry with them.

He did not speak at supper, though his face was calm. The whole area seemed subdued: no one was willing to break his silence.

At the end of the meal, Ehrle whispered with some of the others, and said, "Please, König, don't be angry with us. We need help."

König said, "You cannot get help from a prisoner."

She was no longer imperious. "We are prisoners—of—of ourselves and them. Give us a little time, tell us what can be done. Then we will let you go. You have a ship and a radio, and can bring help."

"We don't *know* he has a ship and a radio," said young König. "Might be he was dropped here."

König said, "I have a ship and a radio, and you have a strategy." He stood and began to gather empty dishes. "You are playing hard against soft, and that is a very old game. It is no longer clever. It is against Galactic Federation's rules for me to tell you where my ship is, because there is no one to guard it, and if you try to force me to tell my conditioning will break my mind and you will be left with a real drooling idiot. I will tell you where it is not: it is not in the hangar with Halvorsen's bones and the remains of her ship. Nothing else is."

"Hangar! Bones!" Surprise and horror swept the vault.

"You didn't know! I see, I'm glad to see that." And he was, for no lie could be so well orchestrated. "And yet you have pieces of her equipment in your stores."

Ehrle's arms went out involuntarily. "You—" it began as a yell and she brought her voice down, "you think we, us down here, killed her!"

The movement had pulled the collar of her shirt apart and

he saw the silver glint on her neck. The last thing. He sat down. "None of *you* killed her. She stayed quite a while—perhaps more than a thirtyday—and then what became of her?"

"One morning she was gone."

"As you had been told . . . and the ones here, did they think she had gone in her ship?"

It was someone else who muttered, "Until the broken pieces were found on a midden heap."

"The Youngers would have used the radio to call for help, but the Elders smashed it," König said. "Vervlin never did care for radio . . . and I suppose the young ones thought she had run away, and eventually died somewhere on this world." Slow nods. He was giving an out which both parties needed very badly. "But she was stabbed with a pitchfork. No one knows who killed her, and I don't want to know."

"Someone on Vervlen killed her," a hardy soul ventured, reaping black looks.

"Fifty years ago," König said. "Galactic Federation can punish no one here for that."

"But they will not want to help us," Ehrle said gloomily.

"They will want to help. I can swear that." But, the one last thing. "You are also wearing something on your neck, Ehrle." Halvorsen's recorder. He could not do what he had never done before: find a way to be alone with her and take it by seduction or force. There was no time, no room, and he had no talent for it.

She said nothing, but pulled up the chain slowly, unwillingly, until she had the silver locket in her hand. Then, "This was in the trash, also . . . it did not seem to belong there. We thought it was a thing a leader might wear, and the leader in this group has worn it for many years." She looked up. "Swear again that you will help. You lied to the Elders."

"About the men to the east? How many ears you do have! There *are* many men to the east, Ehrle, all over the universe. But I do swear. That is the recorder from Halvorsen's ship. Would you like to hear what she has to say?"

"Starwoman's voice . . ." Whispers spread.

"Will she tell who killed her?" young König asked.

"I doubt she would have been recording then. If you let me have that I will show you how it works and give it back to you."

Slowly she drew the heavy chain over her head. "I often

thought this was some kind of instrument but I push this button often and nothing happens." She gave it to König; her eyes held a trace of fear.

Young König, leader-in-line, said, "We should call all of the others and let them hear Starwoman too."

"When I hear, everyone will know," said Ehrle, rap-on-the-knuckles. "Go ahead, Star-König."

König took the fine chain from his own neck.

"You said that was a Galactic Federation emblem. Was that a lie?"

"No. It is what I said, but also a key, something that opens things. Each one of these is made a little differently, to fit one recorder." He did not know where the fit was on this one, the light was dim. He moved the side of his key around the edge of the locket until it was retarded by slight magnetic force, and pushed. The filigree slipped in with a click. He pushed the button. Silence. "Reversing." Click. He pushed again. Squeals and whines. "Those are coded records of distances and directions; this piece is connected to the controls when the pilot is aboard." Click.

Signe Halvorsen recording . . . The voice was dry and matter-of-fact, but breaths drew in. König held his own.

And Starwoman told what they already knew: that Vervlin were degenerating in the pattern already suspected, and accelerating; that the Elders were unintelligent and almost helpless, and the children astonishingly bright, efficient and well-organized, as well as self-sacrificing—the voice wavered and lowered a bit . . . *and very brave* . . . a pause. *Halvorsen recording* a new day, voice crisp and cool, describing organization and communal practices . . . slightly longer pause, and König said, "I think it needs rewinding," pulled the key half out and pushed it in again. Nothing else then, except a faint buzz and crackle. "No . . . it's very old, and probably broken." Not really; he had wiped it. Halvorsen was dead and he was alive and he truly did not want to know more about her death.

"Very brave," Ehrle whispered. Leave it at that. "I wonder why she was killed?" Question asked for the first time.

König thought he knew. That cool fact-gatherer would not swear to bring help. König had sworn to try, because he was a Vervlin. And they were brave. He pulled the key out and gave it to Ehrle with the locket. "You can listen to the beginning again."

• • •

When the table was cleared he took his dried underwear and
went behind the chimney to put it on. He had suppressed evidence and did not care. He doubted the missing parts were of
much value and he had already allowed the most explosive
information to surface and dissipate. Halvorsen could not describe her own death; he believed he could reconstruct it.

Would the Youngers have used the pitchfork? They had
more subtle ways. Perhaps they had manipulated the Elders
who must have seen Starwoman as an only too obvious foreign
body, with her ship, instruments, authority—all things Vervlin
in their right minds avoided and twisted ones hated: they had
smashed them.

Children locked in cellars. Halvorsen had more sense than
to decry them openly, but her attitudes would speak: *very
brave* . . . But to the young, the leaders among them, her very
unwillingness to rebuke their elders and make promises to themselves would speak even more loudly. If he judged it right she
had unwittingly fed fears and prejudices until she became to
each party the ally of the other: a mutual enemy. And she had
not come back, and the youngest had been allowed to build a
legend.

A conjecture. Director, you decide.

He came round the chimney to find a group of younger
adolescents choosing straws for baby-sitting and guard duties.
The bells began to ring, old church bells struck with broom
handles. The hammering of their clappers in confined spaces
would have loosened teeth.

"Put your robe on, Star-König. It's cold, the night," young
König said.

He did not want to watch the Elders degrading themselves,
and he did not think he would be given the opportunity to
escape. The young knew the night terrain better than he did
without his direction-finder, and he wanted to leave freely with
their good will, and keep his promises. He doubted GalFed
would expend another search team for dead König. He tied the
drawstring of his hood beneath his chin and accepted the loan
of a pair of mittens. Except for the very young, all Vervlin had
big hands like his; most, like him, were left-handed.

He thought Willi was a certain candidate for guard duty,

but he was among the dark bundled figures shifting aside a
cupboard at the back wall. There was a niche to get through
on hands and knees for a few meters until the ground lowered
and allowed standing; the natural cleft had not been dug, though
a few heavy uprights and crossbeams warded off collapse. The
passage curved down for twenty meters into a shallow puddle,
and rose sharply until a cold wind flowed in from the starry
opening and the lantern was blown out. The children were
quiet, almost solemn, like a tribe preparing for religious rites
themselves.

They squatted in the brambles of a hillside looming over
a trampled area back of the sheds where the tanning and smoking were done. Beyond them the houses crouched like tame
beasts; above, the two bright planets moving among the stars
had made the long wars of fifty years ago.

König was relieved to find that the ceremony was no orgy.
In the center of the trampled area a larger carved ape crouched
on the edge of a much wider basin in which something was
burning, and around it a circle of fifteen elders was moving
slowly in a simple dance, shuffle-hop, shuffle-hop, each dipping a stick with its end wrapped in rags into the basin until
all carried lit torches. The wind carried an aromatic breath of
the burning stuff, perhaps a psychotropic; after some minutes
the dance quickened, though not greatly: the bodies were thick
and graceless, the legs crook-shanked. The faces only firelit
blobs.

The children did not giggle or whisper but remained silent,
crouching, arms on knees, chins on arms. The jigging torches
dropped sparks that shook themselves off clothing almost miraculously without scorching their bearers.

In the distance among branches König could see three more
circles of dancing light from far houses. He was squatting
among thorns, shouldered by bodies. The area was bordered
by sheds, houses, hill-slope and crest, only a thin wedge of
forest visible to his left. He thought for a moment that he heard
the *chirr* of one of the blue apes, and the hairs prickled on his
neck, but there were no trees for them here.

The dancers started to sing tunelessly, "Ay-yeh!" shuffle-
hop, "Ay-yeh!" shuffle-hop. König was wondering how long
it lasted, how long he would be forced to last it out, when a
figure behind his shoulder sprang up with a yell of *"Ay-yeh!"*,

ran down the hill in leaps and grabbed a torch from its bearer, joining the chanting circle.

The children called in low urgent voices, "Willi! Willi!"

Ehrle said hoarsely, "Shut up! Just let him go!"

König realized why Willi had been allowed to come. Ehrle, after all, knew her limits.

The dancer deprived of his torch staggered round outside the circle for a moment and sat down scratching his head in great puzzlement, but Ehrle was already slipping down into the opening of the hill and summoning others after her in silent procession.

No one reproached her aloud; a few hard looks were directed at her. In the cellar each child seemed to want to get as far away from any other as possible.

Ehrle threw off her mittens, hooked legs over a bench, sat, propped elbows on the table and covered her face with her hands.

König dropped his borrowed mittens beside hers and loosened his drawstring to pull back the hood. "They all go that way?" he asked, very quietly, to let her ignore the question if she chose.

She pulled her hands away, down the length of her face; the displaced flesh suggested more age than she had or he had allowed her. Her eyes were a bit reddened. "Everyone chooses . . . what seems the best way." Then her eyes lit with anger and she pounded both fists on the table. "König! Star-König! Tell us about the Ninety-nine again, the normal ones!"

There was a little stillness following her change of mood, a stopping of motion by König and everyone else.

He heard the *chirr* again.

A few more children had come into the room, and one, an older girl, he thought, was wearing what seemed to be a blue fur collar. He watched, he could not turn his eyes away, as the blue fur sat up on her shoulder and began to eat some morsel it held in its claws. He stood very still.

"What are you looking at?"

"What do you call that blue animal?"

"An ape. Why?"

"We also called them apes. Is it dangerous?"

"Only if a bite or scratch becomes dirty, and they don't bite or scratch often. We bring one in sometimes to feed."

They were immune. It seemed it had come with the genes. And they had playfellows.

"Why are you afraid, König?"

"In the beginning—" Dared he give them the weapon? The story would be a lie without it. "In the beginning a bite or scratch would kill."

The girl launched the ape: it leaped from shoulder to table to shoulder toward him. He did not move. "Dead Königs don't help much, not?"

Ehrle snapped, "Helig, take that thing away!"

Someone grabbed it, it chattered wildly, and the girl retrieved it sullenly, muttering disgust to match; it disappeared into the cleft.

König folded his arms. "I don't like that. It is not a joke."

"There is not much joking here."

"That I agree with . . . The story is not long or complicated, and it has little to teach. The first settlers were used to cold weather, but not all year round, as here, and they were given a body inheritance of even colder-weather peoples, so they could hunt and fish and work in the woods if crops were bad. They trained with those Solthree peoples to learn the work before they came. They found the land quite good here, and the farm animals grew well, but they took care of the forests as they had been taught in case of hard times. Some grew to enjoy that very much: they cut wood, replanted trees, gathered what they could eat, fished and hunted. They left their land shares to the ones who preferred farming and went on living in the woods. That was a mistake."

"Why, Starman? It seems well-thought."

"Because the Vervlin forgot what they had learned in their histories and holy books. Among many Solthree peoples, and others for all I know, free-living hunters and herdsmen don't get on well with farmers who stay in one place. Not if a hunter chases some great roaring beast out of the woods, breaking fences, trampling crops, galloping through the sheds sending the pigs running squealing their heads off and scaring the milk out of the cows—I'm glad to see you laugh, but where would you be for all your work without the farms?"

"I want to see the roaring beasts," said Mooksi, chin cupped in hands.

"Long gone," König said.

"Were the Ninety and Nine farmers, then?" young König

asked. "I thought they were not, but you seem to feel sorry for them."

"They were hunters and woodsmen. But Vervlin have always been respected for their honesty, and these ninety and some wrote down what had happened in their journals as honestly as they could. They had no wish to hurt the farmers. There were no apes here then. Galactic Federation knew about them, but they lived far across the continent and bothered nobody. Then something happened to their forests—disease killed the trees, or earthquakes disrupted them, or they caught fire—or all of these things. The apes moved and settled here. They disturbed the woodsmen, scared the big animals, and whenever they scratched or bit, people and animals died. Their spit was poison—then. Careless children . . . dead in a few hours. Men, women, animals. Not so very many; enough to frighten them out of the woods, back to the land. But the farmers were angry and told them . . . told them it was the wrath of God upon sinners . . . and would not let them on the land, even to hire out for their keep . . ."

"Another mistake," said Ehrle quietly.

"And when the Colonial census people came the woodsmen asked to return, and made still another. They had become very angry. They didn't tell about the poison deaths. A few of them hoped the apes would attack the farmers. I know this because I've read what was written . . . and they were very ashamed of it later . . ."

"If they had told? What difference would that have made to us?"

"Very little. GalFed would have moved the colony or destroyed the apes, the woodsmen would have stayed and kept fighting the farmers."

"Why did they want to come back later?"

"I think they enjoyed the free way they had lived here before the trouble. They got over their anger, and thought they might fight the apes, or the farmers, to a standstill, or find other land here. But the colonial Vervlin thought they wanted the original land, and threatened to abandon the whole colony and go before the law and demand reparations—"

"And that was a mistake," said Helig bitterly. "They should have abandoned. Because you were saved and we not."

"There was really only one mistake," said König. "The first one made by Galactic Federation when they believed they could join parts of seed to make people who could live comfortably on this world." He was beginning to droop from lack of a good night's sleep.

"And how can they repay *us*? Your fathers were normal when they left here."

"No. The ones who mated with normal people right away had mostly normal children, but some were not, and those were discouraged from having children." Forbidden. "And a few had abnormal grandchildren. They would have liked to stay together as a group, but could not last without bringing in new blood. The ones who tried to intermarry, about a third of them, had to give up. They were given land and money and whatever else they needed." Like sterilization. "Very few were lucky." When his raw energy was spent he wearied quickly and completely, and he was very tired now.

"But some were, like you," Ehrle insisted. "What can be done for us?"

He took a deep breath. Halvorsen would not have touched this one with a pitchfork. "You would have to stop mating among yourselves and take the seed of normal people, or give it to normal ones. That would not help you at all. It might help a few of your children. Changes in diet with some hormones— the chemicals the body makes to control growth and function— might help you a little, might help your children more." But not untie that unholy knot in the chromosome. "Your children's children's children might be pulled up little by little." The silence tightened like parchment and he let his arms drop. "You are young. It's hard for you to look ahead to the hope that you might have a few normal great-grandchildren . . . when I can only ask Galactic Federation for help." He was nearly asleep on his feet.

"How long do *your* Vervlin live, König?"

"To our fifties. It is a short life for Solthrees."

"We die before forty," said Ehrle.

"You are the adults here."

"Yes. We have four or five years of that."

"What shall I tell you?" There was nothing. He was desperate. "GalFed will come here with medicines that will make you three times taller and handsomer than I and you will live to be three times my age!"

"Perhaps it would have been better if you had, Starman," Helig said.

"A child's story? Broken promises and battered hopes make people sick and cruel and ugly." And how far they had been driven along the road, the brave children. "Youngers, am I on trial, or may I sleep? I got very little sleep last night."

The lamps were guttering, and upstairs the floors were creaking as the Elders stumbled into their beds. König smelt once again a cold drift of aromatic herb washing in through the screened conduits. Thunder whispered far away, rain pattered softly. The youngest children were being put to bed, the oven fires banked down with ashes.

But Ehrle and the other eldest ones surrounded him, heads tilted, eyes far away. Duty had burdened them; as soon as they could walk or grasp they had been made to heed. If they were by some miracle created whole down generations, how many more generations would they need to recognize an instant of happiness? Even he had had to learn his meager share through outsiders. He said in a low voice, "If I don't go back no one will come here again. No one will help."

The children turned away and began to blow out lamps; a few murmured together. One pulled down the shelf that had been Willi's bed and piled blankets on it, motioning to König.

König lay down on his side, facing inward, and through half-closed eyes watched the shadowed figures moving. It was cooler by the wall, he warmed his hands between his knees and let sleep gather in him. Sentence in suspense. He wondered how long Halvorsen had really endured this place, and how to break the flesh-and-blood prison wall . . .

"König!" Intense whisper. Ehrle. Hand on his shoulder.

"Let me sleep," he begged.

"König, you!" The hand became a fist that shook and pounded. He cared little for touching, and surely not like that.

"Oh God, what now?"

"Quietly."

"Mustn't wake them up there," he muttered and tried to turn away. The grip held.

"Down here you must wake now!"

He pulled himself up on one elbow, his head was sagging. "What then?"

"König, I am eighteen years old, and I have had my bleedings for over a year. Helig is half a year younger than I, and there are two other girls in this house who bleed. You can give us your seed and we can begin the new cycle of children, even if we never know what becomes of them. It's no use to keep you here longer, but you can do that much for us before you go."

König felt his soul shrivelling and the flesh withering on his bones. "Good God, Ehrle! I'm not some kind of—some kind of animal you can use to improve the stock! That's a dangerous idea."

"We don't care about that! No one who comes here will know of it."

He sat up. "I cannot . . . I cannot service a bunch of you like—"

"We will wait as long as need be," said Ehrle, every word a bell tolling.

"I'm so tired . . . I can't think straight. Please let me sleep and we'll discuss it tomorrow."

"We will discuss it when you have agreed, König. A grown man like you must still have—"

"It's impossible. I can't—"

The hand had never left his shoulder. "Why are you shivering?"

"I told you," said young König. He was dipping a stick into the fire to light a lantern. "A man grown for nearly twenty years and he has no children, when his people are dying out." He came holding the lantern before him, face lit yellow from below. "He knows how to care for children and seems to care about them but he has none. He is telling the truth at least this time. He cannot."

"Maybe he is one who goes with men," Ehrle said.

"He would still have the seed," said Helig.

"This one has none," said young König.

"Goddamn it, if I did such a thing I'd lose my—"

"I think you have already lost," the boy said.

"You cannot have children. Not at all," Ehrle said, and took her hand away at last.

He yelled, "I told you there were those who were not allowed—"

No one woke. He wondered if they had been drugged, if there had been a plan. The faces of Ehrle, König, Helig, others surrounded him. Hard composed faces.

Ehrle said flatly, "Those who were not allowed, you said, were defective ones or had made defective ones. Do you have brothers or sisters, König?"

"No."

"But you are a normal grown man of thirty-five."

His face was beaded with sweat, he wanted sleep as if it had been a drug in his own system. "I made promises, I will keep promises. But I will not make children."

"Why can you not make children?"

No promises were enough for them, for that accumulation of anger and frustration. These would kill, if others had not. The smooth fresh faces. He had no ghost to give up. He had never been quite alive. Hands gripped his shoulders, each finger pitting through the cloth layers.

"Goddamn you, I'd run through the lot of you and the cows too if it would do any good—and don't think I'm joking, you don't have to put on the laugh this time! I am not normal, damn you! I am not a man. I am a clone, a being in the shape of a man, made from a store of cells kept alive for two hundred years. That was the kind of reparation we got! Without internal sexual organs, that means no seed at all, only hormones to make us look like men and women, perform like them, only it doesn't work quite that well and oh God this is the first bloody time I'm glad I never took a clone woman and raised a clone child and my family weren't part of those—"

"There were none! There were none! And you made promises to us!"

"There were a few of them! There were! I told you the truth!"

Helig sneered. "And the truth is, if men come here from your damned filthy Galactic Federation they will not let us have children at all! And we will *all* live as idiots in filth until we die with Vervlin! And then they will sell it all over again!"

The hands pulled, tore, dragged him from bed. He beat about him with his fists. "I told you—" He did not know if more had gathered or it seemed so; the hard bodies walled him, drove him the length of the vault, into another opening, this uphill, tripping on hard granitic edges; his head knocked against the ceiling, he was dizzy.

And out into the forest trampling moist dead leaves. The rain had stopped, but wind still rustled the trees and the blue apes woke and chittered.

They pushed his back to the trunk of a great conifer, plucked the cord from his hood, dragged his hands around the tree and tied them, ripped down his clothes to bare shoulders and chest, the cold struck him. One of them, he could not see which in the dark or in his terror, shinnied up the tree to grab boughs and shake them, mimicking obscenely the noise of the apes, jumping down and pulling back. All of them in a circle about König and the trunk; and the apes dropped squalling, scratching, biting at his head and shoulders, tangling their claws in his hair, in as great a panic as he; left him clawed and bitten, scampered to find other trees.

There was no mercy to beg for. He had stormed, cajoled, commanded in his life, never begged. Never died. The lantern disappeared and the children were absorbed in darkness. His mind twisted like a worm in contemplation of dying, he sagged against the trunk. He was not a man for contemplation and had never studied the holy books of Vervlen. Had not the farmers driven woodsmen back into the forest to die?

He let himself slip downward until he was sitting, in order to shrug his body into his clothing against the cold. He was still bare about the head and chest and the wind plastered dead leaves on his sweating skin. His nose was running, his breath rattled. He waited for cramps and retching and hoped they would bring death with them quickly. His stomach knotted sooner than he had expected and he twisted grotesquely in order to vomit on the planet rather than himself. So much for revenge. *Murdered for a pair of boots.* That was simpler. And he had turned his eyes away from Halvorsen and the pitchfork. That had been quicker. Cramping and vomiting drew up his legs and wrenched his arms again and again until his mouth ran with bile. The wind stung the sores on his bared skin, the trees whispered in darkness. He thought he heard laughter, but it was only the barking of blue apes and the hooting of strange birds he had not had time to notice. He had never feared the entity Death but was often afraid of dying. Now it was only a matter of waiting out the pain. He was terribly angry, but not afraid at all. The anger dulled at last and the world turned black.

"Oh ay, Master König, what y' doin' here?"

He knew the voice: Willi.

"Willi," he whispered. His eyelids were cemented shut. He forced them open, blinking away crust and film. His mouth was dry. Alive again? Maybe.

"What y' doin' here?" Willi repeated. He was bending over König, head against black trees and gray sky, one hand holding a string of fish.

König did not say, *What the hell you think?* but only repeated, "Willi," as if he were as stupid.

But he was unjust. Willi dropped the fish and knelt beside him. The sun was about to rise, the forest blew and flittered and spoke the sounds of its creatures. The boy reached into his tackle bag and pulled out a knife to cut the cord. He dragged the limp hands about until they rested, two hairy purple things, on König's knees, and rubbed them between his own warm ones; then paused a minute in thought as visible as if his skull were transparent, pulled his mittens from his pocket and forced them over König's hands.

"Thank you, Willi." He was alive. He was immune. He was a true citizen of Vervlen, the blind gut of humanity.

Willi flushed with pleasure at thanks from a man half dead and wholly stupefied. "Y'r hurt. Come with me to home and get help."

König shuddered. "No thanks. Just help me up, please."

His legs shook. He clung to the trunk and giggled helplessly because if he had been a fearful man he would have killed himself with the poison of his expectations. He pulled the clothes about his neck and the hood over his head. His shoulders ached, his hands were turning hot and stinging. "Where was the stream you were fishing in?"

"There," Willi pointed. "It's the only one about."

"Good. Here's your mittens."

"Oh no! Y' keep those." Willi picked up his fish, odd shapes with fins like wings. He drew close to König and said in a loud whisper, "But watch out. They're a bad lot, them, sometime. I know. I was a leader."

"Yes . . . good-bye, Willi."

He staggered from tree to tree, working life into his fingers, easing it into his shoulders. He did not touch the crusted cuts on his flesh. On the way there was a little valley, like the dip of the forest floor where he had landed, but not the one. The sun was up.

He sat on an outcropping in the valley's shadow to rest, and though he still felt like giggling he began to weep. He had often cursed himself for whining at his own fate. It was at least permitted to weep for them, the Elders turned useless and the

Youngers already warped in every part of their lives, in intelligence, determination, bravery. And cursed both them and those who had created him. The apes threw pods at him and the wind sang an old song his people had found somewhere:

> Yellow leaves are flying, falling
> where the King sits, lonely one
> flocking birds are crying, calling:
> withered, wasted, dying, done...

He pulled himself up the hill and across the wooded land to the cliffside, slithered down vines and saw the pool Willi had fished in where the half-winged creatures leaped and flopped gracelessly splashing; followed the stream upward until he reached the hangar wall. He did not go near the hangar. He regretted not having taken the pitchfork from Halvorsen so that he might arrange her bones with dignity; likely they would merely have scattered.

He found the flat stone and examined it: one among many, it did not seem to have been moved. He worked his fingers inside the mittens. The stinging and the heat were going with the stiffness. He heard footsteps in the leaves above, looked up and saw Helig, ape on her shoulder. He clenched and stretched his fingers, and stood still. So did she, a few meters away from the cliff's edge. The ape leaped from her shoulder to the fir above, ran cackling to its topmost branch.

König did not take his eyes off her. Squatted and dropped the mittens. She took a step forward. He flung the stone back, grunting. From the corner of his eye he caught a glance of another figure on the cliff, upstream. Young König. No sign of Ehrle. He whipped his head about and back: no one across the stream.

Eyes on Helig he groped for the bag, found it, ripped it open, plunged his left hand in, the stunner seemed to leap into it. Helig took another step forward. Young König took two steps toward her.

The stunner was a little thing, standard issue for colony-shifters. König had practised much and seldom needed it.

Helig stepped nearer. "Can you kill us all, König, before we find your ship?"

König aimed dead on and thumbed the stud.

The tiny nerve-poison capsule burst in the corner of the blue ape's eye. The animal squawked horribly, seemed to try to keep balance for a moment, fell sliding down the eaves of the conifer and landed with a thud at the girl's feet.

She gave a little shocked cry, grabbed up the bruised and paralyzed creature and ran sobbing. König was more shocked than she. "Dear Lord, you can cry for *that!*"

He shifted aim to young König, gloving his gun hand with the other: a gesture; his stance was as hard as a rock. "Which eye do *you* want it in?"

Let him believe it kills. Let him believe.

Young König stood a moment, empty hands at his sides, and backed away. He would not run.

"—alone!" a voice rode on the wind. "Leave us alone, König!" Deeper in the forest he saw Ehrle, hands resting on the tines of a forked tree. Her cheeks were reddened with wind, a wisp of hair blew across her forehead. She had not come forward, not to lead here.

"Alone," the wind cried.

"You will be left alone." Against his will he saw her in a year, a little more, waiting in line awkwardly with head down, splayed thumbs hooked over the tops of the dishes.

His mouth tasted of bile, of failure. He supposed that was a common perception. The shadows moved and she was gone.

He put the stunner on the rock, pulled the recorder from the bag and looped the chain over his head, slid the chronometer with the remotes over his wrist, pressed a colored button for the thin beep of the direction-finder; shoved stunner and bag into his pocket, scrambled up the vines, panting and clumsy. He follwed the cliff-edge, gun in one hand and infrared scanner in the other. Its light-strip flickered with the movements of small animals.

When the hypnoformer was reversing he waited listening and scanning for the moment it took the field to dissipate. The shuttle broke like sun through cloud, white dappled with shade, gold numbers burning.

He saw no more Vervlin, and when he had climbed in and locked down looked no more on the world. The ship lifted its feral beak to part the sky, pulling after it a whirlwind of yellow leaves that reached the tops of the trees before they drifted in slow circles downward to the forest floor.

ELIZABETH A. LYNN: AN INTERVIEW

by Vonda N. McIntyre

As our nonfiction offering this issue, we have an interview with one of the fastest-rising science fiction and fantasy writers by an award-winning writer of the field whose own reputation is still growing. This is a light, delightful piece and shows both interviewer and interviewee to have an attitude about their work which we think will be very interesting and appealing to our readers. It is very obvious that they both had fun doing the interview, and we're sure you'll have fun reading it.

Most SF writers start out as SF fans—readers of science fiction, to be sure, but members of the worldwide convention attending and amateur magazine publishing SF community, as well. Elizabeth A. Lynn is one of the few exceptions to this tradition. She sold two stories before she even discovered fandom. While studying aikido (in which she has a brown belt), she met writer David R. Mason, who in turn introduced her to Fritz Leiber. Leiber lent her his copies of the SF news magazine, *Locus*, and the *Bulletin* of the Science Fiction Writers of America, both of which contain reports of markets open to original story submissions. Lynn began sending out her stories—including one to *Aurora: Beyond Equality*, which I co-edited. I remember the story very clearly, and my reasons for turning it down equally clearly, though as time goes on the reason seems less and less good. So someone else gets the credit for buying Elizabeth A. Lynn's first story. However, I seem to get the credit, if that is what it is, for introducing her to SF fandom. I got her in touch with other writers in the San Francisco area, and they introduced her to the late lamented Magic Cellar, a unique night club that became a hangout for SF people, writers and fans. Lynn was actually in Cleveland the year the World Science Fiction Convention was held there, but she didn't know about it; her first convention was the Oakland Westercon, in 1975.

Like many SF readers, she discovered the genre, if not the community, at a very young age. (As Terry Carr says, "The golden age of science fiction is twelve.") Lynn, however, began a little earlier, at eight. She recalls *More Than Human* in particular, and then *Childhood's End* and *The Stars My Destination*. After that, she says, "I just went apeshit, and read everything I could get my hands on." Her mother reads SF, so it was in the house, and when she got to high school she, like so many of us, combed the library for books with the little atom-and-rocket sticker on the spine. Unlike many young girls who like SF, she was not afflicted with a school librarian who decreed SF to be "boys' books." But she did find it annoying that the books were always *about* boys. There were some notable exceptions, such as Tigerishka in Fritz Leiber's *The Wanderer*, but ordinarily when women existed in SF novels at all, they were "wimps." It seemed like they should be *doing* things. Still, Lynn identified with any character who was intelligent. "We like to think SF isn't escapist literature," she says, "but for me, in high school, it was. I saw it as almost a literal escape."

Having been convinced by a "helpful" high school English teacher that she was utterly talentless as a writer, she went on to Western Reserve University, where she took a double major in English Literature and philosophy. Advanced placement tests in English got her directly into junior-level courses, "Taught by professors who were good teachers and who genuinely loved their jobs." She discovered philosophy when she took the required History of Philosophy course. She became interested in the philosophy of language, studying the revolutionary field of transformational grammar at a time when the rest of the department was interested in the philosophy of science. "It was fun to be in on the ground floor," she says, "even if we didn't know at the time that that's what it was."

While taking two majors—and completing college in three years—she also worked at a number of different jobs. She was a switchboard operator at her dorm, an usher at the Cleveland Symphony, and cashier and cook at a coffeehouse that turned out to be a major dope center. The management eventually got busted. "It was an education in itself," Lynn says. "Employees got $1.25 an hour and all they could steal." But singers such as Tom Rush, and the Youngbloods, appeared there: she got to hear a lot of neat music.

One semester, she took twenty-one credits (and earned all A's). "I work well under pressure," she told me, when I cringed with sympathetic exhaustion. Even the coffeehouse job had its points: "Drinking 3.2 beer from eleven to one and spacing out on music kept me sane. But the beer was like horse piss. Or possibly not as good."

After receiving her Masters in English Lit at the University of Chicago, she taught in a ghetto school that had (for example) six sets of books for eight first-grade classes, and a single set of magnets for sixteen-hundred students. Later, in San Francisco, she worked as a hospital ward manager. Once she had finished her first short story—and realized she could do it again—she knew it was only a matter of time before she would become a professional writer. It took her several years to save enough money to stop working and write full time, and another couple of years before she began making a living wage as a writer. But since then she has hardly looked back. Since 1978 she has published four novels: *A Different Light*, and the Chronicles of Tornor trilogy: *Watchtower*, *The Dancers of Arun*, and *The Northern Girl*. Berkley will publish *The Sardonyx Net* in 1981. Currently she is working on a sword and sorcery novel, *Kyri of the Wolves*, for Pocket Books. She has been nominated for the John W. Campbell award for best new writer (twice), and all three pieces of work that she published in 1979 was nominated for the World Fantasy Award. *Watchtower* won for best novel and "The Woman Who Loved the Moon" [from *Amazons*, edited by Jessica Amanda Salmonson] for best short story.

As she says, she works well under pressure.

VNM: Did you always want to be a writer?
EAL: Yes and no. I was—and am—a voracious reader. My parents had a massive library, and I read everything in it, plus

everything I could get from the school and local libraries near my home. I was fascinated with words and with the process of putting words on paper, but the few times I tried to do it, in high school, even I could see how imitative the stories were. My teachers said flatly that they were bad. Sometime in college I accepted what others told me, that I would never be a writer, and I stopped writing. It wasn't until I got out of graduate school and had worked for three years doing other things that I realized the desire to put words on paper was still there.

VNM: Did you ever actually take writing classes in high school and college?

EAL: No. In college I just didn't have the time to do "creative writing." Besides, I *knew* I couldn't.

VNM: Who was it who—

EAL: A ninth-grade English teacher.

VNM: Argh.

EAL: Yes. After that it seemed kind of pointless. I did a little poetry in college. But poetry was different. Besides, everybody was doing poetry. I'm not quite sure when it became clear to me that I was, dammit, going to write. But I do remember finishing that first story. I was so happy: I'd never finished any piece of fiction before.

VNM: It is kind of neat, that first one you finish.

EAL: Then you have to go and do the next one. At that point I was working full time as well. It was hard. I didn't realize how tough it was going to be when I first started writing and thinking of myself as a writer. I was working full time in a hospital and in doctors' offices, and even when the doctors were real nice and let me use the typewriter, which they did, the energy that it took to go from doing one kind of work to writing was like changing energy levels in an atom.

VNM: Really. Even more so...there are more atoms to move. I admire people who can do both—work full time and write. Like Gene Wolfe.

EAL: I don't understand how anyone can keep it up. When I quit work it was with such a sense of freedom—when I actually started making a living as a writer I knew I would never do both again. Either I was going to write or I was going to stop writing and take a job, but I would never try to do both. It was killing.

VNM: But you haven't had to stop and take a job since you started writing full time.

EAL: No.

VNM: You write to contract: first you sell the book, and then you write it. How is that working out?

EAL: It keeps me fed! But I am getting pretty tired of it— lately I've been missing deadlines, which tells me it's time to start doing things differently. After these contracts are completed, I want to do some short fiction, and then I want to rest for a while. I have another project in mind—a non-science-fiction book. But I don't really want to talk about that.

VNM: You seem always to have several projects planned ahead. Do you ever worry that you'll eventually burn out?

EAL: No. If it happens, it happens. I don't want it to, of course, but I certainly can't see how I'd stop it. I do plan to slow down.

VNM: Do you want to talk about what you're working on now?

EAL: A book called *Kyri of the Wolves.* Alicia Austin will illustrate it.

VNM: What is it about? Is it a lost child story?

EAL: No—it's a woman warrior story. It's a story in which "The Woman Who Loved the Moon" is a myth. In fact Kyri, who is the hero of the book, comes from the same family as Kai Talvela, from the short story. It's very different from what I've done before. It's sword and sorcery, so it's got real witchcraft, not just telepathy and whatnot. It's got magic and a religious structure, and a complicated mythology which I had great fun working out and then had to write down so I wouldn't forget it.

VNM: When will it be done? Or do you know?

EAL: I don't know when it'll be done. I've given up giving myself deadlines. For one thing I can't seem to meet them. I'm finding it more and more frustrating every time that happens, so I've just given up. But the book feels like it's going well. I'm at chapter eight, just about the halfway point.

VNM: That will be your sixth novel. What was your *first* sale?

EAL: Oh, God, it's been so long, I don't remember—

VNM: You don't remember your first sale? Come on, Lynn!

EAL: My first sale was "We All Have to Go." I sold it to *Future Pastimes*, edited by Scott Edelstein, and it was reprinted in *Tricks and Treats*, the Mystery Writers of America anthology for its year. The next story I sold was to *Antaeus*, for their popular fiction issue. You remember their popular fiction issue.

VNM: Yes, I was thrown out of their popular fiction issue.

EAL: Then I found out about fandom and *Antaeus* ceased to look at my stories. I wonder if there's a connection?

VNM: Unclean! Unclean!

EAL: The next thing I sold was to *The Magazine of Fantasy and Science Fiction*. That's not so bad.

VNM: Good old F&SF, no, that's pretty good.

EAL: It's funny—I keep writing stories that are in bits and pieces of categories, but not quite. I've written two pseudo-mystery stories that have no mysteries in them, and are not quite crime stories. I don't know quite what to call them, but they've been published in mystery anthologies. I wrote a horror story that F&SF published, and another that was published in a Doubleday anthology. I think of them all as SF. Categories confuse me.

VNM: I think all of us have had the experience of sending stories to mainstream markets and getting them back with reject slips that have a definite looking-down-the-nose tone to them. You've studied English literature—do you think there's a qualitative difference between SF and "mainstream"? Do you think the SF designation is useful or just a publishing/marketing convenience?

EAL: I do think there's a difference between SF and mainstream; or, to put it another way, I think science fiction is a particular kind of mainstream literature. I first heard this theory from Philip Klass, who is also the writer William Tenn, and it makes more sense to me than any other theory I have heard. It states that science fiction is the literature of the era that developed the scientific method: that it came out of a way of looking at the universe in which process and inquiry are central, that it developed as the religious explanation for the creation of the universe, and human beings, was being abandoned in favor of a mechanistic one, and that the first SF book, *Franken-stein*, by Mary Shelley, is concerned precisely with the first science fictional theme, the place of human beings in a world which has suddenly lost its philosophic center. I like that theory; it makes sense. It explains why science fiction appeared so suddenly in the middle of the eighteen hundreds: it was a literary response to a climate of ideas. *Frankenstein* was published in 1818; forty years later came Darwin with "On the Origin of Species."

VNM: The publishers don't seem to look at SF that way.

EAL: American publishers don't, certainly. But American publishers when they think of SF don't think of Shelley and Verne and Wells, they think of *Thrilling Wonder Stories*. I have great admiration for the vigor of the pulps, but in some ways they did a great disservice to SF, by ghettoizing it in the minds of writers *and* readers. It's easy to name "mainstream" writers who have written SF: Gore Vidal, Cecilia Holland, Shirley Jackson, Marge Piercy—and the list grows when you include fantasy. But the publishers think they can sell more SF by sticking the rocket-and-atom on it, and by now they have created a self-fulfilling prophecy.

VNM: It seems to me that about half your work is very definitely science fiction, and the other half very definitely fantasy. Why don't you talk about the difference between the two?

EAL: Oh, great.

VNM: "Oh, great, groan," or "Oh, great, great"

EAL: "Oh, great, groan"—because that's real hard. People have been running around that one for years.

VNM: Yes— "Define the difference between SF and fantasy," and then they write twenty pages and never come to a conclusion. But you do write both, and none of your work straddles the border—wherever the border is.

EAL: Except one story that people insist on thinking does, and that's "The Gods of Reorth."

VNM: I thought that was straight science fiction.

EAL: So did I. But it does have a fantasy tone to it.

VNM: That's true. Whenever you do a science fiction story that deals with myth, people assume it's fantasy.

EAL: My standard definition when someone asks me the difference between SF and fantasy is to say, "SF has spaceships and fantasy had swords."

VNM: And then you giggle.

EAL: And then I giggle. But then I also quote a definition that I think Norman Spinrad first gave, which is that SF *creates* a suspension of disbelief in the mind of the reader, while fantasy *requires* the suspension of disbelief.

VNM: I like that.

EAL: I like it, too, so I stick with it. What it means is that you don't have to explain what those elves are doing there in your fantasy story. That makes sense to me. It's a good working definition and I'm not sure I want to get any more detailed than that.

VNM: The more detailed definitions always eat their own tails anyway. But I wondered if you felt different when you're writing SF from when you're writing fantasy.

EAL: With SF I have to do more research. I want to try to make sure that my science, even if it isn't totally up to date, at least isn't dead wrong. With fantasy, it depends on what I'm writing. With the more realistic fantasy of the Chronicles I did a fair amount of research just to find out how things were made and how long it took and what level of technology existed at a certain level of history. And how likely it was that certain types of technology existed at the same time as other kinds. With what I'm working on now, sword and sorcery, I find I'm making more of it up and playing more games with it. I guess what I'm doing is depending on my background in literature to give me both the knowledge of the mythological structures I'm playing around with and the sense that I'm not using them wrong.

VNM: The *Chronicles of Tornor*—your trilogy—has been described as historical fiction about an imaginary country. Would you comment on that?

EAL: I think *I* said that. It's pretty good, anyway. A review in *Foundation* took me to task for juxtaposing cultures in *Watchtower* that in real life could never have co-existed. The reviewer said that was cheating, somehow. The review annoyed me strongly, much more strongly than any other review I've had, because it assumed that the historical motivations which *did* exist *must* exist; furthermore, it assumed that I didn't bother to do any research and simply went blithely on making stupid assertions about history. What I did with the trilogy was set up a country, Arun, and try to show its culture in various periods and in various locations throughout the country. In *Watchtower*, the earliest of the books, I tried to show a barbaric and somewhat backward milieu being impinged upon by a new philosophic and cultural development; in *The Dancers of Arun* I showed the flowering of that development 100 years later in another part of the country; in *The Northern Girl* I show the major city of the country at a period of corruption and change.

VNM: It must be irritating to be trashed for your cultural extrapolations—to be told "these two cultures *could not* have existed at the same time"—especially since in so much SF the reader is presented with a whole world that contains a single culture.

EAL: Precisely. I just got a letter from someone who wanted me to tell him all about the world, and tell him what its name was. What I wrote back to him was that I'm not writing about a world. I'm writing about one land mass, and one country on that land mass, and the people in that country don't know very much about the world. I'm trying to stay within their frame of reference. It very much bothers me, especially when fantasy writers write about whole planets as if the same stuff was going on all over the planet.

VNM: It bothers you more in fantasy than in SF?

EAL: Yes, it does. In SF I'm willing to accept that at least in some instances those planets may have been colonized, so you could have a monolithic culture.

VNM: On a colony, sure. But usually, it's "Take me to your leader," with the assumption that there is a single one.

EAL: And they all speak the same language. Yes—when that occurs it bothers me just as much in SF.

VNM: How do you go about doing research?

EAL: It depends on what I'm writing about, of course. For example, I wrote a story called, "I Dream of a Fish, I Dream of a Bird": it was about artificial skin, and it was published in *Isaac Asimov's Science Fiction Magazine* in 1977. I went down to the science room in the San Francisco Public Library and read everything I could on artificial organs, on skin, and on proteins. I also talked to a biochemist. But most of that never got into the story; I simply needed to know it so that I could feel confident that I wasn't fucking up and making a stupid scientific mistake. By now, of course, half that research is obsolete. In the novel *Watchtower* I described the making of a bow: I spent hours looking that up. On the other hand, some things I don't look up at all: in a story called "Circus" in *Chrysalis 3*, all the detail came out of my head. I later got a letter from someone who'd spent a lot of time around carnivals, complimenting me on how well I conveyed the authentic circus flavor!

VNM: Speaking of letters, what kind of fan mail do you get?

EAL: After *A Different Light* came out, in 1978, I got some hate mail: How dare you write about those filthy godless homosexuals, etc. Now I get about a letter a week, and it's pretty complimentary stuff. I've got a fair amount of mail from gay men who say thank you for putting someone like me into a fantasy novel; I've also gotten some letters from women who want to know why none of my novels has a female protagonist. I tell them to read *The Northern Girl*, when it comes out.

VNM: Returning to writing, did you always write science fiction?

EAL: In high school I started an Ayn Rand-type novel about a sculptor. Ayn Rand is fascinating—when you're in high school. It got as far as forty pages before I abandoned it. It was terrible. But since 1971 I've always written SF, fantasy, or stories with elements of SF or fantasy. Both the "mystery" stories have science fictional elements in them.

VNM: Who's the most influential writer on your work? Or is there one?

EAL: That's a difficult question. I'm fascinated by different styles of writing and by the way style changes from genre to genre. Modern writers I like: Lawrence Durrell, Doris Lessing, Gore Vidal (the essays more than the fiction), Thomas Disch (I think *On Wings of Song* is a brilliant book), Joanna Russ, Cecilia Holland, Toni Morrison. That's a short list. I don't read a lot of fiction anymore—when I do, it's mostly historical fiction and mysteries. I read a lot of history; right now I'm working my way through a book on the Bronze Age of China, with pictures.

Who would I say influenced me? I don't know. I could point at some of the writers whose works I admire tremendously. They tend to be the stylists, like Disch, and Russ. And Lessing, because when she does it right, it's perfect. It's almost like watching somebody do a piece of three-dimensional art. She takes an image and builds it and builds it, and you can see her slapping on the clay from all sides. Of course when it doesn't work, her writing gets unbearably clunky. Everything slows to a creep, and you wish she'd hurry it up. But I find her style fascinating. It's very different from mine.

VNM: Reading your work, I don't feel intense echoes of other writers. That is, reading some work you often feel, oh, this person just finished reading a Delany novel.

EAL: When I was working on *Watchtower* I was very consciously trying to use some of the lessons I learned in reading

Cecilia Holland's historicals: the way she uses her verbs, the whole structure of her paragraphs. I was trying to use some of her stylistic . . . peculiarities? Her stylistic methods.

VNM: The short sentences?

EAL: The short sentences. The sense of action, the constant movement. When she's describing something, it's very textured. I don't know if it worked in *Watchtower* or not. The rest of the trilogy, I tried to loosen it up progressively so that the second book is more flowing and complex. On the simplest level, the sentences are longer than in the first book, and, similarly, the third as compared to the second.

VNM: I didn't think that it didn't work in *Watchtower*, but I did find myself occasionally wishing there were a compound sentence or so just thrown in there for fun once in a while.

EAL: It's funny, because when I look at it I can see the choppiness, but when I read it either aloud or to myself, it flows. I'm not quite sure what that means, or even if it makes any difference.

VNM: The process of oral reading and the process of silent reading are very different—or anyway the process of story-telling and the process of reading are. Did you mean to do it like that, as if it were somebody sitting by a campfire telling a story?

EAL: Not consciously, no. I'd love to be able to say yes.

VNM: In *Watchtower* and *Dancers*, the protagonists of the story are men; in *The Northern Girl*, all the viewpoint characters are women. Did you plan this? Was it meant as a comment on the world and culture, or did it just turn out that way?

EAL: I planned it; or at least, when I realized what the order of the books was going to be, I planned it. The novels were not written in the order they appeared. *The Dancers of Arun* was written in novella form in 1971, and I stuck it in a drawer, not knowing what to do with it. I mean, it was a love story about two brothers! Years later I realized that it was a middle story, that something happened first and something else came after it. I sat down and wrote the novella *Watchtower*. Since *Dancers* was about men loving and nurturing other men, and *Watchtower* came one hundred years before *Dancers*, it was pretty clear to me that *Watchtower* had to show the foundations of the cultural change that led to such behavior. And though the point of view character in *Watchtower* is male, the central relationship of the story, the pivotal relationship from which Ryke learns who he is, and isn't, is the relationship between two women.

VNM: That was a deliberate theme.

EAL: Certainly. I believe that if men are going to learn to care for each other, to give each other the emotional support and nurturance that they now expect to get *only* from women, they are going to have to watch women to see how we do it.

VNM: Writing about a society in which the people behave differently from today's status quo is the sort of thing that gets one accused of putting politics in one's fiction—and of "proselytizing."

EAL: That's true, But everyone does it, whether they know it or not. I try to do it consciously because at least then I know what I'm saying. You can't *not* put your social and political beliefs into your work; you can merely be unaware that you are doing so. As Paul Novitski said in an article, all fiction is political in that the writers' unconscious assumptions reflect themselves in the work.

VNM: Why do you think that so many women write novels with male protagonists?

EAL: One reason is, I think, that women are taught more about men than they are taught about themselves. As Suzy Charnas has pointed out, in a patriarchy women survive by knowing as much about men as they can. There's another reason, too: one learns to write by reading what has been written, and most literature is by men, about men. Anything men do in this culture is considered to be more exciting, more valuable, and more a fit subject for fiction than what women do, and it takes a certain amount of psychic and psychological work for women writers to get past this belief, to just set it to one side.

VNM: What's going on in the field these days that you really like?

EAL: I guess it isn't enough just to name names, and it seems somewhat trite to say I like people who are shaking things up.

VNM: Who do you see as shaking things up?

EAL: Tom Disch, a lot, as in *On Wings of Song*. Suzy Charnas, with *The Vampire Tapestry*, taking that whole traditional structure of vampires and turning it inside out and doing what she wants with it and making a nice gloss on civilized structures at the same time. I really enjoyed that. *Wild Seed*, by Octavia Butler—I thought that was tremendously interesting.

VNM: So did I.

EAL: Those are three of the more interesting books I've read recently.

VNM: You teach SF at a university: what do you think of the current academic interest in SF?

EAL: I think most of the time the academics don't know what they're talking about on any subject. But my class is somewhat different from the usual SF class: it's in the Women Studies program at San Francisco State, and I teach specifically feminist books and feminist theory.

VNM: What books do you teach?

EAL: It changes. This year I'm teaching, in order, *Dreamsnake*; *The Kin of Ata Are Waiting for You*, by Dorothy Bryant; *Juniper Time*, *Woman on the Edge of Time*, *Les Guerrilleres*, *Titan*, *The Two of Them*, and *Motherlines*.

VNM: Have you ever taught a book you hate?

EAL: Not hate. But I taught *Beyond This Horizon* by Heinlein once, and I decided not to do it again next semester.

VNM: Have you ever taught one of your own books, or let your students discuss one of your books in your presence?

EAL: No. I won't, either. I do spend one class session or part of it talking about *writing*: what it feels like, how I do it, what happens to a manuscript after it leaves my hands, stuff like that.

VNM: You said earlier that you didn't ever want to *have* to hold down a job and write at the same time.

EAL: Yes. I teach for fun. I enjoy the teaching. If I had to do too much of it I'd go bonkers. But as it is, what the hell, it gets me out of the house, it gets me talking to whole bunches of people. I learn things from my students. And they're incredibly supportive. The seven months I was writing *The Sardonyx Net* was probably—I say this about every book—one of the hardest periods of time I ever spent. It was like constantly beating my head against a wall. And I was teaching at the same time. I would walk into my four o'clock class, after a day at the typewriter, going, "Bdee, bdee, bdee," and they'd talk to me and pat me on the head and hand me glasses of milk and pull me out of it. They were wonderful. I owe so much to that year, to those women, for being supportive and not giving me a hard time about the fact that I came in cross-eyed every week.

VNM: One last question: "Ms. Lynn, where do you get your ideas?"

EAL: From Schenectady, of course—just like everybody else.

BIOGRAPHICAL NOTES

PAT CADIGAN was born in New York, grew up in Fitchburg, Massachusetts, and now lives in Kansas City, where she writes for Hallmark Cards during the days and stays up late at night working on a novel. She has been a clockcase sander, disc jockey, belly dance teacher and Tom Reamy's typesetter. "The Pathosfinder" is her third professional sale, the first two being to *New Dimensions 11* and *The Magazine of Fantasy and Science Fiction*.

RONALD ANTHONY CROSS seems to enjoy a very involved, not to say crowded life. In addition to selling a series of highly experimental and fantastic fictions to ORBIT, FUTURE PASTIMES, NEW WORLDS, OTHER WORLDS, and *Charlie Chan Mystery Magazine*, he writes music and is a practicing lacto-vegetarian. Otherwise, he writes, "biographical stuff is very difficult here, as something weird has happened to the memory."

JACK DANN has made his reputation in the field as both a writer and anthologist. His stories have appeared in *Playboy*, *Omni*, *Penthouse*, *The Magazine of Fantasy and Science Fiction*, and *Orbit*. His novels are STARHIKER and JUNCTION, with a third, THE MAN WHO MELTED due out next year. He also edited three very strong anthologies, WANDERING STARS, FASTER THAN LIGHT (with George Zebrowski), and FUTURE POWER (with Gardner Dozois). He lives in Johnson City, New York.

PHYLLIS GOTLIEB is a Canadian poet and novelist. The three works she is best known for in the United States are science fiction novels: SUNBURST, O MASTER CALIBAN!, and A JUDGMENT OF DRAGONS. She has also written a novel about the survivor of a Nazi concentration camp, WHY SHOULD I HAVE ALL THE GRIEF? (Macmillan of Canada 1969) and four volumes of poetry including DOCTOR UM-LAUT'S EARTHLY KINGDOM and THE WORKS.

R. A. LAFFERTY was born in 1914 and somewhere along the way (apparently he claims correspondence training) he became a practicing electrical engineer. In the early sixties he began bombing (the very word) the science fiction marketplace with a series of short stories which quickly established him in the midst of the New Wave and earned him accolades from Delany and Zelazny. Some of his very best work, widely acknowledged as of tour de force quality, has been in the short story form with such successes as the Hugo Award winning "Eurema's Dam" (1972) and "Continued on Next Rock" (1970). His several novels include ARRIVE AT EASTERWINE, THE DEVIL IS DEAD and the non-genre OKLA HANNALI.

ELIZABETH A. LYNN has lived in New York, Cleveland and Chicago and is now happily settled in San Francisco where, she says, she belonged all along. A DIFFERENT LIGHT, published by Berkley in 1978, was her first novel. Since then she has published the critically acclaimed and very successful Chronicles of Tornor, a three-book story: WATCHTOWER, THE DANCERS OF ARUN and THE NORTHERN GIRL. At the 1980 World Fantasy Convention, Lynn was awarded two World Fantasy Awards—one for WATCHTOWER and one for her short story, "The Woman Who Loved the Moon." Her next novel, THE SARDONYX NET, is forthcoming from Berkley.

VONDA N. MCINTYRE is the acclaimed author of the award-winning novelette "Of Mist, and Grass, and Sand," which she expanded into the award-winning novel, DREAMSNAKE. She is the author of many other stories, and currently lives and works in Seattle, Washington.

KEVIN O'DONNELL, JR. is a young writer whose work has appeared in virtually all the science fiction magazines: *Omni*, *Analog*, *Isaac Asimov's*, *Galaxy*, *Galileo*, *Amazing*; and in various anthologies. He is the author of BANDERSNATCH, MAYFLIES, and CAVERNS, with several more titles forthcoming. He has been justly hailed as one of the most exciting and important new writers of the genre to emerge in the past decade, and we are expecting great things from and for him. O'Donnell is also the publisher of *EMPIRE: For the SF Writer* (Box 967, New Haven, Ct. 06504), a little magazine aimed at anyone interested in writing, editing, or publishing SF. He and his wife live in Connecticut.

MARGE PIERCY's most recent novel, VIDA, has just been issued in paperback by Fawcett. Her most recent book of poetry, THE MOON IS ALWAYS FEMALE, published by Knopf, is out in paperback and hardcover. Her only play, THE LAST WHITE CLASS, co-authored with Ira Wood, was published after three productions around Massachusetts by The Crossing Press in Trumansburg, N.Y. She is also the author of THE HIGH COST OF LIVING, WOMAN ON THE EDGE OF TIME, DANCE THE EAGLE TO SLEEP and SMALL CHANGES. Her books of poetry include THE TWELVE-SPOKED WHEEL FLASHING, LIVING IN THE OPEN, TO BE OF USE, HARD LOVING, and BREAKING CAMP.

ALAN RYAN seems to have burst full-grown on the scene in the past two years. He has had stories published in NEW DIMENSIONS, SHADOWS, *Twilight Zone*, and *The Magazine of Fantasy and Science Fiction*. He was nominated for the John W. Campbell Award as Best New Writer in 1980. He writes reviews of the genre for several magazines. His first novel, PANTHER, was published this year. He is currently editing an anthology about the future of religion, called PERPETUAL LIGHT, which should be a blockbuster. His next novel is THE KILL, a horror novel. He lives in New York City.

ROBERT THURSTON is the author of ALICIA II and the bestselling Battlestar Galactica series. His short stories have appeared in NEW DIMENSIONS, NEW VOICES, ORBIT, *Fantasy and Science Fiction*, *Cosmos*, *Analog*, *Amazing*, *Fantastic*, *OtherWorlds*, and CHRYSALIS. Thurston attended the Clarion Writers Workshop in 1969 and again in 1970, where he wrote the prizewinning story "Wheels," the basis for his forthcoming novel, A SET OF WHEELS.

DORIS VALLEJO is one of the most promising new talents to be seen in years. Her first book, a children's novel, THE BOY WHO SAVED THE STARS, was published by Starlog Press in 1980. Her first adult novel, WINDSOUND, was recently published by Berkley Books and Ballantine Books will be publishing MIRAGES: The Fantasy Erotic Art of Boris Vallejo, text by Doris, in 1981. The Vallejos live with their two children in New York.

CONNIE WILLIS lives in Woodland Park, Colorado. She made a great impression on the field last year with her marvelous story in *Galileo* Magazine, "Daisy in the Sun." With Cynthia Felice, she has sold a novel WATER WITCH.